Lift Your Eyes to the Mountains

Mountains of Faith, Book 1

Catherine Barbey

Cover Art by Rebecca Priestley
Cover Design by Rob Richards
Editor: Arielle Bailey

Note to Readers:

As a British author, I've purposefully retained British spellings and grammar throughout, so I hope that's not too off-putting to my readers who prefer to read in American English.

For more from Catherine Barbey join her mailing list at catherinebarbey.com/readerslist

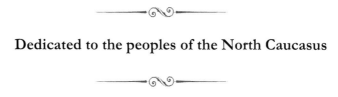

Dedicated to the peoples of the North Caucasus

Prologue

The Caucasus Mountains, Russia

July 1987

"Come on, Bela, not much further now!"

Bela scrambled up one more rock towards where her uncle was standing, at the top of the steep hill.

"My legs are a lot smaller than yours," she panted, smiling up at him. He laughed. She was glad to see him looking so happy. A few more steps and she reached his side. She straightened up and stood, hands on hips, copying him, straining to catch her breath. She looked around at the amazing view that he was already admiring.

"You like being up in the mountains, don't you, Uncle Artur?"

He nodded and pressed his fist against his chest. "They hold a special place in my heart. I feel more alive out here than anywhere else I know."

Out here, in the middle of this beautiful, rugged terrain, her uncle did indeed seem like a completely different person. It was as if the pain in his life had been washed away by the clean, mountain air.

She shielded her eyes from the sun as she looked towards the snow-capped peaks of the Caucasus range. Somewhere behind those jagged mountain giants were the even higher twin peaks of Mount Elbrus, though it wasn't possible to see them from here.

"I think Nana told me a Nart story once about the mountains. I must ask her about it when we get home." She loved hearing Nana tell the stories of the ancient heroes of their people. Nana said that their people had ridden their horses over these mountains and pastured their flocks on these hills for centuries before the Russians came. She could imagine her uncle dressed in a shepherd's black woollen *burka* with a shaggy goats-hair hat, watching over his flock.

"Papa's car looks so far away, Uncle, look." Her father's Volga, which they had borrowed for the day, looked like one of Azamat's toy cars on the stony, mountain road below. Her comment seemed to shake Uncle Artur back to the present moment and his frown returned.

"I think it's time we started heading back home now, Bela."

"Just a moment, Uncle."

Beautiful mountain flowers were scattered over the hillside—delicate little things, white and purple and gold—and Bela ran around gathering up two small bouquets to take back, one for Nana and one for Mama. She knew they wouldn't survive the trip home in the hot car, but she couldn't help herself.

She looked up again and breathed in deeply, filling her lungs until she felt they would burst. Uncle Artur was right;

it was so refreshing to get out of the oppressive heat of the village and come up here where the air was cooler. The long drive from their village had been worth it. Her uncle had already started climbing back down towards the car, but Bela lingered a while longer. She drew in the beauty of the scene around her and tried to impress it upon her memory. The view, the flowers, the sweet, fresh scent of the air. The wonderfully delicious sense of freedom. The majesty and wonder of these towering hills and mountains, which seemed to touch the very sky itself. At that moment, another feeling, or perhaps it was a small voice, flickered inside her. Whatever it was, it was as clear as if someone had spoken the words directly to her.

Lift your eyes to the mountains, my daughter.

1

I lift up my eyes to the mountains –

where does my help come from?

My help comes from the Lord,

the Maker of heaven and earth.

Psalm 121, verse 1 and 2

Chapter 1

2003, March

"Stop, please!" Bela called out to the driver as the *marshroutka* neared the crossroads. The minibus pulled over, and she clambered out, closing the sliding door behind her. She watched it continue down the main street of the village and then, when she was sure all was clear, crossed over to the other side and started to walk down the gravelled road that led to her family home.

The letter she'd picked up at the post office earlier that afternoon was hidden in her handbag, but she couldn't stop thinking about it. Another rejection. Another door slammed in her face. She breathed heavily, struggling to control the disappointment. She was young, intelligent, and ambitious, and her English skills were excellent, even if she did say so herself. But none of that mattered. She'd never have the chance to prove herself, all because she'd not been able to finish her university degree, through no fault of her own. It wasn't fair. She'd be trapped working in the boring mobile phone shop for the rest of her life at this rate.

She glanced down at her work uniform underneath her coat, a smart black skirt with a white blouse. Nothing had changed about her life, really, since the time she was a schoolgirl, wearing similar clothes and trudging this same route back home every day from School Number Two on the outskirts of Shekala. Only now, she had slightly more painful, high-heeled shoes on her feet. She suddenly longed to be wearing her much more comfortable village slippers.

She reached the little shop where she and Zalina used to buy sweets when they were younger. Rima was sitting outside on the wooden bench, wisps of grey hair peeking out from underneath her red, winter headscarf. The sleeves of her winter housedress were rolled up to the elbows as she sat soaking up the last of the day's sunshine, watching the world go by and waiting for customers. Bela nodded a greeting to her as she passed, and Rima nodded back, bobbing out of her seat and flashing a gold tooth as she smiled. Life was so much slower here than in the town of Shekala. People had time to sit on benches and wait for their neighbours to pass by. It was nice, in a way, but it also felt as if the inhabitants were living out their lives a couple of decades behind the rest of the country.

The village of Awush was quiet on this warm spring day. Small mounds of snow still clung to the shady patches, but the days were heating up now, and they would soon melt away. Bela closed her eyes and took a deep breath, allowing the clean village air to chase away the weariness of her working day. The bustle of town life began to fall away from her shoulders, and she relaxed a little. There was a time when she couldn't imagine wanting to leave this place. She had so many happy childhood memories of growing up in this village. True, there were things she'd rather forget too, but this was her home, wasn't it? This was where she felt truly herself.

Then why was she so desperate to get away?

She kept to the middle of the road, picking her way around the potholes and avoiding any patches of ice. A few minutes later, she reached the corner of the road on which her family property sat behind a high, yellow-painted brick wall. She turned to walk towards it. Theirs was one of the larger houses in Awush. The main two-storey house rose in the centre of the property, its silver metal roof gleaming in the sunlight, but the two side buildings were hidden from view: the summer kitchen on one side where Nana often slept during the hot months, and the smaller building on the other side which housed Uncle Artur. Bela paused at the large, ornate, metal gate that guarded the entrance to her home. She smiled as she heard Tuzik whining with impatience inside the yard, waiting for her to appear, his tail excitedly swishing against the concrete slabs next to his kennel. Bela pushed open the gate, closed it carefully behind her, and walked through the front yard. She went over to the large German Shepherd and tousled the fur on the top of his head.

"Poor Tuzik," she whispered as she scratched behind his ears. "Tied up all day. It's not much fun, being a guard dog, is it? I'd love to set you free, but Papa wouldn't like it." She jangled his chain a little, and he nuzzled his soft, wet nose against her hand, grateful for the attention and, albeit brief, human contact. She sighed as she straightened up again and turned to walk up the four steps which led to the main house.

Her mother was in the kitchen, preparing food, as usual. She paused and looked up from her chopping board at Bela, who was lingering in the doorway.

"How was work today?" Mama asked in Circassian. Bela always found it a relief to revert to her native tongue after a long day working in the centre of Shekala, speaking Russian to her customers and colleagues.

"Oh, the usual. Boring." Bela went over to the table, pulled out a stool, and sat down, stretching out her tired legs. She had exchanged her fashionable high heels for some house slippers at the door, and her feet were thanking her for it.

"I'm just not sure it's going anywhere, Mama. I wanted a job where I could use my English, perhaps travel a little, but instead I spend the whole day filling in forms and selling people the same boring mobile phones." She couldn't see the point in telling Mama about the rejection letter. Not again.

"Just be happy you have a job, *lapochka*, and don't worry so much. It's not easy to find good jobs these days."

"I know, I know. You always say that, but I just feel so… restless."

"It won't be forever. Hopefully, soon, you'll…"

"Mama! I'm not having the marriage conversation again!"

She'd been brushing aside Mama's comments on that topic ever since she'd turned eighteen nearly five years ago now. It wasn't that she hadn't had offers. Some of the boys who'd expressed an interest were fun and good-looking, and some even had 'good prospects', as Papa would have said. But she'd been determined for a long time that she would only marry for love, not out of a sense of duty, or fear that she was growing too old and would be left on the shelf, as Mama liked to remind her on a regular basis. She wasn't totally against the concept of marriage, but it scared her. She'd lost faith in the whole idea. If she was going to marry, then she needed to be sure it would lead to happiness. She would wait until her heart told her that she had found 'the one'. She'd already witnessed too many examples in her young life of relationships going wrong when people settled for anything less.

"Do you want me to do anything to help, Mama?" Best to change the conversation.

"Not at the moment. Papa won't be home until about seven. Why don't you pour yourself some compote and go and keep Nana company?"

Bela got up and reached for a couple of glasses from the cupboard above the sink. She found a half-empty jar of homemade blackcurrant compote sitting in the fridge, poured some into the glasses and went through to the back room.

Nana was sitting in her favourite chair, one eye on the television while she knitted away at some garment or other. She had the television on almost constantly, though usually just for the comfort of the background noise. Bela placed the other glass of compote on a coaster on the table beside her grandmother and sat down in the chair opposite. The compote was sweet and tasted delicious. She let out another sigh. She must stop doing that; she was beginning to sound like an old woman.

"Sell many phones today, *si dakhe*?" Nana asked.

"Seventeen today, Nana. My boss was pleased."

Nana nodded and went back to her knitting. Bela sighed again. Seventeen mobile phones? What was the point of that? Would her life would ever be exciting or meaningful?

"Michael!" Jane Gregory called up the stairs to her twenty-four-year-old son. "If you and your dad don't go now, you're going to miss the plane!"

"Coming, Mum!" Michael stuffed the last of his clothes into his suitcase and shoved it down hard. He struggled with the zip, but eventually got it closed. He took one last glance around the room. It hadn't changed much in the five years since he'd first left for university; it was still littered with souvenirs and memorabilia of his life to date. He glanced at the matriculation photograph of the first-year students at his college at Oxford. There he was in the second row, a young and eager fresher, about to embark on his degree in Spanish and Philosophy.

"Don't you think that's a bit of a strange combination, love?" his mum had said when he first suggested it. No, he had absolutely loved it.

He ran his hands along the books on the shelf underneath: Aristotle's Nicomachean Ethics, Descartes, Locke, his large Spanish dictionary, Gabriel Garcia Marquez. He traced his fingers down the spine of the copy of Miguel de Cervantes's Don Quixote which had been his prize book when he'd left his boys' grammar school. Next to it were the pan pipes he'd bought at the market in Cuzco on his third year abroad, and the memory made him look up to the framed photo on the wall of himself and his friend Mark against the iconic backdrop of Machu Picchu, jubilant at having just finished hiking the Inca Trail. He smiled, his heart beating faster at the thought of this next adventure upon which he was about to embark.

Yet there was still something tugging at his heartstrings here at home. He paused as his eyes fell on a photo of him and his sister Claire, taken one summer on holiday in Cornwall before the accident. She must have been about four. He was almost five years older, his arm wrapped around her, every bit the protective, older brother. Her eyes were looking up at him rather than at the camera as she licked her ice cream.

"Michael!" Jane's yells were getting more urgent now. Michael swung his hand-luggage bag onto his shoulder, grabbed his suitcase, and bounded down the stairs.

"You've got your passport and your tickets?"

"Yes, Mum."

"You're sure you haven't forgotten anything?"

"No, Mum. Stop worrying and give me a hug!"

Jane's expression softened. She wouldn't be seeing her only son for at least another six months, probably longer. She pulled him into a tight hug.

"You know we'll be praying for you every day." She pushed him away a little, but still held tightly onto his arms as she looked him in the eyes. "Don't do anything stupid. Be careful, and call us as soon as you can." Her eyes glistened as the first of the tears began its descent down her cheek.

"Of course, Mum." Michael forced back the lump that was forming in his throat. He turned to his sister, reached down, and gave her a hug.

"You take care of Mum, okay?"

Claire looked up at him, raised her eyebrows, and rolled her big, blue eyes. "Don't worry about us, we'll be fine. Just bring me back some souvenirs, okay?"

"Okay."

Michael was silent for the first ten minutes of the journey to the airport. He gazed out of the window, watching seemingly endless green fields lined with trees and hedgerows pass by. He was doing the right thing, wasn't he? Leaving his family. Leaving Claire. He felt guilty when he was travelling, like he didn't deserve to have these kinds of adventures, visiting other countries and cultures. He was grateful for his trust fund that enabled him to spend time doing what he loved. Not every potential PhD student could afford a year abroad to gather their research data, and he was keenly aware that his privileged background gave him an advantage others didn't have. But that wasn't the only reason he felt guilty.

He checked the front pocket of his rucksack once more for his passport and plane tickets. There they were, next to his Bible and his Russian phrasebook. He laughed a little as he thought of all the hours he'd clocked up trying to learn this difficult language. Spanish had been a lot easier!

His dad heard him laugh and glanced over. "Who'd have thought it, hey? Russia, of all places! I can't say I've ever wanted to go there for a holiday, although people say St Petersburg is quite an impressive city."

"Do you think you and Mum might come and visit me?" Michael asked tentatively.

"Oh, I don't know. We'll think about it."

Michael watched his dad at the steering wheel, his hands dutifully in the ten-to-two position. He knew his parents wouldn't come. It would be difficult anyway, with Claire. Suddenly, the familiar doubts and the feeling of loneliness rose up again in his gut. He knew no one in Russia. What was he doing, leaving everyone he loved behind?

I will be with you, son.

There it was again, the familiar, comforting voice of God's Spirit inside him. Michael turned and looked out of the window once more, his heart strengthened. God had a plan for his life. God would watch over him. He didn't need to fear the unknown. It wouldn't be long before the landscape of Russia would become as familiar to him as that of the green, rolling hills of the English countryside.

Papa hadn't shown up for dinner after all. He'd had to meet some colleagues in town, Mama had said in her resigned voice. It was something that happened often and was to be expected, given his important role in the regional government. Uncle Artur would show up later, no doubt, swaggering unsteadily on his feet, his eyes glazed over and his breath stinking of vodka. Bela missed the old Uncle Artur, the one who used to take her to the mountains. The one who smiled at her and told her stories. The one who brought back sweets from his job at the confectionary factory and delighted to see his niece's eyes light up each time he handed them to her. He was the one who had taught her how to light a fire and how to cook *shashlik*. Now, he was just the family embarrassment, the black sheep that they tried to hide away when any guests came to visit. As for Azamat, no one quite knew where he was, but then her older brother was used to doing what he liked, regardless of the worry or extra work it might cause Mama.

It had been a subdued dinner, Bela, Mama and Nana picking at their fried chicken and potatoes in relative silence. There wasn't much to talk about. In a month or so, once the last of the frosts had gone, they'd be busy in the garden. Mama would cajole Azamat into digging it all over, and then Bela and Nana would get to work raking it all down and sowing the seeds. Bela was looking forward to that. She'd always enjoyed working alongside Nana in the garden, although it was hard work. Nana was keen to use every inch of space. "Why spend money in the market when you can grow your own?" she would say, although it seemed to Bela that the little money they saved from not having to buy potatoes and carrots in the market was hardly worth all the sweat and blisters involved in digging them up in their own back yard each September. However, it was nice to have home-grown tomatoes, cucumbers, dill, and parsley, since they were so much tastier when freshly picked. The pumpkins were very easy to grow, spreading their tendrils around the edge of the vegetable plot, and the fruit trees and bushes weren't that much work once they had been pruned in the spring. Nevertheless, there was certainly enough work to fill the awkward silences all summer long.

They cleared the meal away, and when all the chores were done, the three of them settled in the living room in front of the television. It was at times like this that Bela most missed Zalina. It had been eight years since her best friend had left the village, and it was hard not to be able to talk about it. There were so many unspoken conversations hanging in the air, not just about Zalina, but about other things too.

Tuzik started barking, and a minute later, the front door slammed. Azamat was home. Mama got up to go and fix him some food. It wasn't long before the voices wafting through from the kitchen started to grow louder and angrier. Bela's predictable conversation with Mama was about marriage, whereas Azamat was constantly nagged about his lack of a proper job. Blocking out the sounds coming from the television set, Bela concentrated on the conversation taking place in the next room.

"I have got a proper job, I don't know why you don't think that!"

"Tinkering about with car engines down at Tamik's house doesn't count as a proper job."

"I'm learning the trade, Mama. It takes time."

"It would be nice to see you making some money out of it, that's all."

"It's not like I need to. Our family's rich enough."

"I'm thankful for Papa's job, yes, but I'm thinking of your future. One day you're going to settle down with a nice girl and have a family of your own. You need to have a job to support them."

Bela smiled to herself. At least she wasn't the only one getting hassled about not being married. There was a brief silence, presumably as Azamat tucked into the plate of food Mama must have just put down in front of him.

"Are you sure you don't want to reconsider Papa's offer of a job at his office?"

"No, Mama. Stop bugging me about it. I'm not the office type. I like working with cars. I'm happy with my life, so just let it go, okay?"

Bela turned her attention back to the television, but she'd lost interest in the programme.

"Nana?" she asked. "Are you happy with the way your life turned out?"

Nana slowly put down her knitting and thought a while.

"If you chase after happiness, *si dakhe*, you will always be disappointed."

"Was life always hard for you, Nana?"

"Oh no. I've had many happy moments in my life, yes, of course. Marrying your grandfather was one of them. He was a good man. And handsome too." She smiled, her eyes taking on the faraway look of fond memories.

"But, things didn't quite turn out as you expected, did they?"

"We must expect hardships in this life, *si dakhe*. What counts is the way you rise above them. Don't forget the good times, and don't let the difficult times quench your spirit. Just take what comes along and make the best of it. There's always something to be thankful for."

"But you make it sound like nothing is in our control, Nana. Maybe there are some things we can change? Maybe we can change our lives and make the happy times come along more often, like Uncle Albert did?"

Nana was silent for a moment, focussing back on her knitting, her eyes narrowed and thoughtful. Perhaps Bela shouldn't have mentioned Uncle Albert. She knew Nana missed her eldest son and his family.

Nana set her needles down again and looked at Bela. "All you can do is try to make wise decisions when you need to, but you can't always control what happens after that. And you can't control the decisions of others. You can try to influence them, but at the end of the day, everyone walks their own path."

Like Uncle Artur. How unhappy Nana must feel to see her middle son like that. How her heart must ache for him, for the troubles he'd had to bear.

Would Mama have the same heartache over her son? What lay in store for Azamat? Perhaps he would turn out all right in the end and make Mama proud, the way he used to.

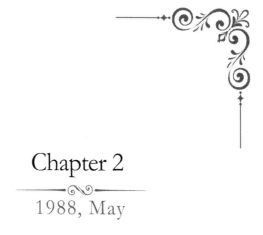

Chapter 2

1988, May

Bela woke up early with a smile on her face and her body trembling with great excitement Today was the ninth of May—Victory Day—and soon the whole family would be heading into Shekala to watch the parade and walk in the town park. She lifted up her net curtain and looked outside. It was a beautiful, sunny day. *Perfect*. She glanced in the mirror and grinned at her reflection. Just another week and she would be eight years old, and then it wouldn't be much longer until her first year at school would be coming to an end, with three whole months of summer holiday looming deliciously on the horizon.

She dressed quickly and went to the kitchen, where she found Nana standing over the stove, cooking breakfast.

"Are you looking forward to the parade today, Nana?" she asked, grabbing a chunk of bread from the basket in the middle of the table.

"No, *si dakhe*, I'm not coming this time."

Nana pushed the scrambled eggs around with a spatula. She added a dollop of *smetana* and a pinch of salt and stirred the mixture again before dishing it out onto the plates and sitting down at the end of the table.

Bela got out two forks, gave one to Nana, and then sat down opposite her. "Does it make you feel sad? Because of Grandfather?"

"A little, but only because it reminds me how handsome your grandfather used to look in his uniform when we went to the May Day parades together. He was very fortunate to survive the war, you know. He was just twenty years old when victory was declared in 1945. Men as young as that rarely returned from the front."

"Did you know people who died, Nana?"

"Oh yes, many. There wasn't a street in this village where someone's son hadn't been killed in the war. Freedom must never be taken for granted. We must always remember the dead and be thankful for their sacrifice."

Nana's words made Bela feel sober during the short car ride into town, but as soon as they parked, her heart lifted again. They found a good spot to watch the military parade as it passed in front of the main government building on Prospect Lenina. Bela was transfixed, staring in awe at the tanks and other military vehicles as they passed just a few metres in front of her. Behind them came the ranks of war veterans, all marching perfectly—if a little stiffly—in step, their faces held high and their war medals displayed proudly on their chests.

During a lull in the ceremony, Bela looked around her. The sycamore-lined streets were crowded with other excited families just like hers, everyone wearing their best clothes and waving flags.

After the parade, several important people gave speeches. She dutifully stood still to listen, but she didn't understand everything they said. The speeches were all in Russian, and she'd only really started learning Russian properly since she'd been at school, something she was a little ashamed of. But Nana had insisted that her children and grandchildren should first know how to speak the language of their people.

Eventually the long speeches were over, and Bela made her way through the park with her family, a happy skip in her step. Papa bought her, Azamat, and Madina a handful of sunflower seeds each, wrapped in a little newspaper pocket, from an old lady who was selling them by the side of the path. Bela munched contentedly on these, spitting out the shells and secretly hoping that there might be ice cream at some point later that day.

The town park was one of her favourite places. There was always a holiday atmosphere about it. Shekala was a spa town, and many people came from all over Russia to enjoy the mountain air, the warm climate, and stay in the *sanatoria* hotels, which were built around the two man-made lakes. Mama said that there was even special spring water available that was supposed to cure many ailments.

They reached the square at the far end of the park, where a troupe of Circassian dancers were preparing to entertain the crowd. Bela grabbed her sister's hand, and they raced to get a good viewing position. Madina helped her shuffle her way to the front of the crowd, where they waited with eager expectation. First came the group dances. Bela loved the traditional clothes the dancers were wearing. The men looked so handsome in their black shirts, tight black trousers, and black boots. On their heads, they wore old-fashioned, square-shaped, grey hats made of soft wool, and over their shirts they wore long-sleeved, long-tailed, grey coats, secured at the waist by leather belts, each sporting a silver dagger. The breast pockets of the grey coats were a series of smaller pockets, each containing a silver-topped cartridge meant to hold gun powder. They looked so proud and magnificent.

However, it was the women that Bela admired the most. They were so elegant and graceful in their long, red and gold gowns which hid their feet, leaving her wondering whether they were really hovering an inch above the ground as they floated effortlessly around the dance floor. Their hands were hidden underneath long, flowing sleeves, and they wore ornately decorated, cone-shaped hats, each with a white veil trailing behind. The dancers' sleek, black hair was woven into two long plaits each, which hung down their backs, some all the way to the waist.

The band struck up: two drummers, an accordion player, a man shaking wooden clackers, and another man playing the traditional stringed instrument that looked a little like Bela's violin but was played resting on the lap. Suddenly, the dancers started to move gracefully around each other in long lines, the men and women passing and twirling round each other but never touching. The men pounded their arms in and out and stood on the very tips of their toes, and the women hovered gracefully, looking meek and demure and never meeting the men's eyes.

Azamat's favourite part was the solo men's dances, which involved lots of jumping, spinning and leaping, and at one point, throwing and dancing around real knives. Watching displays such as this made them all proud to be Circassian. All three of them were learning traditional dancing at school, and Azamat had been chosen to be in a special dance troupe, for which he worked hard after school three times a week.

At the end of the day, Papa announced that he was treating them all to a meal at a nearby café. Bela chose her favourite: the *khichini*, cheesy pancakes smothered in butter.

Azamat preferred the *cheburyeki*, deep-fried meat pies, and Madina settled for a tomato, cucumber and dill salad mixed with sour cream. Bela sipped her fizzy pear drink through a straw. When Papa allowed them each to choose an ice cream after the meal, she couldn't believe there could be a more perfect day.

Azamat stepped outside. It was a warm, muggy day at the end of May. Summer would be here in full force soon, and school would be over. He couldn't wait. He crossed the yard and pushed aside the thin, net curtain which hung in the doorway to the summer kitchen. Nana was dozing on the old mattress that rested on top of the iron bed frame in the corner of the small room.

"Are you coming to the show, Nana?"

Nana heaved herself up and swung her legs over the edge of the bed. She tucked a stray strand of greying hair back underneath her headscarf and smoothed her hands down her faded summer housedress. She slowly straightened her brown, woollen sleeveless cardigan, placed her feet on the floor, and went over to the stove.

"I'm not sure there's time for a cup of tea, Nana."

"There's always time for a cup of tea, *si dakhe*."

"But Papa said we have to go now. Are you sure you're not coming, Nana?"

"I'll stay and look after the house. You go on and have a good time. I'll look forward to hearing all about it when you get back."

Azamat walked back out into the yard and checked that his dance outfit was all in order. His palms felt a little sweaty, and his heart was racing, as it usually did before a dance show. Papa, Mama, Madina, and Bela were just coming out of the main house, and Bobik was on his feet, wagging his tail vigorously and straining at the metal chain which tied him to an iron ring set in a patch of concrete near the crude wooden kennel that grandfather had made many years ago. Bela ran over and patted his head. Azamat never could understand why she was so soft with him; he was just a stupid guard dog after all.

He walked up to the large, ornate metal gate at the entrance to their yard, undid the bolt and pushed the gate open to allow Papa to drive the car out. The gate next door opened too, and Zalina ran out, no doubt to see what was happening. She was all right, Zalina, but she was Bela's friend, not his, even though he and she were in the same year at school. He nodded at her but didn't say anything.

It took only fifteen minutes to drive to the *Dom Kulturi* building in town. Today there would be dance troupes from each of the schools in Shekala, all performing and hoping to win prizes. Azamat's troupe was one of the best, and they were in for a chance of winning a medal. He loved the feel of dancing on stage, holding his head up proudly, beating his arms in and out and spinning round on the tips of his toes. Most of all, perhaps, he loved knowing that his parents were proud of him, as they sat there watching him with big smiles on their faces. To see Papa on his feet clapping loudly as Azamat finished a complicated twirling sequence made his chest puff out with happiness. This year his eyes would also be searching for another person who might be watching him: a pretty girl he'd seen at the last show. She'd been dancing with her school troupe, and he hadn't been able to take his eyes off her. He had no idea if she'd noticed him staring at her, but at least he'd managed to find out her name: Milana. Would he ever get to talk to her? He certainly hoped so.

One day.

Chapter 3

2003, March

Michael stepped through the glass doors and out into the main airport hall. Immediately confronted by a sea of unfamiliar faces all jostling behind the barrier to welcome the new arrivals, he lowered his gaze and moved forward as quickly as he could, pulling his suitcase behind him. Once he was away from the main crowd, he stopped and scanned the placards for anything recognisable. Finally, he noticed his name written in marker pen on a piece of white cardboard and made his way towards the bearer.

"Hi Michael. I'm Cody. Did you have a good flight?" The tall, athletic American shook his hand vigorously and took his suitcase from him. "Hey, you sure travel light!"

"Hi, yes, it was good, thanks." Michael glanced around again at all the signs written in the Cyrillic alphabet and tried to identify some words that he recognised. 'Taxi' was one. Fortunately, Cody, the language school student who would be rooming with him, had come to collect him. At least he wouldn't have to navigate the cluster of taxi drivers who clamored around the tourists, vying for their attention. One of them asked him if he needed a taxi as he passed by, but he held up his hand to brush the man off as he focussed on keeping up with Cody, who was striding towards the door. They walked out into the airport car park and located the driver who was waiting for them. Cody easily lifted Michael's suitcase into the boot of the car and indicated that Michael should sit in the back.

"This your first time in Russia?" asked Cody once they'd set off, turning around in the front seat to grin at Michael.

Michael gave up trying to find any seat belts in the back of the black BMW and returned his attention to the American.

"Um, yes. Looking forward to it though. You been here long?"

"About six months now. It's been a cold winter up here. A pity there aren't any mountains nearby for snowboarding. Still, St Petersburg's a beautiful city."

Michael nodded, taking in the scenery around him. They passed rows of austere grey apartment blocks. Outside many of the identical windows hung simple wire washing lines, clothes pegged and waving in the breeze, even though the weather was far from warm. Snow covered much of the grass verges, but the roads and pavements had been swept clear and gritted. People hurried about wrapped in heavy coats and fur hats. Michael had planned to buy some Russian-looking winter clothing once he'd arrived, so as to fit in better, but Cody was wearing a bulky Western-style puffer jacket, so now he wasn't sure he'd need to.

Cody and the driver were saying something in Russian, and soon they turned off the main road and navigated around the back of some apartment blocks. The driver stopped outside one, and they all got out. Cody reached into his wallet and paid the man before grinning at Michael.

"Home sweet home!" he said cheerily, as the driver left them standing next to Michael's luggage outside a drab metal door. The apartment blocks were built around a central courtyard, where there were two swings, a slide, and a roundabout that all looked as if they'd seen better days, as well as a couple of wooden benches, the blue paint faded and flaking. There were no children using the playground—most of it was buried under snow.

"We're on the third floor. No elevator," said Cody, as he punched a code into the door's keypad and pushed it open. Inside was a dark stairwell with rows of battered mailboxes lined up along one wall. Michael waited a few moments for his eyes to adjust to the dim light, his nose screwing up at the rather unpleasant smells of rotting food scraps, cat pee, and discarded beer bottles. Cody grabbed the suitcase and bounded up the stairs. Michael followed close behind. On the third floor, Cody inserted a key into the door on the far left and opened it. Once inside, Michael followed Cody's lead and took off his shoes in the narrow hallway, hanging up his coat next to that of his new roommate.

"You want to borrow some slippers?" Cody indicated a pile of cheap-looking slip-on shoes of various sizes.

"No, I'm good, thanks." Had he packed his slippers? He wasn't sure. Perhaps he should buy some soon.

The apartment was small and rather basic but not unpleasant. Cody gave him a quick tour. There was a small kitchen, a living room, a rather narrow toilet room, and a slightly larger bathroom with a bath and shower attachment.

"Once you've seen one Russian apartment, you've seen them all!" Cody said.

There were two bedrooms. Cody was clearly already ensconced in one of them, so obviously Michael's would be the other.

The room was a little dark, probably because of the enclosed balcony at the end of it.

"That's full of the landlord's junk," said Cody casually, noticing the direction of Michael's gaze. "No point getting excited. There's not much of a view."

He pulled Michael's suitcase into the room, while Michael dropped his rucksack onto the bed.

"I'll let you get settled while I go and make us something to eat."

Michael gazed around the room, noticing the slightly dirty net curtains, the wooden wardrobe, the chest of drawers with a few handles missing.

Home sweet home indeed! Michael thought wryly.

This was certainly going to be an adventure.

It didn't take Michael long to work out the metro system, and soon he was travelling back and forth from the language school, hopping on and off trolley-buses and *marshroutkas* like he'd been living there for years. There were so many people in St Petersburg that the public transport was always crowded. If he was lucky, he might get a seat, but then the unwritten laws of courtesy dictated that he give up that seat immediately to any elderly person, woman over a certain age, pregnant lady or mother with a child. Eventually he got in the habit of just standing up anyway. If he manoeuvred himself correctly, he could stand with one foot down on the step and not have to stoop over for the entire journey. In the beginning, he'd hated calling out his stop to the driver, since his clumsy, foreign accent would immediately identify him as a tourist and draw stares from the other passengers. But he began to develop a thick skin and gradually got used to the unwelcome attention. It became another motivation to improve his Russian as quickly as possible.

He studied three days a week at the language school. On his first day, he'd had a short interview to ascertain his level of Russian, and then he was placed in the appropriate level class. There were three other students in his assigned class: two Germans and an American. Cody had been moved up to a higher-level class, but Michael was determined to join him there as soon as possible. Michael's teacher, Valeri, had a constant, cynical smile on his face, as if he found the concept of foreigners trying to speak his language highly amusing. His constant use of the word '*Konechna*!', meaning 'Of course!', turned out to be a common Russian habit rather than a term of disdain or frustration, but Michael only realised that after a few days of wondering if Valeri really thought he was completely stupid.

Outside of lessons, Michael enjoyed roaming the streets of the city, visiting all the tourist sights, coffee shops, and restaurants. Sometimes Cody would accompany him; other times he was joined by Katja and Daniela from his class. One Saturday, the four of them made their way to the famous Catherine Palace at Pushkin.

"This has to be the most beautiful palace I've ever seen!" exclaimed Daniela in awe as they walked through the main gate and beheld the impressive blue and white building for the first time. Katja, the quieter, more studious of the two, nodded in agreement and immediately reached for her camera.

After an informative tour of the inside of the palace, during which Cody had drawn many a stern look from the *babushkas* guarding the rooms by illegally trying to skate down the tiled corridors on the obligatory soft slipper covers they all had to wear over their shoes, the four of them hunted out a suitable place to have their picnic lunch.

"So, Cody," began Daniela as she munched through her salami and salad roll, "why are you studying Russian here in St Petersburg? Are you a linguist like Michael?"

Michael had already explained to his class that he was planning to study some of the minority languages of the Russian Federation as preparation for his PhD in Linguistics.

"No, not at all!" Cody laughed good-naturedly. "You won't catch me stuck at a desk with a pile full of books longer than is absolutely necessary!" He gave Michael a friendly pat on the back. "I'm looking to set up a business."

This clearly piqued the interest of both the girls, who stopped munching and looked at Cody with newfound respect.

"What kind of business?" asked Katja.

"Outdoor tourism. Mountain climbing, hiking, skiing, and snowboarding—that kind of thing."

"Here in St Petersburg?" asked Daniela in disbelief, wondering, no doubt, how far it was to the nearest mountain.

"No!" Cody laughed again. "Once I've got a good level of Russian under my belt, I'm planning to head down to the Caucasus."

"The Caucasus. You mean, like, Chechnya? Isn't that really dangerous?"

"There's a lot more to the Caucasus than Chechnya. The east side is a bit of a no-go, *konechna*, but the west, towards the Black Sea, has a lot of great potential for attracting foreign tourists. Places like Krasnodar, Sochi, Pyatigorsk, Kislovodsk."

"Have you been there already?" asked Katja.

"Sure, yeah. I took a trip there last September, before coming here. Amazing place! The mountains are incredible. Bet you didn't know the Caucasus has the highest mountain in Europe? Five thousand, six hundred and forty-two metres."

"I thought it was Mont Blanc?" objected Katja.

"No, Elbrus is taller by about eight hundred metres. I've heard it's not too difficult to climb either. I can't wait to have a go myself."

"The Caucasus are a linguist's dream," said Michael. "There are over forty different languages spoken there, all completely unrelated to Russian. They're some of the hardest languages in the world." He stopped short of explaining exactly why, since he didn't want to bore his friends, but his mind was already swimming with facts about ergativity and all those interesting ejective consonants. He'd sat in on a lecture about it at Oxford once.

"Hey, you two could move down there together then!" suggested Daniela.

Cody and Michael looked at each other and grinned.

"Yep, we've already been talking about that." Michael admitted. He still felt a little unsure about it. What did Cody really think about having Michael as a roommate for the whole year? Was he thinking that he was too boring? Too British? Stuffy? No fun? Not sporty enough? What kind of impression had he managed to give Cody over the last few weeks of sharing an apartment together?

Cody broke into a broad grin. "It's going to be great fun!" He gave Michael another friendly slap on the back.

"I guess I'll have to get used to those!" Michael joked, pretending to be in pain. The others laughed.

Bela rested her head against the window, watching the policemen outside making their way slowly through the queues of vehicles checking documents, passengers, and goods. With everything apparently in order, her bus passed through the checkpoint which signalled the end of one republic and the start of a neighbouring one and continued on down the road. It wasn't a long journey, but it was a difficult one to make when you didn't want your family to know what you were doing. She had told her mother she was going out to dinner with some friends after work, but truthfully, she'd taken the day off work altogether and headed straight for the bus station. How long had it been? At least a year, probably more like two. Angelina had just been learning to walk.

Eventually, the bus drew to a stop, and the passengers stepped out into the sunshine. Bela immediately spotted the familiar face waiting for her.

"Zalina!"

"Bela! It's been too long!"

They hugged each other firmly, then Bela bent down to greet Zalina's children, who were looking up at her with enquiring eyes.

"How you've both grown! How old are you now?"

"Adam's five, and Angelina's three," Zalina answered for them. Bela gave them each a hug and a kiss and then produced two identical bags of sweets, which they grabbed eagerly.

"Let's go. Ruslan's waiting for us by the car."

Zalina's husband, Ruslan, shook Bela's hand and took her bag. "Welcome!" he said, opening the back door of the car for the two ladies and Angelina. Adam got to travel in the front seat, his face and hands pressed up near the windscreen with the excitement of this unexpected privilege.

Zalina and Ruslan's one-storey home, which they shared with Ruslan's mother, was modest but clean and well-kept. It was too early for the flowers planted along the borders and in the window boxes to be blooming, and the large garden was also waiting for the last frost to be over before planting would begin, but inside it was warm and cosy and a vase of beautiful yellow daffodils stood on the dining room table. Bela removed her shoes, slipped her feet into a pair of house-shoes, and went straight into the kitchen where Zalina had already filled up a kettle with water and was just putting it on the hob.

"So, what's new in Shekala?" asked Zalina, as she fetched the cups and tea bags from the cupboard.

"I don't think much has changed. There's a new supermarket with proper checkout tills and trolleys. Rumours are a few foreigners have started coming back."

Zalina nodded soberly. "That's a good sign. It's been a while since we've heard of any Westerners getting kidnapped. I'm not surprised they all left."

"We haven't seen many Russian tourists either, since the war in Chechnya. But Papa says that the President is clamping down with a heavy hand and peace is being restored to some extent."

Zalina took the kettle off the stove and poured boiling water into each cup. She prodded the tea bags with a spoon, letting the tea infuse the water. "How's your family?"

"They're all well, thank you. Everything's the same, really. Papa's still working for the local government. Mama and Nana are still busy at home. Madina's still miserable in her marriage, although her daughter Alyona is such a sweet girl."

"Is she at school already?"

"Oh, yes, this is her second year. She's doing really well and gets good grades."

"And Azamat?" Zalina gave Bela a knowing smile before opening a packet of biscuits and spreading them out on a plate.

"He says he's training to be a car mechanic, but really he just messes around with Tamik all day. I see lots of beer bottles and not many customers!"

"And you? How's the mobile phone business?"

"It's really taking off. We're busy every day. But..."

"But?"

"Oh, Zalina, I really don't want to be doing this for the rest of my life! I hate being stuck in a shop filling in forms and restocking shelves. It's just so boring!"

Zalina laughed. "A free spirit like you shouldn't be cooped up all day in a city shop!" She removed the tea bags, sat down at the table and stirred sugar into both cups of black tea before handing one to Bela and offering her the plate of biscuits.

"I love our village, but working in Shekala every day, well... I guess it just reminds me of how quickly things are changing, and I feel like I'm missing out on something, somehow. I feel like an insignificant nobody. At least while we were growing up in Awush, most people knew my name."

"I miss Awush so much. I was happy there, for the most part." A look of pain flitted across Zalina's face momentarily, but then was gone.

"What do you miss the most?"

"Oh, let's see. Buying ice-creams from Rima's shop on hot summer days and trying to lick it all up before it melted. Chasing the chickens and the geese."

Bela laughed. "And trying to stop the boys from throwing stones at the stray dogs."

"Do you remember the *babushka* who lived on the corner? We were all so frightened of her."

"And the village doctor who gave us our injections when we were little. I was terrified of her for years!"

"Oh, and there was, gosh, I've forgotten his name now. You know, the dance teacher at the *Dom Kulturi* who would shout at us because we weren't able to keep in time properly. *Raz, dva, raz, dva!* One, two, one, two!"

Bela clapped her hands, laughing, and then took another sip of her tea. Those had been happy times. What would they both be up to now, if Zalina had been able to stay?

"Do you remember that time when Azamat ran off with my doll?" Zalina smiled, wiping the biscuit crumbs from her mouth.

"Oh, my goodness, yes! It's all coming back to me now!" Bela smiled. Zalina, an only child, had often been round at Bela's house, and Azamat and Madina were almost like a brother and sister to her too.

Zalina's children raced into the kitchen, chasing each other with their stuffed animals. Adam's green dinosaur was trying to eat Angelina's brown bear, and she was shrieking with fear. Zalina swept Angelina up onto her knee and tousled Adam's hair.

"They seem to be very contented children."

"They're wonderful." Zalina gave them each a kiss and then pushed them off back towards the living room.

"And you? Are you happy?"

"Yes. Yes, I am." Zalina smiled, but then her smile disappeared. "I miss my family sometimes. In fact, I think about them a lot, always wondering if I did the right thing, you know?"

"Zalina, you had no choice. You had to leave."

"I know, but if I'd known my parents would never speak to me again, never want to see my children…" Her eyes welled up with tears, and she stared into her tea cup. Bela placed her hand on her friend's arm.

"But you're safe here. And happy."

Zalina looked up. "I know. The life we have here is so good. I'm so grateful to God. Ruslan is a wonderful husband and father, and our children are happy and healthy. I'm so blessed."

"I take it you're...?" Perhaps it was a bit awkward to bring up the subject, but Zalina *had* just mentioned God. "You're still into this whole Christianity thing?"

Zalina's expression softened. "Yes. Absolutely. It's the truth, Bela. It's everything to me."

"You still don't regret it? What it did to you?"

"No, not at all. I had to follow God's call. I had to do what was right." Zalina reached across and squeezed Bela's hand. "I'll never forget what you did for me that night."

Bela nodded. "I promised you I'd always be there for you. No matter what, I'll always be your friend."

The time passed too quickly. After a simple but delicious lunch, it was time to go back to the coach station. Ruslan went out to get the car ready, and Bela pulled her boots back on and took her coat down from the hook. She turned to give her friend a goodbye hug but instead, Zalina pressed a book into her hand. "It's a Bible, Bela. A gift for you. Please read it. I pray for you all the time."

Bela took the book hesitantly. It would be rude to refuse the gift, but she felt uncomfortable accepting it, as if she were conspiring in a crime somehow. Christianity might make Zalina happy, but it wasn't for her, she knew. It was a foreign religion, for Russians and Westerners, not for her people. She looked at the small, leather-bound book. It was unlikely she would ever read it, but she didn't want to hurt

Zalina's feelings. Perhaps it wouldn't do any harm if she just put it in her handbag for now.

Chapter 4

1988, November

It was a wet, grey November. The days were shorter and colder, but the snow would not come for another month. Mama had given them strict instructions to wear coats, hats, scarves and gloves should they want to play outdoors. This particular Saturday was a dull, cold one. Zalina had come round from next door to show Bela her new doll, and Madina had, unusually, finished all her chores and her homework, and was admiring the doll too. It was a beautiful doll, with a painted, porcelain face and silky brown hair that hung around its face in gentle, perfect curls. Her dress was dark red, with a white petticoat peeping out from underneath, and her hat, in matching red, sported a long, white feather. Bela thought the doll was the most beautiful thing she'd ever seen and couldn't believe that Zalina was allowing her to hold it.

Suddenly, the door opened and in burst Azamat. Before she realised what was happening, he'd grabbed the doll out of Bela's hands, and was holding it tauntingly, above their heads.

"Give it back, Azamat, you idiot," demanded Madina, rising to her feet.

Azamat froze for a moment, and it looked as if he might hand the doll back after all, but then he turned and raced out of the room. Bela and the others were so shocked that it took them a few seconds before they chased after him, and by the time they'd reached the front steps of the house, he was nowhere to be seen.

Bobik, sensing the commotion, lifted his head and considered barking and joining in the fun, but he thought better of it, as if he were too old for this sort of thing, and just wagged his tail instead.

"Azamat! Azamat!" they all shouted.

"Uggh! Why are boys so stupid!" complained Madina.

Zalina was too upset to respond. She began to cry. Bela made up her mind there and then that she would get the doll back for Zalina, no matter what. She raced down the steps, round the house and into the back yard. She couldn't see him anywhere, even amongst the apple trees at the back. She did notice, though, that the little wooden gate that separated their property from that of Zalina's family next door was open. Perhaps he'd gone through there. Bela ran through the gate and glanced around, anxiously. She often played at Zalina's house, and she knew their buildings and their yard as well as she knew her own.

"Azamat!" she shouted again, unsure of which way to go next. Unexpectedly, Azamat appeared from around the front porch. Bela quickly glanced at his hands. They were empty.

"Give back the doll, Azamat," she pleaded. "Don't hurt her!"

Azamat's smile was playful but malicious. "She wants to play 'Hide and Seek' with you, Bela. She's hiding, and you need to find her." Then he turned and ran out onto the street.

There was no point chasing after him now. He wouldn't come back until all the fuss was over. She started looking around for the doll, relieved that at least the doll was all right. It was just a matter of finding her. Wouldn't Zalina be happy when she brought the doll back?

Bela searched around the concrete yard, in the dog's kennel and then around the back of the property. She even opened the door to the little wooden hut and peered down into the pit latrine, though surely even Azamat wouldn't be so cruel as to drop the doll down there. At last, she saw her. She was lying at the bottom of the concrete steps that led into the cellar underneath one of the out buildings. She'd been down into the cellar many times before, helping Zalina and her mother store their jars of pickled tomatoes, cucumbers and fruit compote down there for the winter. Strange, though. There was usually a little, metal ladder at the side which Bela often used to get down, as it was quite a jump from the first step to the second. She didn't have time to look for it now. She could see the poor doll, lying with her feet and arms spread out, her hat a small distance away. She would get to her as quickly as possible and sweep her up in her arms.

Bela attempted to jump down the first step, but in her haste, she slipped a little and fell, landing awkwardly on her right ankle. A sudden pain shot up her leg, and she gripped her ankle, tears brimming in her eyes. She reached out and grabbed the doll, reunited her with her hat, and cradled her for a few moments. It was such a relief that she was safe and not damaged. She rubbed her ankle, but the pain was still there. She might be the youngest of the family, but she could be just as brave as her older brother and sister. She didn't usually cry when she hurt herself, but this time she couldn't help letting out little sobs.

After a while, she tried to stand on her feet, ready to climb back up, but immediately, she fell back down again in pain. She couldn't walk. And if she couldn't walk, it meant that she couldn't climb out again. She was trapped.

Bela started to cry louder. How long would she be down here? It seemed like a very long time had passed already. She shivered and hugged her arms more tightly around her legs. She could feel the cold now. Usually, she would have been wearing her coat and hat on a day like this, but because they'd all rushed out of the house so quickly to chase Azamat that she was only wearing a polo-neck top, a thin dress, and a pair of tights.

The sky outside looked very dark and foreboding. She clutched the doll close to her body as she looked first at the grey sky above and then into the blackness of the cellar in front of her. Her heart began to pound, and her hands felt clammy as her mind raced through images of all the scary things that might emerge out of that blackness to capture her now that she couldn't run away. Her cries turned into desperate shrieks. Panic swept over her, and she trembled uncontrollably. She had to get away, she had to, but she couldn't.

"Bela?" It was Azamat. "Are you still here? We were wondering where you'd got to. What's the matter, are you hurt?" He jumped down and tried to pull her to her feet, but she cried out in pain again as her ankle folded underneath her body.

"I'll get help," he told her gently, and in a second, he was gone again. A moment later, there was the sound of more footsteps approaching, and the face of Zalina's father appeared, peering down at her. The next thing she knew, she was being carried out of the stairwell, out of the yard, and into her own house, where she was gently laid down on the sofa. Mama's face came into view, white with worry. Madina was standing close by, looking concerned. Bela turned her head and saw Zalina.

"I found her. She's alright," she announced weakly but triumphantly, releasing the doll from her fierce grip and handing her back to her rightful owner. Zalina took the doll gratefully and then stepped back to make room for the flurry of grown-up concern that needed to attend to Bela and her ankle.

Zalina perched herself on Bela's bed next to her friend. It had been a month since the accident, and Bela's ankle had healed nicely, although the doctor had said she should still be careful with it for a while longer. Zalina ran her hand along Bela's soft blanket. She was glad to see her friend up and about again.

"How's first grade going?" she asked.

"Oh, good." Bela smiled brightly.

"Favourite teachers?"

"I like my English teacher. It's fun learning another language."

Zalina groaned. "Just wait till you're in the third grade. I'm sure the novelty will have worn off by then!"

Already, Bela seemed to excel at school, unlike Zalina. Why wouldn't she? She was bright, endearing, and eager to please. Bela's favourite subjects were history and English, the two subjects Zalina struggled with the most, alongside maths, of course. It was ironic, really, that she didn't enjoy history more, given her parents' job at the museum. Zalina had taken Bela to visit the museum last year, and Bela had been completely transfixed by all the ancient artefacts and costumes belonging to the Circassian people of old. It didn't interest Zalina in the slightest. She was more interested in enjoying the present rather than focussing on the past. Which reminded her...

"Oh, it's the anniversary of my grandmother's death today. I'm supposed to help my mother make the *lakom*. I would ask you to help me, but... your ankle."

"I'm fine, really, it's okay. Of course I can help you. It's been three years since she died, hasn't it? I did like her, she was a nice lady."

"Zalina! Your mother's calling." Bela's mother's voice rang out along the corridor and the girls scrambled off the bed.

"Can I go with her, Mama, please?"

"Alright, as long as you're careful with your ankle."

"Yes, Mama."

A few moments later, they arrived in Zalina's mother's kitchen and set to work, helping to knead and roll the dough and drop the little ovals into the frying pan of sizzling oil, then flipping the *lakom* over until they puffed up and turned a delicious, golden brown colour. Zalina's mother had nearly finished the fried chicken, and she began to make the *ships* sauce by mixing some of the chicken broth with fried onions and sour cream. She dished some of it up into small, decorative bowls whilst Zalina and Bela prepared the first tray: a plate of four *lakom;* a bowl of *ships*; a plate of fried chicken legs, and a bowl of various wrapped sweets. When Zalina's mother was satisfied everything was as it should be, she sent them out to deliver the tray to the first neighbour.

"Let's start at the top of the road," Zalina suggested after they'd put on their coats. They walked up to a small house built of grey concrete blocks and banged on the blue, metal gate. They waited for one of the occupants to emerge. It was a young woman wearing a thick, dark green winter house coat and garden slippers. Her long black hair was loosely tied back in a knot, and she looked tired. She smiled kindly at the girls.

"God give rest to her soul," she muttered respectfully and took the tray into her house. A moment later, she returned with the tray, bowls and plates, which were now empty, the contents having been tipped out into her own bowls, and the girls returned down the street to prepare the next tray.

When all the trays were delivered and returned, Zalina and Bela helped wash up the bowls and plates, and then they were free. They walked up the village road together to the top of the hill, Bela leaning on Zalina for support, and stood by the side of a large walnut tree, one of their favourite places in the village. Before them, in the distance beyond the village of Awush, stretched the foothills of the mountains, and behind those, many miles away, the snow-capped peaks of the Caucasus mountain range. There were few sounds in the village that day due to the colder winter weather. Just the odd squawk of a chicken or bark of a dog. All the inhabitants seemed to be indoors.

"Have you ever thought it strange how much we focus on death?" asked Zalina.

"What do you mean?"

"Well, I mean, I loved my grandmother, and I was very sad when she died, but why do we have to commemorate the anniversary of her death every year? Do you think it makes any difference to her, wherever she is? Paradise, I suppose. Do you think offering gifts of food to all our neighbours really makes her more comfortable in Paradise?"

"I've never really thought about it," admitted Bela. "I guess I don't really know much about what happens when we die. Have you asked your parents?"

"Oh, they don't like to discuss such things. I don't think anyone really knows. Maybe there's no such thing as Paradise. Maybe you just go to sleep and never wake up."

"I like to think there is a Paradise. I like to think that it's full of beautiful mountains, and flowers, and no one is unhappy, and there are no chores."

"Or school!" Zalina grinned.

There was a pause. Then Zalina broke the silence with a tentative whisper. "Do you believe in God?"

Bela dropped her gaze for a moment. "I know we shouldn't. Religion is supposed to be for weak people, that's what our teachers say. Mama and Papa say there's no such thing as God, but I don't know. When I stand here and look at the mountains, something deep inside me tells me that there is something or someone out there who made all this. Do you ever feel that when you look at the mountains? There's something about them; I'm not sure what it is."

Another pause. "I had a dream," Zalina offered hesitantly.

"What kind of dream?"

"It was strange. It was so real. I was at school, and there were lots of people around, but I was feeling really scared for some reason. Then suddenly, there was this bright light at the end of the room. It was beautiful. So white! The rays of light seemed to reach me and fill me with warmth. Then I noticed there was a person standing in the middle of the light. I couldn't see properly, but I think it was a man who was also dressed in bright white. The light seemed to be coming from him. He looked at me and held out his hand, as if I should come towards him. I felt this amazing sense of peace. All the fear had gone, and all I wanted to do was go towards the man and take his hand. Then I woke up. But it was so vivid, so real. Not like my usual dreams."

The girls stood in silence for a while.

"I don't know what it means, but it sounds like a lovely dream," said Bela, squeezing her friend's hand. "Maybe one day you'll understand it."

"I hope so," agreed Zalina. "I really hope so."

Chapter 5

2003, August

Michael emerged from the stairwell and pulled his baseball cap down a bit further as his eyes adjusted to the light. He was glad there weren't too many other people out and about at seven o'clock in the morning to watch some strange foreigner go for a run. He broke into an easy jog, and it wasn't long before he'd reached the entrance to Shekala's town park.

He and Cody had moved down to the Caucasus just a couple of weeks earlier. St Petersburg had been a great experience. He'd worked really hard at his Russian, even hiring a private tutor in addition to his class studies. Cody had continued to laugh at him for being such a bookworm, but it had paid off, and now Michael's Russian was even better than Cody's. The two of them had hit it off, fortunately, and Michael had readily agreed to be Cody's flatmate when the subject had come up of them both moving to the southern town of Shekala.

Michael jogged along the wide, paved path leading down the centre of the park towards the first of the man-made lakes. He liked Shekala. It was much smaller than St Petersburg, and that suited him. He liked the friendliness of the locals, the breath-taking beauty of the mountains, and the warm climate. There were so few foreigners here, though, that he and Cody attracted quite a bit of attention. Sometimes that attention was welcome. People readily chatted with them, wanting to know all about where they were from and what they were doing here. However, the heightened police presence and scrutiny of the local officials made him nervous. Of course, it was to be expected. This was a volatile, politically unstable region. Why wouldn't they be suspicious of foreigners? However, knowing this still didn't stop him feeling a constant level of stress and unease whenever he set foot outside of his apartment. He was used now to carrying his passport with him wherever he went, and he knew how to explain quickly that he was enrolling to study Russian at the local university. The officials looked at him warily, as if they believed he was really a spy, but they always let him go in the end.

Running helped him leave that all behind and just enjoy the mountain air and the slightly wild, unkempt nature of the vast town park. He couldn't see the snow-capped mountains in the distance from here, since the summer air was too hazy, but he knew that Elbrus was just a few hours' drive away, and he and Cody had already talked about attempting to climb it together one day.

"Yes, of course, no problem!" their new friend Ivan Ivanovich had promised them when they'd mentioned it. "I take tourists up there all the time. Two strong guys like you will climb it easily. You just need a few days to acclimatise at base camp, then you can climb to the peak in one day."

They had already taken a day trip out there and enjoyed amazing views of mountain peaks, flowering meadows and distant holiday chalets from the chair lifts on the neighbouring mountain of Cheget. The air had been so fresh and clean that Michael could well understand why people came here to improve their health.

Cody had been scouting out possible places to bring clients, and Michael had been more than happy to tag along and experience it all. He'd bought a stack-load of souvenirs, including a traditional, shaggy Caucasian hat made of goat hair. He imagined Claire laughing out loud at the sight of him wearing it when he eventually returned home. She'd asked him to bring her back something. This would be much better than a set of Russian nesting dolls.

He always felt closer to God when he was out in nature. He breathed deeply as he fell into a natural rhythm with his running and opened up a silent prayer conversation with the Maker of the universe.

God, thank you so much for bringing me here. I love this place already. I feel in some ways that it's a dark place that needs your light, but that you have great purposes at work. I know you love this place too and the people here. Please help me to get to know them and make friends. Direct me to the people you want me to talk to. Give me wisdom. Help me to learn all I can about the language and the culture, and show me what you would have me do as a result of my time here.

He sensed God's presence and God's power, and that was enough for him. He didn't need to be afraid when God was with him.

Bela glanced up as the door opened and two young men entered the mobile phone shop. Something about them made them stand out immediately as being foreigners. One was tall with blond hair and a strong, angular jaw-line. He looked confident and self-assured. American, probably. The second one was slightly shorter with dark brown hair. He looked less confident than his friend, but his face was kind and friendly. Probably also American.

The two men started looking at the range of mobile phones on the wall, studying the price and details of each one. She allowed them a moment to peruse on their own, and then approached them to offer her help. At last, a chance to practise her English.

"You want to buy a phone?" Her English immediately sounded rusty to her own ears. Would they notice she was trembling a little? She stood up taller and tried to look professional.

"Yes," the dark-haired man replied, turning to her with a slightly quizzical look. What had he thought of her English? He paused a moment and then asked in Russian, "What do you recommend?"

His Russian was accented but surprisingly good. Nevertheless, she wasn't going to let this opportunity pass her by. She would stick to her English. Chances like this didn't come along often, if ever.

"This one here is quite popular." She motioned to one of the most expensive phones. Her boss would have wanted her to try to sell the more pricey brand. And besides, surely Americans had plenty of money, didn't they?

The man laughed a little and then admitted, "Actually, we were looking for something a bit cheaper. Maybe something similar to this?" He pointed to one of the mid-range phones.

Bela was surprised that his accent had a definite British lilt to it. Not American after all. She took the phone off the shelf and handed it to him. "Yes, this one is good too. It's a good brand."

She brought out a range of possible phones. The two men thought for a while, glancing at the features of each phone and weighing each one in turn in their hands. Eventually, they decided.

"Okay, we'd like one each of this one, please."

"Great," said Bela, smiling. She didn't normally smile at customers, but their smiles were infectious, and it reminded her of the Westerners she'd met while she was studying in Moscow. She took the phones over to her desk, and the two men followed.

"We'll need SIM cards too," said the blond-haired man. There was no mistaking his American accent, so her intuition had been right on that one.

She found the correct boxes belonging to their new phones and placed them on the counter. She then produced a couple of SIM cards along with a clipboard.

"I'll need to take your details, please. Can I see your passports?"

Both men felt around in their pockets and produced their passports. It took Bela a while to fill in the details of each one, but she was fascinated to look at the documents. The American was called Cody Eriksson. She wrote down his date of birth, quickly doing the calculation that he would now be twenty-six. The Englishman, it turned out, was called Michael Gregory. He would have a birthday soon, making him nearly twenty-five, just a couple of years older than her. She copied down their passport numbers and then asked for their address. She instantly recognised the street, just a couple of blocks away, near the entrance to the town park. Which floor would they be on? Why was she thinking all of this? She needed to refocus.

She handed over two forms. "This one is for Mr Eriksson, and this one is for Mr Gregory. Sign here, please." She liked the way they each signed their names with a flourish in Latin script. She rang the money up in the till, placed their purchases in small plastic bags, and handed them to the young men. "Here you are."

"Thank you so much." The Englishman lingered a little, his eyes meeting hers. She turned quickly to the American, who nodded his thanks and began walking out of the shop. The Englishman followed, turning to look at her one more time as he closed the door behind him.

Bela watched them cross the street and then disappear around the corner. She let out a sigh. She hadn't noticed she'd been holding her breath. So, there were Westerners again in Shekala. Were there more than just them or perhaps more on their way? She smiled to herself and felt a tingle of excitement pulse through her body. She would find a way of using her English again, at long last. She would just have to work out how.

September came, muggy and dry. Children returned to school, leaves began to turn on the trees, and Bela and Nana were busy in the garden harvesting the last of their summer crops. It was the apples that kept them the most busy. Nana had a little stall at the Saturday morning market in Shekala, and each week, Bela would accompany her to help sell their produce. Nana probably didn't need the extra income, since Papa had a good salary, but it was hard to know what else to do with all the apples from ten trees. There were only so many neighbours in Awush that didn't have at least one apple tree of their own, so Nana figured that perhaps the apartment-bound residents of Shekala would appreciate their homegrown produce more. Nana's apples certainly tasted wonderful. The blackberries had done well this year too, and they had a couple of bowls of those to sell alongside the apples.

Bela loved the smell of the Saturday market. They sat amongst the fruit and vegetable stalls. The fresh citrus smells of oranges and lemons mixed with the fragrant herbs of dill, parsley, and coriander. Further down the row stood tables selling cheeses and sour cream, and beyond those were the nuts and pulses. Occasionally, Nana sent her to walk around a little, either to check the prices of their competitors or to change some money with them, and Bela would nod at the people she recognised from their village.

One Saturday in early October, Papa and Uncle Artur decided it was time to harvest the grapes from the vine in the front yard. It was a family affair. The men balanced on their ladders and carefully cut down every bunch. Mama took them and laid them out on a sheet of plastic on the ground. Bela and Nana's role was to pluck each individual grape from the stalk and place it into the grape-press. This was a long and arduous job, so Nana hummed a little as she worked. Bela sat mostly in silence, though she wasn't unhappy. It was good to be together as a family. Well, without Madina, of course. And Azamat was, unsurprisingly, nowhere to be found.

Mama helped out where she could in the beginning, but eventually, she needed to go inside and make a start on the midday meal. Papa and Uncle Artur would keep working until it was all done, and the grape vine would be pruned back so drastically that Bela always wondered how it survived each winter. But by the beginning of the following summer, its large leaves would stretch out again and provide welcome shade for Tuzik and anyone else sitting out in that part of the yard.

When she was little, Bela had loved working alongside her father picking the grapes. It was so rare that she got to see him in ordinary work clothes during the day, getting his hands dirty and stained purple. He seemed to enjoy it too, as if the true Papa had emerged from his official, important cocoon and was enjoying fluttering around in the light, free from the usual cares and worries. In those moments, Bela glimpsed how Papa must have been as a boy, running around the village with his brothers, chasing stray dogs and kicking stones. Now that she knew him better, knew what he had done, the kind of man he was, that innocent closeness and infantile admiration had gone, but he was still her Papa and there was still that familiar bond.

They worked hard all day, plucking and squeezing the grapes, taking turns to crank the handle on the old wooden press and see the liquid pour out into the buckets. By the time it started getting dark, they had filled two large, plastic barrels. Papa carefully measured out the amount of sugar and stirred it into the grape juice with a long, wooden paddle, while Bela and Nana swept up the debris from under the grape vines. The barrels were left to begin the fermentation process, and the happy party celebrated with a rigorous washing of hands and welcome cup of tea. There would be more work to do in a few weeks' time, transferring the wine into glass containers and storing them in the cellar, but for now they had done all they could do. Mama produced a celebratory layered honey cake she'd bought from the market first thing that morning, and as Bela observed the happy banter around the kitchen table, she savoured the warm, happy glow, pretending that things might, just for one moment, be like they used to be. How they ought to have been, according to her naïve, younger self. Back in the days when she assumed nothing would ever change.

Chapter 6

1989, November

Bela entered the kitchen to find Mama and Papa huddled around the radio, listening intently to a news broadcast.

"Has something happened, Papa?" she inquired. Papa flapped his hand at her without turning his face, as if to say, 'Don't disturb me, I'm listening'. Bela looked at Mama.

"It's nothing to worry about, *lapochka*. It's just some news from Germany."

"Germany?" She remembered the reason for the Victory Day parade each May. Could they be at war with Germany once again?

"The wall in Berlin has been breached. People from the East are flowing over to the West, and no one is stopping them."

Bela didn't really understand either what was meant by a wall in Berlin or the implications of people being able to climb over it, but it was clear that her parents felt this was an important event. Nevertheless, how could something happening in a place so far away affect their daily lives down here in the Caucasus? Perhaps it was important for Papa because of his job.

Bela studied her father's grave face, his eyes frowning a little as he listened intently to the news report. Papa was a well-respected man, both here in their village and also in the main town. They were one of only a handful of families who owned a car, and Papa also had a driver who would take him to work and back. He always took care to look smart and well-dressed. He wasn't at home much, working long hours in town instead, sometimes even having to stay the night, but when he was here in the village, everyone wanted to shake his hand and bring him gifts of vodka or homemade wine. Sometimes, he brought colleagues home for dinner, usually without any warning, and Bela, Madina, and Mama would race around the kitchen trying to put together a respectable meal of fried chicken and *ships*. There would also have to be green salads, pickled vegetables, rye bread, salty Circassian cheese, fruit, sweets, and biscuits, and of course, wine and vodka.

Mama and the girls served the meal, and sometimes Mama would be invited to stay at the table, but the children would always eat separately in the kitchen with Nana, who, Bela suspected, had usually chosen to stay away rather than been made to. Sometimes Bela, Azamat, and Madina would be called in to be admired, kissed, patted on the head and talked about, and often they would be given gifts of toys or sweets, but then eventually they would be ushered out of the room again, leaving Papa alone to talk to his friends.

Bela was a little afraid of her Papa and certainly in awe of him. He could be harsh with the children, and Azamat had received more than one beating at his hands, although probably justifiably. When Papa had had a bit too much to drink, he could get angry and start shouting at Mama. The children knew then to keep their distance, and it was left to

Mama to try to appease him and calm him down. However, Bela also knew that her father was proud of his family, and there had been many occasions on which he'd come home from work and showered them with gifts or whisked them all out for a meal somewhere in town.

Someone else who also seemed to keep their distance from Papa was her Uncle Artur. Papa often invited Artur to eat with him and his friends, but Artur rarely did. Bela knew that Uncle Artur was very sad inside. He'd been married once, before she was born, but his wife had died giving birth to their first child, and the child didn't survive either. Nana said that Artur was still grieving, and he liked to keep himself to himself. He had a good job at the local sweet factory, which supplied a delicious array of chocolates and caramel sweets for the whole region, and certainly kept Bela and her siblings in good supply, but when at home, he preferred to stay in his room watching television. Bela wondered whether he was watching the news about the Berlin Wall on his television right now, and what he was thinking about it.

"Does this change anything for Albert, do you think?" Mama asked Papa, when the report was over.

"No, I think they'll still go ahead."

"Go ahead with what?" asked Bela.

Papa looked at Bela briefly but then got up and left the room, no doubt preparing to go to work. He probably had to have lots of important conversations with the people he worked with in the government building. Bela turned her inquiring gaze to Mama instead.

"Uncle Albert and his family are planning to move to Germany." Mama explained.

"For a holiday?"

"No, *lapochka*, for good. Your aunt has relatives there."

"But why? Don't they like it here? Why don't they want to stay?"

"It's complicated, Bela. They just feel that things are changing. They think they'll have a better life in Germany."

"Oh." Bela let the force of Mama's words sink in for a moment. What did Germany have to offer that they couldn't get here? She thought of her cousins. They were a bit older than her, but they'd seemed happy in Shekala. It must be awful to have to leave your own country and go somewhere completely different. With a different language and everything. To leave your own people. Nana would never have gone.

Zalina sighed as her eyes moved between the empty page in her maths exercise book and the questions in the textbook she was supposed to be answering. This homework was particularly difficult, and she was bored of having to work when it was such a crisp, sunny day outside. She could hear Bela next door chattering away to her Nana as they tended to the chickens. She quickly shut her books and ran out into the back yard to peer through the thin wire fence that divided their properties.

"Hi, Bela!" she shouted across. Bela turned and ran up to the other side of the fence, a big smile on her face.

"Hi, Zalina! Have you finished your homework? Do you want to hang out?"

"Oh, my homework can wait. It's so boring. Do you want to walk with me down to the shop?"

"Is that okay, Nana?" Bela eagerly enquired of her grandmother.

Nana nodded. "Take some kopecks from the jar in the kitchen and buy us a loaf of bread and some butter."

Zalina made her way around the house to the front yard, slipped through the front gate and waited for her friend. She'd had a special fondness for Bela ever since Bela was a tiny baby and Zalina herself was just three. Zalina had no brothers or sisters of her own, and she'd loved rocking Bela to sleep in the little wooden cradle into which Bela was swaddled and gently tied. One of their favourite things to do when Bela was very little was to recite nursery rhymes and songs together. They both loved one about a bear called Mishka who went to collect pine cones in his basket and got hit on the head by one. Bela always laughed and clapped her hands when it was told.

Zalina got on well with Azamat and Madina too, but she loved the way that Bela looked up to her, with her beautiful, large brown eyes and long eyelashes. Anyone could see that she was going to be a real beauty one day. Zalina couldn't help thinking of her still as 'little Bela', but in fact, her friend was now nine years old. She was such a loving, trusting little girl. Zalina, on the other hand, was more like Azamat in temperament. They were both twelve and a bit wild and rebellious at heart. Her wilfulness and reluctance to toe the line was a disappointment to her parents. They had such high expectations for her, being an only child, but she wasn't going to win any medals at school any time soon. School bored her, and her teachers were always shouting at her to pay attention or to do better. Her history teacher had even thrown a piece of chalk across the classroom at her on Tuesday because she was staring out of the window instead of copying down the dreary chalk scribbles on the blackboard.

If only she were a boy. Boys seemed to get away with it, somehow. It was just expected that they would be more interested in wrestling each other in the playground than learning history. Her father was quite open about the fact that he wished he'd had a son. She didn't blame him for that. Sons were more valued. Her duty was to be a respectful daughter, marry well, and somehow find a way to provide for her parents in their old age, since she had no brother to take on that role. She knew her parents worried a little about the future, but they would be all right. The state would look after them, and they would get a good pension once they'd retired from their job of managing the town's museum and its regular influx of visitors. She could try harder to be a dutiful daughter, she supposed, but she wasn't interested in getting married. Certainly not yet, anyway.

Bela's gate opened, and the two of them set off down the street towards the village shop. It had rained the day before, sending streams of water down the stony streets, but today there were just large puddles left. They turned the corner. A few yard dogs were crouched on the paving slabs next to their owners' gates, and in the distance, a man was walking beside a donkey, which was pulling an empty cart. Two elderly ladies were sitting on a wooden bench under a tree outside one of their homes. The girls nodded to them as they passed, and the ladies nodded back, raising themselves slightly out of their seat but continuing their conversation with each other.

They reached the shop, and Bela skipped in, with a happy smile on her face. Rima, the shop owner, knew them both well.

"How are you today, girls?" she asked them, handing them each a sweet from the nearest jar.

"Good, thank you," replied Zalina and Bela in unison.

The shop was small but well-stocked with sweets, chocolate, fresh fruit and vegetables, cheese and *kolbasa*, bottles of fizzy drinks, tins of various kinds, baskets of freshly laid eggs and a choice of freshly baked white bread or brown rye bread, which smelt delicious. Bela asked for what she needed, and Rima carefully handed her the warm loaf of bread and the packet of butter. Zalina bought a couple of lollipops, unwrapped them and handed one to Bela. As the girls emerged from the shop, a black Volga drove past.

"Wasn't that your father?" asked Zalina, puzzled.

"I think so," said Bela, sucking her orange lollipop, her tongue turning the same colour.

"Who was that lady with him; do you know her?"

"No, I don't think so. I didn't really see."

Zalina frowned. Perhaps Bela hadn't seen what she had seen, and that was a good thing. The lady, whoever she was, with her dyed blond hair and bright red lipstick, had been laughing in an obviously flirtatious way, and Bela's father had taken one hand off the steering wheel and placed it around her shoulder.

Chapter 7

2003, October

"Madina! What a lovely surprise!" Mama bounded down the steps and gave her eldest daughter a hug as she entered the front gate. "And Alyona too! Let me look at you. You're getting taller every time I see you!" She enveloped the young girl in a close hug and kissed her on the cheek.

Bela was watching from the bottom of the steps, giving her mother time to make the first greetings. Now it was her turn to move forwards and hug her sister and niece. "It's good to see you, come in!"

The four of them climbed the house steps, Madina and Alyona removing their outdoor shoes and slipping into a couple of pairs of house-shoes. Mama hurried into the kitchen and put the kettle on the stove.

"Sit down, sit down!" She waved her hand, motioning at the table. "Bela, get some food going."

Bela, anticipating this, had already reached for a bag of dried pasta and was beginning to hunt around for some cheese and cooked chicken.

"You're looking well, Mama. How is Nana and the rest of the family?" Madina asked politely.

"We're all well, thank you." Nana appeared at the door, having risen from her nap. She gave Madina and Alyona a hug and a kiss, and Madina gave her seat to Nana and moved to another stool further away.

Madina lived in a village about half an hour's bus journey away, further up towards the mountains, so it wasn't often that she made visits home. Nine-year-old Alyona looked shy at first, but Bela knew she would soon relax and open up a little. She regretted not visiting them more often.

The conversation centred mostly around how Alyona was progressing at school, and then moved on to the usual village gossip. Bela watched Madina closely. She seemed to be smiling and happy, and she looked well-dressed and well looked after, but it wasn't the full story. There was something sad behind her eyes. Perhaps she'd get a chance to talk to her sister about that later, to find out how she really was. What was troubling Madina? Something bigger than the usual marital problems that Madina had been living with for a while now?

After the meal, Nana took Alyona out to visit the chickens and look around the garden, and Mama, Madina, and Bela settled down to talk. There was a pause as Madina slowly stirred sugar into her mug of tea, clearly thinking about where to start.

"He wants me to leave. It's over, my marriage. He doesn't love me anymore."

"Oh, Madina!" Tears came to Madina's and Mama's eyes simultaneously, and Bela stared in shock.

"We hadn't realised it was that bad. Are you sure?"

"He told me yesterday. After years of fooling around with other women, he's finally found one he wants to settle down with."

"What do his parents have to say about it?"

Madina laughed scornfully. "Oh, you know Galina. She doesn't think her son can put a foot wrong. She says it must be my fault for being such a bad wife. I must have done something to make him unhappy." The tears started freely flowing now.

"And Alyona?"

"He wants me to take her with me. He always wanted a boy, I knew that."

"But he can't just pretend that she's not his daughter!" Bela blurted out. Anger at the injustice of the situation welled up inside her.

"He says he'll send money, but he thinks she'll be better off living with me."

"Well, where are you supposed to go?"

Madina wiped her eyes and looked up at her mother. "I... I was hoping we could stay here for a while. Just until I work out what to do."

"Of course, of course!" Mama was adamant. "And your father will hear about this, of course. Hopefully, he can knock some sense into that spineless husband of yours."

Michael loved the crisp, autumn days in Shekala. After the heat of the summer, walking around the town was now much more pleasant. The leaves had turned beautiful shades of orange and red, and best of all, on a clear day, the majestic, snow-capped peaks of the Caucasus mountains could now be seen towering over the city in the distance. It was funny how you could be here all summer and never see them, be oblivious to the fact that these huge giants were standing watch. Only now, after the summer haze had dissipated, was it obvious that they had been there all along. It was a bit like that with God, really, he mused. So many people just carried on their lives without realising that the Creator of the universe was within their reach, waiting for them to see Him fully for who He was. Longing to reveal Himself to them and cause them to marvel in awe and wonder. If only people would look up and see through the haze of their busy day-to-day lives. The words of Psalm 121 came to him:

"Lift your eyes to the mountains. Where does your help come from? Your help comes from the Lord, the maker of heaven and earth!"

Michael arrived at the entrance to the university. He and Cody had registered there a few weeks ago. They were enrolled on a special Russian course for foreigners, led by a teacher called Raia. He still couldn't quite work Raia out. On the outside, she seemed strict and aloof, as Russian teachers usually were, but he wondered if she secretly enjoyed the cultural quirks of the students in the class. He and Cody were the only Westerners, but there were two Korean couples and a few young men from Central Asia and the Middle East. Michael's plan was to study Russian at the university for a year to fulfil his visa requirements but then also study the local Circassian language during that time, with the help of local speakers. He was looking forward to getting started and learning something of this fascinating language. Very few Westerners, it seemed, had studied it properly and knew how to speak it. He hadn't yet got a topic for his PhD, but he would do as much research here as he could.

He followed the stream of students into the building and along the corridors. A local girl, with beautiful, long, black hair and dark brown eyes that were heavily embellished with eye shadow and eye liner, gave him a long, coy glance and smiled. In the far corner, near the door, another group of girls were giggling and glancing at him. Word had spread quickly that he and Cody were here, and within a couple of days from the start of the term, they had attracted a lot of attention. The guys were cool but generally friendly. He passed a couple that he knew and paused briefly to shake their hands and ask them how they were. But he felt uneasy about the girls. They were very attractive, he had to admit. He would have to be careful. The last thing he wanted to do was get involved in a relationship here. Not only did he not want the distraction, he also didn't want to lead the girls on, for them to start hoping for something he couldn't, or rather didn't want to, deliver: a rich, Western husband.

Mama looked tired. Bela watched her mother wearily move around the kitchen clearing up the remnants of the previous meal and no doubt beginning to think about the next. She was looking older too. Wrinkles were forming around her eyes, and there were a few streaks of grey appearing in her fine, black hair. Perhaps the recent revelation from Madina had accelerated the aging process. It had been a week since Madina and Alyona had come to live with them, and the situation with Madina's husband was far from resolved.

"Is everything okay, Mama?"

Mama turned to her youngest daughter and smiled, but it seemed to be a smile that masked the deeper sadness.

"There's always so much to do, *lapochka*. It's been a busy summer. I'm glad we've finished bottling the last of the compote. We've got nearly forty jars of pickled tomatoes too, so that should see us well through the winter, even with a couple of extra mouths to feed."

"Mama, you need a rest. You need to get out of the house. Get a hobby, go travelling, do something! Don't you get bored of just doing housework all the time?"

Mama laughed. "Oh, you young people, you're always so idealistic. There's too much for me to do here without thinking of going away somewhere else."

Bela paused a moment. "But are you happy, Mama? With your lot in life? With how things have worked out for you? Did you ever dream that they might be different when you were my age?"

"Maybe. But dreams rarely come true, I've had to learn that." Mama sat down at the table and looked at her dishcloth. She seemed to be thinking of something from her past, something that was troubling her, maybe.

"Did you... Did you think that things with Papa would have been different?"

"Your Papa is a respected man and provides wonderfully for our family. I'm happy with that."

"But did you ever think when you married him that... that he would cheat on you?"

Mama flashed Bela a look of anger and annoyance. "I don't think it's respectful to talk about that, Bela. He's a good father to you; you should be thankful."

"I know, I know, but... I'm scared, Mama. I'm scared that if I get married, then the same thing will happen to me. I look around me, and I don't see many happy marriages. Perhaps they're happy on the surface, like you pretend to be, but underneath... I know that Papa's not the only husband that cheats on his wife. And look at Madina's marriage."

Mama's eyes softened and filled with compassion and concern. "I don't want to lie to you, Bela; marriage is hard. And yes, you don't know if your husband is going to be faithful or not. In fact, some men are even openly beginning to take a second wife these days. But you have to learn that it's just part of life. Marriage gives you security and social standing, and most importantly, children. I don't regret marrying your father for one moment, especially since it meant I could have you and Madina and Azamat. Children are everything, Bela. You'll learn that someday."

"Did you ever try to confront Papa about it? Did you try to get him to stop? Did you fight for him?"

Her mother sighed. "No, I was too afraid I'd lose him. I felt it was better to turn a blind eye. Oh, he knew that I knew, but if I didn't make a fuss about it, then I felt pretty sure that his affairs would never go any further. Divorcing me would have hurt him as much as it would have hurt me."

"And so, you resigned yourself to cooking his meals and washing his clothes and keeping his house for him." Bela pursed her lips and furrowed her brows, her stomach knotted inside her. Was this the lot of all women? Would this be her life too? Perhaps it was better never to marry at all. As she allowed her mind to dwell on this, the old feelings of betrayal and anger began to resurface as she thought back to that day that seemed to change everything for her. The day when the wall that had been keeping her safe and innocent had come crashing down and revealed what the world outside was really like.

Chapter 8

1991, November

Life was changing all around them. The great lime, sycamore and horse chestnut trees that lined the avenues in the town park had been turning into a blaze of reds and oranges, yellows and browns; and now, as if in sympathy, were shedding their leaves like tears along the paths and pavements. A younger Bela would have been tempted to play in the large, crunchy piles where some park employee had diligently swept the leaves away from the path, but today this eleven-year-old Bela hurried past them without a glance, clutching her violin case in one hand and her bag of music scores in the other. Just as these tall, silent occupants of the town park had been casting off their possessions, leaving behind bare, empty branches, so the shops in town had been doing the same thing. Goods were being snapped up and not replaced, leaving bare, empty shelves. Papa went to work each day with a worried frown on his face, and Mama struggled to feed everyone in the house with her diminishing supply of provisions. They were lucky that out in the village of Awush they were able to grow and bottle their own fruit and vegetables, but the queues for bread at the local shop were growing longer, and on a few occasions, the shelf had been utterly empty by the time Bela reached the front. Rima would give her a sad, apologetic shrug as Bela placed her coins back in her pocket and turned to walk away.

There were rumours of more people being laid off from work, and Uncle Artur had reported that it looked like the sweet factory, where he'd worked for twenty-one years, ever since he'd left school, might even close down completely. Bela noticed that he had been trying to wash away the uncertainty and worry with an increased amount of alcohol. At first, she had observed him helping himself to more and more refills of glasses of their homemade wine at mealtimes, but now whole bottles of vodka had started appearing, empty, in the yard by the rubbish bin. Mama, tight-lipped and powerless to do anything, had been silently collecting these bottles and washing them, hoping either to use them again or to sell them for a few roubles.

Uncle Albert had been right to leave when he did. From the snippets of conversations she'd overheard between her parents and Nana, she understood that the family had settled into their new life in Germany and her cousins were now fluent in German and doing well at school there. Uncle Albert had found work fairly quickly and the family probably had no worries about where their next meal was coming from or whether there would be any bread in the shops that day. She'd been wrong to think he was making a bad decision, she could see that now. She envied them in many ways. If only Papa had decided to leave at the same time, but then that would have been impossible. And there was Nana to look after, too.

Mealtimes were much quieter and more solemn now. Bela, Madina, and Azamat knew better than to make trouble for their parents, and they spent their days busy with school, chores, and homework. Even Azamat seemed to be working harder than usual, as if it were beginning to dawn on him that he might now need an education to be able to have any hope of finding a job when he left school. But that didn't stop him still getting into scrapes. Bela still remembered the first time he'd come home from school with a black eye. Mama had questioned him about it, but he'd just shrugged his shoulders and stayed quiet, looking down at the floor. Later, when Bela had asked him what had happened, Azamat had explained that boys were supposed to be tough and fight. Just like boys with well-respected fathers who worked in the government offices didn't need to worry too much about their grades, he had implied.

Until now, that is.

Bela looked up at the large white building that stood proudly on the other side of the main street, opposite the entrance to the park, which was marked by a large statue of Lenin and a series of fountains. Papa worked there during the week, although she couldn't say which floor his office was on. Or what exactly it was that he did. She turned to look down the long, broad road, lined with lime trees, waiting for her bus to appear to take her back to the village. Prospect Lenina ran the whole length of Shekala, from the train station at one end far into the distance towards the mountains at the other end, as if to propel the tourists and holidaymakers as quickly as possible straight to their desired destination of forest views, clean mountain air, and health-promoting *sanatoria* hotels. There had been noticeably fewer visitors this summer. Everyone had been talking about it, and a few hotels had even started boarding up their windows.

Bela shivered as a gust of wind caught hold of her and made her pull her woollen coat closer around her neck. Winter was coming. At least that meant that there wasn't much work to do in the garden at home. The potatoes and carrots had all been dug up, the tomatoes and cucumbers had been pickled and sealed in large glass jars, and the grapes were fermenting in enormous barrels in the cellar, slowly turning into next year's homemade wine. A few apples were still falling from the apple trees, and of course the chickens and the cow still needed feeding and looking after. Recently, Bela had noticed that there were fewer and fewer cows joining the cowherd each morning because their owners had had no choice but to sell them for less than half the price that they would have reached just a year earlier.

The bus arrived. Bela jostled on board with a crowd of other schoolchildren, women carrying market bags, and men with their black caps and briefcases. She recognised a couple of friends who'd been with her at the music school that afternoon and nodded to them, but they were too far away and the bus too crowded to allow for conversation. Bela steadied herself on her feet, leaning against the railing of the seat behind her and holding onto the pole in front. She tried not to lurch into her fellow passengers as the bus swung away from the side of the road. She gazed out of the window as the bus turned down Red October Street and rumbled on towards the outskirts of town. She saw her school pass by just before the bus crossed over the train tracks and began its ascent towards Awush.

After a meagre and disappointing lunch, Bela went outside to give Bobik his daily meal. No meat today, just some bread soaked in milk and a few vegetable scraps. Everyone in the family was having to go without, even Bobik.

It was Bobik who heard the woman coming first. He stopped licking around the bowl Bela had just given him, raised his head and pricked up his ears. A moment later, a long, low warning growl started to rise in his throat. He tugged on his chain. Bela glanced up at the gate, wondering who the visitor might be. She got up and started walking across the yard, but whoever it was got to the other side first.

A series of loud bangs echoed around the yard, the noise rippling through the metal gate right to the hinges.

"Aslan! Aslan!"

Bela stopped in her tracks. Should she open the gate? The woman, whoever she was, sounded angry. Bobik was barking fiercely now. Before she had time to decide what to do, Papa came running down the steps and out into the yard. He looked both angry and terrified at the same time. Bela looked up in time to see Mama's face appear at the kitchen window and then disappear again.

"Maria! What in God's name are you doing here? Are you crazy?" Papa opened the gate a crack and glanced worriedly up and down the road. He must have been satisfied that there were no onlookers because he relaxed a little and then faced the lady again, grabbing her by the shoulders and speaking directly and firmly to her face.

"You have to go. Now!"

Bela could see the woman now and shrank back behind Bobik's kennel so as not to be seen. The woman was tall and slim, with dyed blond hair. She looked Russian and was well-dressed. She immediately and defiantly shook herself free from Papa's grasp.

"I need money, Aslan." She had a wild look about her that was both accusatory but desperate. "You promised to look after me and Pavlik. I need money! It's all gone. All my savings, everything, gone."

"Hush now," Papa responded, lowering his voice and removing his hands from her shoulders. He was half inside the gate and half out on the street, and clearly couldn't decide whether to bring the woman into the yard or leave her outside. He glanced again up and down the street.

"We'll talk about this later. This is not a good time."

"It's never a good time, Aslan. I'm fed up of waiting for you to come. I've got Pavlik to think about. How am I going to feed him? He needs new clothes and…" The lady finally broke down and sobbed. Bela backed even further behind the kennel, feeling very awkward that she was witnessing all of this. She ignored the myriad of questions beginning to run through her mind and just watched and listened. It was then that she noticed the small boy clinging to the lady's leg, terrified. He couldn't have been more than about two years old.

"Let me speak to Boris," her father suggested, now trying to gently push the woman back onto the street. "Perhaps he can give you an advance on your pay check."

"Pay check?" The woman paused in her sobbing to let out a cynical laugh. "I guess you haven't heard. Boris let me go. He let all of us go. Says he can't afford to pay us anymore. I don't have a job, Aslan. There's no money. You promised. Don't I mean anything to you? Or were you just taking advantage of me? Having a little bit of fun." Now her eyes were burning with anger and contempt.

Papa got angry and became more forceful. His voice rose, and his eyes flashed in response to the woman's goading.

"I said this is not the time, Maria. You must go. Now." Bela saw Papa pull some money out of his pocket.

"Take this. I'll drive you home, but you must never, never come to my house again, do you understand?"

The woman made no acknowledgment but grabbed the money and stuffed it quickly into her handbag.

Papa stepped out onto the street, grabbed the woman's arm firmly and steered her and the small boy towards the side of the gate, now out of Bela's view. Stepping back inside the yard, he closed the gate behind him and quickly ran around to the door leading to the garage. Bela heard him open the garage door. There was more muffled, angry talking, the car door slammed, then the engine revved to life and the car tyres crunched on the gravel. After a moment or two, Bela left her hiding place and crept into the garage just in time to witness Papa's car disappear around the corner.

She closed the doors quietly and allowed the disturbing thoughts that were whirring around her mind to speak up now. Papa had another lady. Her name was Maria, and Papa had promised to look after her and was giving her money. But there was something else, something she wasn't quite ready to deal with yet. Maria had a son. Papa's son? Which meant... her mind reeled at the truth dawning on her.

She had a half-brother?

A half-brother she had known nothing about.

She walked back up to the front steps of the house, glancing up at the kitchen window. Mama's pale face had reappeared, and she was staring blankly in the direction of the front gate.

Chapter 9

2003, November

Bela hurried through the town park on her way to work. She was going to be late for work, and she didn't like being late. She pulled the collar of her coat closer around her neck and hurried on. The air was chill and crisp, and she could see her breath in front of her. The leaves were almost gone now on the trees, but the first snows had yet to fall.

She pushed open the door and was surprised to see her co-worker Zulieta behind the counter.

"You're late," Zulieta remarked tersely.

"The *marshroutka* broke down," Bela explained, hanging up her coat and scarf and taking her place by the till. "Where's Diana?"

"Didn't you hear? She's been made manager." Zulieta nodded towards the small room off to the side, where, sure enough, Diana was arranging piles of paper on her new desk. Bela was astonished. Diana had been hired after her, and she was much less qualified.

"How? Why?" she stammered.

Zulieta glanced around, leaned in towards Bela and announced in a whisper, "Her father was in here yesterday talking to Irina Petrovna, and the next thing I knew, Diana was being called in to see Irina, and they were smiling and shaking hands like they were long-lost cousins."

Bela nodded and sighed. She had a good idea of what might have made Irina suddenly warm to Diana, who'd never been a very competent salesgirl. She could easily ask Papa to make Irina Petrovna a visit too, on her behalf, but she dismissed that temptation quickly. She wanted a job on her own merits, not because her father was in government, or because of any little 'gifts' he might be able to offer. He was probably the reason she'd got the job in the first place, she knew that, but she was determined to make it the rest of the way on her own. It just seemed so unfair. All that hard work at school, studying hard to get the top grades by her own efforts and no one else's, and then the year she'd studied at Moscow university. If it wasn't for… Well, there was no point dwelling on all that again. She'd ended up having to return to Shekala while her student friends had carried on with their degrees in Moscow. Most of them were now graduates able to chase wealthy jobs in multinational corporations. If she'd been able to stay in school, she could be making trips to Europe right now, entertaining rich clients and using her English.

The bell on the door tinkled to announce a customer, breaking her reverie. She put on her professional pose and went out to try to make a sale. This was her life now, and she just had to live with it.

Michael walked into the living room carrying a bowl of microwaved popcorn. There were eight guys and three girls there, all crowded around the small coffee table, chatting happily. He and Cody had been trying to get to know some of their fellow students a bit better, as well as other locals they'd met around town. Cody also wanted to identify any potential partners for his tourist business. He would need local guides and drivers, as well as people to man a local office and liaise with the authorities about granting invitations for tourist visas. He wanted capable people whom he could trust and get on well with.

Michael looked around the room at the people who'd come. The three girls were all dressed a little provocatively in their tight jeans and low-cut tops. They were all wearing a lot more makeup than he was used to seeing on girls back home in England, but although he questioned whether their motives for being here were entirely innocent, they were just wearing what all local girls of student age seemed to wear here. He inadvertently caught the eye of one of them, Larissa, and quickly glanced away.

The young men were all grouped around Cody and laughing. Cody had a real knack of drawing people to himself and making them feel at ease. Some of the guys looked strong and street-wise. He wouldn't want to get on the wrong side of any of them, but for now, they were giving all the indications that he and Cody were accepted into their inner friendship circle. Michael also had an ulterior motive for wanting to get to know these guys. He was looking for a potential language helper. He would need someone who knew their mother tongue of Circassian well enough to help him navigate through the initial stages of trying to make sense on the alphabet and verb structure, although he doubted whether they'd be able to explain how their language actually worked. Few native speakers could.

One of the young men was someone he didn't recognise. He set down the bowl of popcorn on the coffee table and held out his hand.

"Hi, I'm Michael."

The young man looked up. He shook Michael's hand a little shyly. "Azamat."

"Are you studying at the university?" Michael asked.

"No, I lift weights with Cody at the gym. I came with Vadim," he replied, pointing with his chin in the direction of the tough-looking guy on the sofa.

Michael nodded. He'd met Vadim once or twice already. He was a big Circassian lad who had a hot temper but seemed friendly enough once you got to know him. Michael wondered if Azamat was the same.

"Are you from Shekala?"

"No, from the village of Awush."

"Oh, how far away is that?"

"Only about twenty minutes on the *marshroutka*." Azamat nodded again, this time pointing out of the window towards the west.

"Did you grow up speaking Circassian or Russian?"

"Circassian, until I was about seven, when I went to school. That's what everyone in the village does."

"I'd love to learn a few words, could you teach me some?"

Azamat's expression brightened, and he looked pleased. It probably wasn't every day that a foreigner was interested in learning his language.

"Like what?"

"Um, okay, like... How do I say hello?"

Michael tried to copy Azamat's words. He seemed to have said it well because Azamat grinned broadly. One more test, just to check that this guy knew the language as well as he said he did.

"And what are the days of the week in Circassian?"

Azamat didn't hesitate and reeled them all off in order.

Michael was impressed. He wasn't about to try to copy what Azamat had just said, but it showed that Azamat really knew the language well. Other Circassians he'd met who'd been brought up in Shekala naturally used the Russian words for the days of the week and seemed to have forgotten the original words in their own language.

"Listen," said Michael, "would you be interested in meeting up sometime to give me lessons in Circassian?"

Azamat looked a bit taken aback, not sure what to say.

"There would be no preparation. I'll tell you what I want to learn. All you'll have to do is just turn up. I'll pay you, say, a hundred roubles each time?"

Azamat's shoulders relaxed, and his broad grin returned. He shook Michael's hand. "Sure, okay."

Chapter 10

1993, February

Mama's voice was angry now, and Bela could hear her berating Azamat for his latest report from school.

"You can't afford to mess around, Azamat! Your grades are falling, your teachers say you are lazy and disrespectful, and there was that incident last week about the broken window."

"I told you, it wasn't me."

"Well, who was it then? Was it Vadim? He's nothing but trouble, Azamat. I don't want you hanging around with him."

"I wasn't, Mama; I was with Tamik."

"Tamik, hah! He's not much better."

Bela wandered back towards the bedroom that she shared with Madina. She would let Mama worry about Azamat. She'd long since given up trying to make her wayward brother see sense. It was a shame. He was bright when he put his mind to it. It was just peer pressure from the other boys in his class that made him act stupidly.

Madina was at her desk. She was eighteen already and would be finishing school soon. She spoke without turning around. "Azamat in trouble again?"

"Yes." Bela sank down onto her bed and picked up a school book. "He could go really far if he just worked a bit harder."

"Well, maybe there's no point."

Madina's answer took Bela by surprise. "What do you mean?"

Madina turned around and looked at her sister. "I mean, maybe it doesn't make a difference whether you do well in school or not. It doesn't mean anything anymore. There are no jobs, no money."

"You don't mean that, do you? You've always worked so hard. You're top of your class, you always have been."

"Maybe I've just been wasting my time."

Bela was shocked. "Of course not! You'll get a great job when you leave school, everyone knows that."

There was a pause. "Actually…"

"What?"

"I think I might get married instead."

Bela was completely stunned into silence. No words came out. Did her intelligent, hardworking older sister just admit that she was going to throw away her chance at a career just to get married?

Madina glanced down and fiddled with the sleeve of her blouse. "I think that Musabi might ask me soon."

"Musabi! Really?"

"He's decent and hard-working. I could imagine being happy with him."

"But, do you love him?"

"I don't know; I think so, maybe."

"Does Papa know?"

"Not yet, but I think he'd approve. Musa comes from a good family."

Bela paused to take in what Madina was saying. Maybe it wasn't quite so unexpected after all. Madina was right, the chances of finding a job after school were really slim, no matter how good your grades were. And even if you did, the pay would almost not be worth it. It just seemed such a shame, that's all. To throw away all that hard work just to cook and clean and raise babies.

Madina looked up, her eyes shining. "Just think, Bela. A wedding! I've started thinking about the kind of dress I'll wear. And of course, you'll be my bridesmaid."

Bela's face brightened as images of beautiful dresses, perfectly coiffured hair, and immaculate make-up started to race through her mind. She might not think much about marriage, but weddings were certainly fun. A wedding would bring so much joy to the family after the last couple of years they'd gone through. There'd be three days of celebration. All their relatives would come. There would be a wonderful feast and music and dancing.

"Really? I would be your bridesmaid? You'd choose me over your best friends?"

"Of course, you're my sister!" Madina reached out and squeezed her hand.

Later that night, Bela lay on her bed, thinking about what Madina had said. She was happy for her sister, but she couldn't help worrying about her too. What if Madina thought that getting married was the answer to all her problems? What if she was simply using it as an excuse to escape the uncertain world around her, the world that no longer held promises of secure jobs and a good income? Did her sister really know what she was getting herself into?

Bela thought of Mama and Papa's marriage. There had been no mention of that woman, Maria, since that fateful day last year, and Bela hadn't mentioned what she'd witnessed to anyone, not even to Madina. In some way, by not speaking about it, she could pretend that it never really happened. Maybe Papa didn't have a mistress after all, or another son somewhere in Shekala. Maybe Mama and Papa's marriage was a happy one, and they were all one big, happy family. Should she tell Madina about Maria now? Would that change Madina's mind about marriage? Should she know that men could be unfaithful? Surely, she was already aware of that? Surely, she wasn't that naïve?

That Friday, Bela came home from school to find Uncle Artur crumpled in a heap outside their front gate, an empty bottle in his hand. She stood there for a moment looking at him, her head tilted to one side, her heart heavy. Poor Uncle Artur. There was no work at the factory and no chance of anything anytime soon. He had no wife to comfort him, just memories of what he once had and thoughts of what could have been. His little boy would have been fourteen years old by now, if he had lived. The same age as Azamat. How often did Uncle Artur think about him? Did it pain him to see Azamat and imagine his own boy at that age?

She sighed and knelt down next to him, gently removing the bottle and shaking him on the shoulder. He was unresponsive. She tried to lift him to move him inside the gate, but she couldn't; he was too heavy. She needed to go into the house and tell Mama instead. It was cold, and it would be dangerous for Artur to stay here much longer. His hands were already freezing. Besides, Papa wouldn't want the neighbours gossiping about this drunken black sheep of the family any more than they already were doing.

Uncle Albert had done the right thing, moving his family away once they'd realised there was little future left for them here in Shekala, although they couldn't have known that the rouble would collapse and everyone would lose their savings. Life in Germany must be so much better. If only that could have been her. It must be so wonderful to travel to another country and experience a different kind of life. Her cousins must be speaking fluent German by now and enjoying luxuries she couldn't afford. She took one last look at Uncle Artur before she went to fetch help. Probably not many people in Germany had drunk uncles lying outside their front gates.

Zalina sat in front of the mirror brushing her hair forward so that the bruise on her cheek would be less noticeable at school. She'd tried to cover it with make-up, but there was only so much she could do. It wasn't her father's fault, really. He'd been angry with her school report again and had lashed out, but she understood that he was just scared about the future. He and her mother hadn't been paid by the museum for months now. There was just no money around anywhere. Her mother had managed to scrape in a few roubles here and there by doing some sewing for friends and neighbours. Yesterday, she'd mentioned a possible job cleaning other people's houses once a week, though Zalina knew that it would be a humiliating step for her. Her father had more pride and fewer options. It was so important for him to be the provider of the family, and now he was helpless and hopeless. No wonder he pinned all his hopes on Zalina getting a good job to support the family. But with her dismal grades, it wasn't looking good, and her family didn't have the kind of money or social standing that would enable her to bribe her way through university.

She'd tried hard the last few months at school, but it seemed that the teachers were already against her, and nobody wanted to give her extra help, not without a little extra payment. She wasn't stupid, just not academic. But then she wasn't terribly pretty either, not like Bela or Madina, so it was unlikely she'd be able to hook a wealthy husband. Besides, hopefully, even *her* father would realise that fifteen was still a little young to be thinking of marriage.

She looked in the mirror one last time. She'd better just keep her head down and avoid eye contact. She touched the spot gently and little sparks of pain stabbed through her cheek. It wasn't the first time her father had hit her, and it probably wouldn't be the last. What did worry her was that his anger and frustration seemed to be increasing. It was unfair for him to take it out on her, but as an only child, there were no other siblings to share the burden. At least he wasn't hitting her mother, she was fairly sure of that.

No one said anything about the bruise at school, though a few must have noticed. She walked home from the bus stop with Bela, who'd been looking at her strangely the whole ride home. As soon as they were out of earshot of the other passengers, Bela stopped and turned to look more closely at Zalina's face.

"Oh, Zalina. Did your father do that?"

Zalina hesitated, but she could be honest with Bela without feeling like she was betraying her father. They'd practically grown up as sisters, and Bela knew him almost as well as Zalina did herself.

"I got bad grades again. It's nothing." She shrugged her shoulders. It was true, the pain in her cheek had subsided, but inside she still felt the pain of what it represented. Perhaps her father would get more violent if things didn't change soon.

"Does your mother know?"

"I think she probably does, yes, but she doesn't want to say anything. We're all tiptoeing around my father at the moment. He's so worried about when the next pay check might arrive and how we're all going to manage."

"I can help you with your homework, if you like. Do you want to come back to my house?"

Zalina smiled gratefully at her friend. Bela had often offered to help her with her homework, but she hadn't really seen the point of it before. Her low grades didn't use to bother her too much. But now?

"Yes, that would be good, thank you."

The two girls walked a little further in silence.

"I've been getting friendly with Natasha, recently," Zalina said casually. "Do you know her? She's in the class above me."

"Yes, I think I've seen you two together."

Natasha lived in Shekala and was half Russian, half Circassian, but the thing that Zalina found most interesting about Natasha was that she was quite open about her Christian faith. Having a Russian mother, of course, it was only natural that she should be drawn to the Orthodox church, especially since her Circassian father had died when she was eleven. But Natasha didn't seem to be into that sort of Christianity. When she'd first mentioned that she was going to church on Sunday, Zalina had asked if she was going to light candles and say prayers for the dead. Natasha had laughed.

"Our church is a bit different from that."

"What do you mean?" Zalina had asked.

"We're just a small group of believers, all Circassians. We meet in someone's home. We read the Bible, sing songs, and pray for each other. It's really friendly. You should come."

Now it was Zalina's turn to laugh.

"Oh, I'm not into that sort of thing. Our family doesn't believe in all that."

Natasha looked thoughtful for a moment.

"I didn't either. I think of myself as more Circassian than Russian, even though I don't speak Circassian much anymore. But who you are or what your background is doesn't matter. What matters is what is true. The more I read the Bible, the more I'm convinced that it's true. It's really changed my life. God has changed my life."

Zalina started to feel uncomfortable. She really liked Natasha. The girl was warm and friendly, and there was something about her that Zalina had been drawn to when they first became friends. An aura of peacefulness. Natasha didn't seem to care about what other people thought of her; she exuded self-confidence. She seemed to know what she wanted out of life and where she was going. Zalina had found her fascinating. But now that the conversation was openly turning to religion, there was something in Zalina that wanted to back down and run in the opposite direction. She didn't want to be some sort of religious fanatic. Natasha seemed to sense her hesitation and changed the subject. Zalina was relieved to find herself on solid ground once more.

However, the conversation with Natasha had continued to gnaw at her. She'd watched her friend closely over the next few weeks, looking for signs of delusion or brain-washing, but she'd found none.

Bela gave her a little nudge on the arm, bringing her back to the present. "You were going to tell me something about Natasha?"

"Oh yes. Well, she's invited me to come to her baptism on Sunday. Apparently, she's going to be dipped in the river to declare her faith, or something like that. Her church group will be there. I don't think I should go; I think I'd just be really uncomfortable. What do you think?"

"Would your parents let you go?"

"Oh, probably not, but I don't see any need to tell them. After all, I'll just be out for a walk in the park with my friends, like I usually am on a Sunday."

"But your father would be angry. Are you sure you won't be found out?"

"Okay, now you're making me feel nervous. Maybe you're right. It's probably not worth the risk."

The girls arrived outside Bela's gate.

Zalina gritted her teeth. "Right then. Maths homework, here we go!"

Bela laughed. "I'm sure you can do it. I'll make sure you get through your exams, don't worry."

"I can't believe I'm getting help from someone who's three classes below me!"

"Well, if I get stuck, we'll just ask Madina."

"It would make me feel a little better if you did."

Chapter 11

2003, December

It didn't seem like Christmas Eve, and yet it was. Everyone else in Shekala seemed to be going about their normal working Tuesday, but he and Cody were doing their best to replicate Christmases from home. They'd even managed to haul a small pine tree up their five flights of steps the day before yesterday. The market had only just started selling them, which seemed like rather late timing to Michael until he remembered that they were really selling New Year trees, and New Year was still another seven days away. The decorations they'd found, a few baubles and bits of tinsel, were also technically New Year decorations. Michael had hung some tinsel around the door frames, since they didn't have any pictures on the walls, but Cody had found that a bit strange, admitting, "Yeah, we don't really do that back home."

Michael was doing his best but sensed that Christmas was going to feel quite strange and lonely this year. He made a mental note of things he should have asked his parents to send: a small nativity scene, a Christmas music

CD, more ornaments for the Christmas tree, and a jar of mincemeat. He'd never really thought much of mince pies in previous years, but now, for some reason, he was really hankering after a plate of them. Heck, he'd make the pastry himself if he could.

"Mince pies? That sounds really weird," Cody had commented when Michael mentioned this to him. Apparently, Cody was missing plates of Christmas cookies, candy canes, and cornbread.

After they'd got the tree looking vaguely Christmassy, Michael had headed back out to the market in search of a turkey. A dead one, that was. He'd seen a few live ones and didn't really feel up to the task of dispatching one on his kitchen table. The central town market was bustling as usual, although not overly more so despite the fact that it was the day before Christmas. At least, that was one advantage to Christmas Day being an ordinary working day here—no queues in the shops or mad dashes to get the last Christmas pudding. Mmm, Christmas pudding. He'd have to add that to the list too.

He went through the main entrance, avoiding eye contact with the gypsy beggars that hung around on the pavement outside. One was a girl of no more than ten. She was dirty and scruffy and was kneeling on a piece of torn, brown cardboard. The other was a young mother who was holding a baby wrapped in a rather dirty blanket. He wondered what the gypsy men did. "Probably hanging around the corner in their shiny, clean cars waiting for the women to bring them the money," Cody had said cynically the other day.

Michael pushed past the stream of people hanging around the stalls selling stuffed animals and school books. He made his way into the main market building. Inside, it was packed with more tables and vendors, this time selling cheeses and sour cream, mostly homemade. The local sour cream, or *smetana,* was really delicious, he'd discovered. The local cheese was more of an acquired taste. It was a large, circular shape, a lot whiter in colour than the cheese he was used to, and quite salty. On the other side of the room were the honey sellers. The locally-made honey was so much more delicious than shop-bought honey, and he often enjoyed sampling the different jars before he picked one to buy.

But this time, he was on a mission to buy a turkey, so he kept walking towards the back of the hall. He soon saw tables of chickens, ducks, geese and turkeys. All dead, thankfully, but still more or less intact by the look of things. Their feathers had been plucked, but their sharp beaks were still attached to their long necks, which hung limply over the side of the tables. The smell of raw flesh made his stomach cringe a little, but at least it wasn't as pungent in this room as it had been back in the sweltering days of summer. Michael had never really had to think before where his food had come from back home in England. It was just a case of popping into Tesco and picking up a package of chicken breast all nicely cut up and wrapped up in cellophane. But here in Shekala, there was no Mr-Tesco-middleman to do all that for you. He found a table selling larger birds.

"*Indyeika?*" he asked hopefully, using the Russian word for turkey and pointing at something that looked a little like a turkey might. That is, a dead turkey with no feathers. The seller, a large, burly woman in a white apron, nodded. Michael tried to look as if he was about to haggle and knew what he was doing, but the truth was he'd never bought a turkey like this before and had no idea what constituted a 'good' turkey, if there was such a thing. He hesitated for a moment. Perhaps he should have gone for a chicken instead. It was just him and Cody after all, and there did seem to be an awful lot of meat on the turkey. But then again, there was so little about Christmas this year that was familiar that he was darn well going to get a turkey and roast it with potatoes and parsnips—what was the word for parsnip in Russian?—and even Brussel sprouts if he could find them—*Brussel sprouti*?

Having acquired the turkey, which was now wrapped up in a black plastic bag, Michael pushed his way back out of the building. He glanced around at the other market stalls. Perhaps he should buy something else while he was here. No, he was tired and it was best to head home. The market always gave him a bit of a headache, and he was doubtful that he'd find either parsnips or Brussel sprouts anyway.

Azamat wiped his sweaty hands on his jeans. Why did he feel so nervous all of a sudden? Michael, the Englishman, had just gone into his kitchen to make some coffee. Azamat looked around the room from his vantage point on the slightly shabby sofa. He'd heard that Englishmen and Americans were rich, but you wouldn't know that from looking at this apartment. The room was obviously furnished with the landlord's own furniture, and Michael and his American friend hadn't seemed to have bought much of their own. In one corner was a pine tree, decorated for New Year presumably, which was just a couple of days away. There were a few other holiday decorations dotted around the room, and, for some strange reason, there was tinsel over the door frames. Against the wall, on the opposite side of the room from the sofa, was a brown wooden *stenka* with various cupboards, drawers, and shelves behind glass doors. Many of the books on the bookshelf looked to be English, but he couldn't read their titles. He'd never been good at English at school. Or at anything else for that matter. Apart from sports, perhaps.

There were some figurines in the display case above the books: a couple of traditional Circassian dancers, such as were commonly sold to tourists. One was a man in a black *burka* and shaggy goat's wool hat; the other was a woman in a long dress of red and gold with long sleeves and a tall hat on her head, her long, black plaits hanging down her back almost to her waist. The figurine looked so much like Milana. He saw her face everywhere, even now, years later. Random strangers in the street, poster girls advertising make-up or dresses. But they weren't her. He saw her in his dreams too, and sometimes it would be so real that he woke up to find his arms outstretched, trying to reach for her, trying to touch her one more time.

The living room door banged, and Azamat jumped, startled, as if he'd been caught doing something wrong. Michael had returned to the room with a tray, which he set down on the coffee table. He placed the two steaming mugs of black coffee onto coasters and put a bowl of wrapped sweets in the middle of the table. Azamat picked up the sugar bowl and put two spoonfuls into his mug.

"Thank you for coming, Azamat," Michael started.

Azamat nodded in recognition and placed the teaspoon back on the tray. Were all English guys this friendly and smiley?

"Before we start our lesson, I just wanted to ask you if it would be alright if I recorded you?" He placed a small, black recording device on the table. "It's so that I can go over what you've said again and again after you've left, so that I can practise after you've gone. It really helps me learn new vocabulary and get the accent right."

"Sure, no problem," agreed Azamat. It seemed a bit odd, but still, a hundred roubles wasn't to be sniffed at, especially if it didn't require much work on his part.

"Great. Today I'd like to start with some basic vocabulary." Michael reached into a plastic bag underneath the coffee table and drew out an assortment of fruits and vegetables, which he placed on the table. As he pointed to each one, he wanted Azamat to say the word in Circassian, then he scribbled something on a notepad. Azamat looked at what he was writing but it didn't look like either Russian or English. Never mind, he wasn't there to ask questions. He carried on, dutifully saying the name of all the items. Potato, onion, orange, apple… This was easy.

After they'd gone through the words a few times, Michael recorded Azamat speaking those words on his recording device. The food items were put away, and a new set of items were brought out. Azamat spoke out the words as slowly and clearly as he could. Plate, knife, fork, spoon, cup…

This pattern continued, and soon the hour was up.

"Well, that's it for today. That's given me lots of new words to learn! Thank you so much, you make a good language helper. Would you like to continue helping me?"

"Sure. How often would you like me to come?"

"Could you do twice a week? Say, Mondays and Fridays at four?"

Azamat didn't have to think hard. "*Konechna*, no problem." It wasn't like he had a regular job with Tamik. He didn't like to admit it, but Mama was right: he was just tinkering around with car engines and not really doing much each day. Besides, he liked this English guy, and it might be very useful being friends with a foreigner. If he went out of his way to help Michael with his work, then he would be able to call on Michael to help him when he needed it. Friends were assets, particularly wealthy friends. If his father had taught him anything, he had taught him that.

It was New Year's Eve, Bela's favourite holiday. She still remembered the wonder of it all when she was a child, visiting the huge, decorated tree opposite the main government buildings, the lights gleaming off the fresh-fallen snow. Grandfather Frost, *Ded Moroz*, and his granddaughter, Snegurochka, would be there, handing out sweets to all the children. This was a tradition her people seemed to have no qualms about adopting from the Russians. Lately, there had been elements of Western Christmases sneaking into the traditional New Year's celebrations. Pictures of chubby, red-faced Santa Claus in his red and white outfit appeared in shops, in contrast to the tall, slimmer figure of *Ded Moroz* in his blue coat. Some shops were even playing English Christmas music over their loud speakers in the week leading up to New Year. She often caught herself singing along absent-mindedly to Rudolph the Red-nosed Reindeer or Frosty the Snowman.

All her family were gathered around the large table in the living room: Mama, Papa, Nana, Uncle Artur, Azamat and herself, and this year, Madina and Alyona, of course. She hoped Musabi was feeling a pang of guilt over not celebrating New Year with his daughter for the first time. Madina didn't like to talk about it, but apparently Musa's girlfriend had moved in with him and there was talk of a wedding as soon as the divorce had gone through. Still, it had been fun to have Madina there once again to help her decorate the tree. Madina had always been better at hanging the baubles in exactly the right place and making it all look symmetrical, in contrast to Bela's haphazard attempts in recent years.

The television was on in the background, of course, airing the usual celebrity show from Moscow, full of glitter and sparkle and the most well-known Russian singers all sitting around tables, drinking champagne and applauding each other's performances. A comic duo, men dressed as old babushkas, was hosting and making people laugh. At midnight, there would be the chimes from the Kremlin clock, the President's address and the fireworks. They always stayed up for that, even when she'd been very little. Some years, if they were lucky and it wasn't too cold, Papa would set off a few fireworks of their own in the yard. On other years, she, Madina, and Azamat would run up to the top of the hill to get a good view of the fireworks coming from the main square in Shekala, just a few miles away.

Mama was busy putting the finishing touches to the food, and Bela slipped back into the kitchen to help her. The salads were the most intricate. Her favourite was the *ovoshnoy tort*—layers of different-coloured, grated vegetables topped off with mayonnaise. There was traditional Circassian food too, of course. *Ships*, fried chicken, millet bread. And lots of alcohol. Papa was in charge of the alcohol, and Bela knew he'd be keeping a watchful eye on Uncle Artur. For now, though, Uncle Artur seemed to be behaving himself, sitting in the corner next to Nana and watching the TV. Mama had ensured that there would be plenty of juice and compote available at the meal as alternatives to wine and vodka, although of course there would be the obligatory popping of the champagne bottle at midnight.

Bela was busy grating carrots for one of the salads when Papa sauntered into the kitchen. He looked relaxed and happy, and come to think of it, Mama seemed relaxed too.

Bela looked from one to the other. Maybe things were good in their marriage at the moment. Papa hadn't been away quite so much recently.

"So, my little Bela," said Papa, squeezing her shoulder as she worked. "What will the New Year bring for you?"

"I don't know, Papa."

"Maybe a young man?"

Bela winced. *Here we go again.* "I haven't met anyone yet, Papa, but you never know."

"Well, I heard that Alim is quite keen on you," said Papa, winking at her and smiling at Mama. It seemed that Mama was already party to this information. Bela put down the grater and turned to face her father.

"Alim? Alim, son of your friend Boris?"

"That's the one. Boris and I have been having a few chats recently. It seems that he's keen to have Alim settle down as soon as possible, and your name came up."

"But, Papa, you can't surely expect me to marry Alim? He's cruel and conceited and has a reputation as a playboy."

"Oh, but you haven't really got to know him yet. I'm sure he's quite a nice, young man. Besides, think about it Bela, Alim is an only son and is set to inherit everything from Boris. You would live in Boris's house, which we all know is very large and comfortable."

"I don't care about the money, Papa!"

Mama put down her knife and went to stand next to Papa.

"You wouldn't want for anything, Bela. Your children wouldn't want for anything. Isn't that worth thinking about?"

Papa's face got sterner as Bela's opposition clearly started to irritate him.

"It's my duty to see you married off well, Bela. Alim is a good choice."

"Oh, and did you think Musabi was a good choice for Madina?" The words just slipped out of Bela's mouth. Her eyes brimmed with tears. It wasn't hard to see how a marriage to Alim would go down the same slippery slope towards misery and abandonment as Madina's had done.

"Musabi is an idiot. He'll come to regret what he's done to Madina. Alim won't make the same mistake." Papa glared with anger now.

"I'd rather be single for the rest of my life than marry someone I don't love!" sobbed Bela, and she ran out of the kitchen. Just outside, she bumped into Madina. It was clear from the look on Madina's face that she'd heard the last part of the conversation. Bela looked at her and then kept on running down the corridor to her bedroom and flung herself on the bed. Why had this conversation had to take place tonight? It had spoilt New Year for her.

As she lay there, her sobs lessening and her tears gradually drying up, she became aware that she was behaving rather childishly. Why had she flown into such a rage? Why couldn't she just have a calm conversation about marriage with her parents? Why was it all so raw, so full of emotion? Deep down she was scared. Scared that she'd never be happy in marriage. Scared that marriage represented the end of what little freedom she had. Marriage would be the end of her dreams, of her hoping for a better life. She had to do something to make sure that she never had to walk down the path that was being set before her. She must make her own path, preferably one that led away from this place that seemed to be sucking the life out of everyone she knew and loved.

After a little while, she heard the door open and Mama came in. She sat down quietly on the bed next to Bela and put her arm around her.

"I'm sorry, Mama. I know you and Papa just want what's best for me."

"It's our job to see you well set up in life, *lapochka*."

"Even if I'm not happy?"

"I don't see why you can't be both. Just give Alim a chance. I know he seems a bit like a rogue at the moment, but he'll settle down. Especially if he becomes a father. Boris and Raisa are good people. You could do a lot worse for a mother-in-law. Just look at Madina!"

Bela laughed. Madina's mother-in-law had been awful. Raisa, on the other hand, seemed like a nice, kind lady.

"Don't be sad on New Year's Eve, *lapochka*. Let's forget about it all for now. Come back and let's have some food. Alla Pugachova is about to sing."

Bela dabbed the remaining tears away from her eyes, checked her face in the mirror, and followed Mama back into the living room. She would play along for now, so as not to spoil the evening, but there was no way she was going to marry Alim.

Not now, not ever.

Chapter 12

1993, June

The day of the wedding had come at last, hot and humid but dry with clear, blue skies. A week had passed since Madina had been 'kidnapped' by Musabi's cousins. It wasn't a total surprise; she'd been expecting it for a while. Bela had noticed how she'd been paying extra attention to her appearance every time she left the house, just in case. It had happened just outside the town park, when Madina was taking a walk with some friends. They had just arrived at the exit, apparently, when a car sped up and Musabi's cousins got out. She had pretended to resist but had eventually got into the car willingly. Bela's family was immediately informed, and Azamat and Uncle Artur— fortunately sober—had gone round to start the negotiations.

Bela loved all the traditions that their people had around weddings. It was important that the girl was 'rescued', if that's what she wanted, before she'd spent a night there, so as to protect her honour. But Madina had consented to stay and be married, so Artur and Azamat had returned home to inform Mama that the wedding would be held in one week's time. Mama's face had glowed with excitement. She and Bela had made several trips to visit Madina, where she'd been staying, hidden, at Musabi's parents' home. Her future father-in-law had not been allowed to see her before the wedding, according to custom. The women had discussed dresses, hair, and other details, and Mama was busy preparing Madina's trousseau. The family would present Madina with a chest of drawers filled with fine new clothes all ready for Madina's new life as a married woman.

The wedding and the wedding feast itself were the responsibility of Musabi's family, so Bela was not needed to spend hours in the kitchen preparing food. Instead she could enjoy the honour of being Madina's bridesmaid. She had chosen a long, elegant, peach-coloured dress which complemented her complexion wonderfully. The hairdresser curled her long, dark hair and placed small jewel-like sparkles in it. She felt like a princess! Madina had opted for a more traditional-style Circassian wedding dress, with long sleeves and a thin veil tumbling from a tall, beautifully embroidered hat.

Just after midday, the loud beeping of car horns announced it was time to go to the registry office. Outside, in the front yard, the music and dancing had already begun, and the place was swimming with relatives and neighbours. The formal ceremony at the registry office was over quite quickly, as there were three other brides queuing up that day, and the rest of the day was a whirl of photographs, fast cars, and dancing. A whole line of wedding cars sped through the town, jumping red lights and honking their horns, green Circassian flags flapping from the car windows. They drove to all the main sites in town, stopping at each one for half an hour or so to drink a toast of champagne and dance a little. When they visited the war memorial, Madina placed her wedding flowers there as a wreath to honour the dead soldiers. Occasionally they passed other brides and wedding parties doing the same thing.

It was several hours later when they eventually returned to Musabi's family home. Madina was made to stand, veiled and silent, in a corner of one of the rooms, where guests would come and sit, chat and stare at her. At one point, Musabi's mother came in and smeared honey on Madina's lips. If she licked her lips, she would be a bad wife; if she resisted, she would be honourable. Bela wondered how hard it was for Madina to resist, but she did.

Outside in the yard, the men had slaughtered a couple of sheep and were skinning them and preparing them for boiling in large cauldron-like pots over the fire. Inside, the women were putting the finishing touches to the salads and plates of cheese, bread, fruit, sweets and biscuits. The feast began. The main guests squeezed around the table in the dining room. Others ate at trestle tables outside in the yard or in another room of the house. Wine flowed freely, and the guests were taking turns to propose long and elegant toasts, wishing good health and long life to the bride and groom.

That evening, Bela danced and danced, and when she wasn't dancing, she stood in the circle of onlookers, clapping for the couple who were dancing in the middle, keeping time to the music from the drums and accordion. She didn't really notice who she was dancing with; she didn't care. Some of the young men looked at her rather attentively, but she stayed near her closest male relatives, knowing that they would protect her from any unwelcome advances. It wasn't unheard of for a girl to be kidnapped at someone else's wedding.

The end of the evening was drawing near, and the dances would soon be over. Bela watched her sister as she twirled elegantly around. What was Madina thinking? She looked serene and happy. Who wouldn't be when they were being presented with gifts of gold bracelets, necklaces, and earrings, as well as money? At one point there had even been a mock 'selling' of her, where the two families had bartered for her in jest. Large numbers of rouble notes had been stuffed into hands and pockets. Weddings were an expensive business, especially in these uncertain times with monetary reform just around the corner. How many of the guests had had to borrow money so that they could do what was expected of them and be seen to be being generous?

Bela sat down in a corner to catch her breath. This is what Madina had wanted after all. The wedding was always the fun part, but it's what came after that really mattered. Would Musabi be a good husband? Loyal? Would Madina be happy?

Bela desperately hoped that she would, but only time would tell.

The car alarm, if there was one, had not gone off. Azamat shifted his feet nervously, hands clenched inside the pockets of his jeans as he watched Vadim reach down inside the broken window to unlock the door. Vadim gave a muffled yelp and swore deeply under his breath. He'd obviously caught his arm on some of the broken glass, but he had the door open now. Azamat glanced around anxiously. It was two o'clock in the morning and dark, but there was always a chance that someone had seen them.

Vadim was inside now, checking the glove compartment. He pulled something out.

"I thought they'd have more than this," he muttered. "Check the back seats."

Azamat didn't move. Why was he here? Why had he laughed and agreed when Vadim had suggested that they break into a car or two before they went home that night? Vadim had often boasted of the haul of treasure he sometimes came across - cash, watches, CDs, sometimes the odd credit card. It had seemed daring and exciting half an hour ago, but now Azamat wasn't so sure.

"Azamat! What are you doing? Get your ass into the car and see if you can find anything valuable."

Azamat obeyed without thinking, though a quick search told him there was nothing there.

"Check the boot," came the next order. Vadim seemed to be busy dismantling the car stereo.

Azamat went round to the back of the car and lifted the boot. "Hey, there's lots of crap here."

In a moment, Vadim had joined him. They started rifling through plastic bags and rugs, but then the sound of a car engine broke through the stillness, followed by bright lights, a siren, and the screeching of tyres. Both boys jumped back, their eyes wild with terror. Their instinct was to run, but it was too late. Strong arms grabbed both of them. They'd been caught.

It was nearly four in the morning by the time the two policemen left the house. Both Azamat and Vadim were sitting on the edge of the sofa, eyes down, hands fidgeting nervously. They hadn't moved from that position the whole time that Papa had been talking to the cops. Papa had laughed and joked with the men, smiling and shaking their hands. Probably money had been passed across in one of those handshakes. But Azamat knew that for all Papa's breeziness, he was fuming inside. He feared his father more than anyone. Why had he done it? Stupid! If only the car had been alarmed, then they would have just run away, and everything would have been fine. For the hundredth time that night, he asked himself why he'd let Vadim talk him into it. Why hadn't he just stood up to him and told him what he thought. Why did he let people manipulate him like this? He was always the follower, never the leader.

Azamat could hear Bobik barking out in the yard as the two policemen left and got back into their car to drive away. Probably the whole street knew by now that Aslan's son had been picked up by the police. Papa stormed into the room. His expression had changed to one of complete fury.

"Out! Out now!" he growled at Vadim, who promptly leaped out of his seat and ran to the door without a second glance. Papa's attention turned to Azamat. The tirade began.

"You complete idiot! What were you thinking? It's bad enough to be woken up by the police in the middle of the night, but to be told that your stupid son has been caught stealing and breaking into cars… you've humiliated me. You've brought shame on our family. A man in my position can't afford to have his reputation tarnished by some foolish, idiot of a boy. How dare you do this to me!"

Thump! Azamat had expected the blows to come at some point, but he was still taken aback by the force of the first one.

"I'm sorry, Papa. It was Vadim…"

Thwack! The second blow knocked Azamat onto the floor.

"Don't you give me your stupid excuses. This is never to happen again; do you understand me? Do you understand me Azamat?"

"Y…yes Papa."

A sharp kick to the stomach caused Azamat to double up into the foetal position. He heard Papa's steps on the floorboards as he walked out of the room, then the door slammed. Azamat remained where he was, whimpering from the pain, tears in his eyes. As his mind replayed the events of the night, a myriad of emotions surged through his body. Frustration, shame, humiliation. But mostly anger.

Later that morning, Mama found him and woke him up. He had fallen asleep where Papa had left him, still crumpled up in a ball on the floor.

Zalina entered the room nervously. She still wasn't quite sure she'd done the right thing in coming here. She scanned the faces of the eight people already seated, but she knew no one other than Natasha. Natasha sprang up, greeted Zalina at the door and ushered her into the room, indicating the spare seat next to hers. Zalina sat down and noticed that her hands were shaking a little. That was no good, she had to be strong and confident. She was just visiting, after all. There was nothing to be afraid of. She never needed to come back here if she didn't want to. She didn't have to agree with anything she didn't think was right.

The leader, a middle-aged Circassian man, got up and welcomed everyone. Zalina studied his face, looking for evidence of deception, but there was none. This man seemed to radiate a peace and assurance that Zalina hadn't seen before. Well, perhaps only in Natasha. Yes, there was something similar about the two of them.

The man, whose name was Slava, spoke a welcome in Russian, and Zalina could tell that at least some of the

Circassians in the room were more fluent in that language than in the language of their people. It wasn't uncommon, and it was easy to default into Russian since everyone knew it. However, Slava then took out a large, blue book, opened it and started speaking. Out of his mouth came the most beautiful words in Circassian. They seemed to touch Zalina somewhere deep in her soul. They were holy words, read from a holy book, she was sure. They spoke about a man called Jesus, who was full of love and wisdom. He called people to come to him. He would give living water. He was the bread of life.

Zalina was transfixed. She felt that this man Jesus seemed to be speaking directly to her, calling her to belong to him, to accept the gifts he was offering her. Somehow, this man knew her. He knew all about her. He knew she wasn't perfect, that she wasn't worthy, that she often did things that she knew weren't right, but he still loved her anyway. She was known and loved and wanted. She'd never truly felt that before. Her mind flashed back to the dream she'd had several years before, when she was about ten. Had the bright, shining man been Jesus?

At the end of the meeting, Zalina found herself hanging back when the others left. She wanted to talk more to the leader and to Natasha. She suddenly had many questions, and, of course, fears too. If this was the truth, she needed to know. She wasn't ready to commit to anything yet, naturally, but she needed to investigate further.

She thought of her parents, her family. They had their own particular view of God and religion, and it was very different to what she had heard this evening. They definitely wouldn't be happy to find out she was interested in Christianity. Religion was just something to be in the background, something that didn't really impact your life in any way. Religion was about trying to live a decent life. As for Christians, well, Christianity was a Russian religion, wasn't it? Brought by the people who had conquered their people long ago. It was foreign and unwelcome. More than that, it was untrue. But what she had heard tonight seemed to make more sense than anything she'd ever learnt about religion and God before. If anything was true, then surely it was this. And besides, she'd heard these words spoken in her own language. God knew the language of her heart. She had to find out more.

2

He will not let your foot slip –

He who watches over you will not slumber;

Indeed, he who watches over Israel

Will neither slumber nor sleep.

Psalm 121, verses 3 and 4

Chapter 13

2004, January

Bela was nervous and excited at the same time. When Azamat had finally confessed to her that he'd been helping a British linguist with his language studies, Bela had pestered him continuously to introduce her. Azamat had teased her that she just wanted to marry a rich foreigner, but she tried to persuade him that she was simply after a job, that's all. She knew she had a good level of English. Perhaps she could be of use, somehow? Maybe as some kind of secretary or assistant. If not with the British guy, then perhaps with one of the other foreigners he must be friends with. She couldn't stand working in that awful mobile phone shop for another year. Finally, Azamat had given in and had told her about a small party that the Americans, as he called them, were having. He offered to bring her along, and she'd jumped at the chance.

Azamat spoke into the *domophone* outside the apartment block entrance and someone inside buzzed them in. They climbed up to the fifth floor, the heels on Bela's winter boots clicking on the steps. She'd brought chocolates with her, since it would have been rude to turn up empty-handed, but was now wondering whether that was the right thing.

The door opened, and they were ushered in to the hallway. The coat hooks were already piled high with coats, and pairs of boots and shoes were piled up around the door. It was good to see that the Americans had at least known to buy a sufficient number of house slippers for their guests, and she chose a blue pair that looked her size. She turned round and gave a little jump of surprise. Facing her was the same British guy she'd met in the phone shop a few months ago. She had suspected that he might be the same British linguist that Azamat had been talking about, but she hadn't been sure, as Azamat hadn't exactly been forthcoming with details about his employer. He smiled and reached out his hand towards her.

"*Privyet!* Welcome. I'm Michael."

She took his hand and shook it. "Bela, Azamat's sister."

Michael shook Azamat's hand too, then turned back to Bela. "You look a little familiar. Have we met before?"

"You bought a phone from me back in September."

Recognition dawned on Michael's face. "Oh yes, of course. You spoke excellent English, if I remember."

Bela felt her cheeks flushing with embarrassment and pride. She switched to English. "Yes. I was glad to be able to practice on someone at last. There aren't many native English speakers here in Shekala."

Michael smiled encouragingly, clearly impressed once again with her English. Bela glanced behind him and noticed there were quite a few young people gathered in the living room and spilling out into the hallway and kitchen. Michael was still looking at her when she returned her gaze to his face.

"I'm sorry, would you like a drink?"

Bela followed him into the kitchen. The kitchen counter was full of non-alcoholic drinks, which struck her as odd. She had assumed that Westerners happily drank alcohol, and yet Michael and his roommate seemed to be serving nothing but juice and fizzy drinks. Yes, there were a few bottles of vodka and wine over in the corner, but she guessed that these had been brought by guests who didn't know better. Her shoulders relaxed a little. It was good to know that the chances of a drunken brawl developing in this overcrowded apartment were pretty slim. She pointed at the carton of orange juice and waited while Michael poured some out for her. She awkwardly exchanged it for the box of chocolates she'd been carrying.

"Um, these are for you."

"Thanks. I love Russian chocolates."

He put them on one side and steered her back out towards the living room. "Let's find you a seat. Here, do you know Larissa? She's a student at the university."

Bela didn't recognise the girl, but she turned to find that Michael had gone to welcome more guests. Drat, she'd have to find another chance to show him how good her English skills were and persuade him that he could put them to good use somehow. She smiled politely at the girl, but one look showed her that she wasn't the sort of girl she'd have much in common with. Larissa's eyes had also followed Michael out of the room, and Bela could tell that she was interested in him in another way. He'd better watch out. Probably half a dozen girls in here were desperate to become 'Mrs Gregory'. At least Bela wasn't one of them. She was after something else.

Michael stood watching the beautiful Circassian girl from the hallway, where he was pretending to be in a conversation with some guys about the latest performance of the local football team. He'd recognised her instantly, though he didn't want to admit to himself that he hadn't been able to get her out of his mind for the past few months. He'd even been thinking of excuses to go back into the phone shop, but unfortunately his phone had worked perfectly, and he had no need to upgrade it. How amazing that she had turned out to be Azamat's sister. He didn't believe that coincidences like this happened for no reason.

Lord, why is she here? Did you bring her? Are we supposed to get to know one another? Please help me to be careful, she is rather pretty!

She and Larissa suddenly turned to look at him, as if they'd both been talking about him, and he quickly turned his attention back to the guys in front of him. The last thing he wanted to do was to give Larissa the idea that he'd been looking in her direction. That girl was relentless in her pursuit and not very subtle about it either.

Someone slapped him on the back. He turned to see Cody's wide smile.

"Hey, Mike. I don't want to be pre-empting my own birthday surprise, but perhaps it's time to bring the cake in?"

"Sure, of course. Pretend like you don't know." Michael grinned. He hunted around the kitchen for the matches and took the cake out of its box. The cakes you could buy at the supermarket sure were wonderful. This one was covered in delicious-looking vanilla cream icing and topped with chocolate curls and glacéd cherries. He placed the candles at regular intervals and lit them with the match. He nodded at the guy nearest the light switch to turn off the lights, and then picked up the cake and started walking into the living room, praying that he wouldn't trip over anything on the way.

"*S dnyom razhdeniya tebye*… Happy Birthday to you…" he started singing, and was soon joined by a chorus of other voices.

Towards the end of the party, Bela finally managed to find an opportunity to speak to Michael. She might not have another chance to put her services forward. Fortunately, Azamat hadn't shown signs of wanting to leave yet, though some of the other guests had, so there were fewer people now.

"I wanted to thank you for taking on my brother as a language helper," she started, trying her best with her English accent.

"Oh, no problem. He's a great help, actually."

"He's been enjoying it, and it's good for him to have some regular money coming in."

"I'm sorry I can't offer him more sessions, but Circassian is such a complex language that I need a good two or three days in between just to process all the new vocabulary."

"I…er. I was wondering if you might need an assistant. I mean, someone who speaks English and can help you type up your notes or anything else you may need?"

Bela felt her cheeks redden, worrying he might have taken her meaning the wrong way. "I guess I'm looking for a job too." She laughed nervously.

Oh dear, this wasn't going very well. What on earth would he think of her? Would he be able to see that she wasn't just another Larissa, trying to wheedle her way into his life? He looked at her thoughtfully, as if he were trying to determine what her motives were.

"You know, I hadn't thought about it, actually, but I'll certainly bear you in mind. Your English is very good. Where did you learn it?"

"Just at school and then at university in Moscow, briefly."

"You mean you've not been to England?"

"No, unfortunately. I would have loved to have gone. I mean, I always wanted to travel and improve my language skills, but…"

"But your family couldn't afford it?"

"Well, kind of. Something like that. It just didn't work out, that's all."

"And you're not exactly enjoying working in the mobile phone shop?"

She laughed. "No. I want to be somewhere where I can use my language skills. You and Cody were the only foreigners we've had in the shop in months. It was so wonderful to be able to practice speaking with you."

"You seem very different from your brother," he said, looking over at Azamat, who was playing cards with some guys in the corner.

"Yes. Azamat didn't really enjoy school, but I did. He's a good guy though," she added quickly. "Just easily led astray, that's all." She frowned as she noticed Vadim was here. Papa wouldn't like that at all. Vadim was *persona non-grata* in their house ever since that incident with the police.

"Look, perhaps I can find something for you. I do need to turn in a paper for the local linguistic conference in May. You could help translate it into Russian for me."

Bela's face brightened. "Yes, I'm sure I could do that."

"Okay, great. I'll be in touch. Can I have your number?"

They exchanged details, and Bela hoped that he wouldn't see her hands shaking slightly as she punched the numbers into her phone.

Their eyes lingered for a moment longer, as they both wondered what to say. His eyes were a deep blue-green, and she felt a sudden urge to brush away the strand of dark brown hair that had flopped down in front of one of them.

"It's been lovely meeting you, Bela." He held his hand out again. She took it, trying to maintain a formality that suited their potential working arrangement.

"You too, Michael."

Chapter 14

1994, April

Madina gazed lovingly at her baby daughter, rocking the cradle gently from side to side and humming a quiet lullaby. Gradually, Alyona's eyelids drooped lower and lower until she settled into a contented sleep, her lips instinctively sucking every now and again on the pacifier in her mouth. As she watched over her sleeping angel, a tear escaped from Madina's left eye, followed quickly by one from her right. She brushed them away. How could her life be so beautiful and so painful at the same time? How had she so swiftly got to this point? Nineteen, married with a baby, and already her marriage was falling apart.

The first two or three weeks following the wedding had been wonderful. Musa had been loving and attentive, and her new parents-in-law had been welcoming and polite. She had enjoyed her status as the *nisasha* of the family: the new, young bride. Her mother-in-law had gradually eased her into the chores that were expected of her, allowing Madina and Musa to sleep in a little in the mornings. But then the novelty of it all began to wear off and Madina was made to understand just exactly what was expected of her. She was there to cook, clean, and produce children.

Then, just seven weeks into her marriage, she missed her period and quickly went out to buy a pregnancy test from the local *aptyeka*. It took her a bit by surprise that it had happened so quickly, but it was what everyone had been wanting of her and waiting so eagerly for. Everyone except Musa, perhaps.

Galina had been delighted, but when Madina's morning sickness set in with a vengeance, there seemed to be very little compassion and concern coming from any corners. She was still expected to cook and serve the dinner, even though the smells from the kitchen made her retch and run to the bathroom to empty the meagre contents of her stomach into the toilet bowl at least five times a day. After a few weeks of watching Madina throw up what little she was able to force down her throat, Galina had eventually persuaded Musa to send Madina to the local hospital. It had been a welcome rest from having to cook and clean, but the sickness had continued, and after ten days, the doctors had sent her home again. The baby was healthy, and that's all that mattered. She just had to be strong and get through this. It would pass soon, she was told. But to her, it had seemed to go on for an eternity.

At the height of the sickness, Madina had felt so utterly miserable that she had even contemplated getting an abortion just to be free from this horrible, horrible feeling. She looked down at Alyona, asleep now, feeling a mixture of guilt that she had ever considered destroying the life of this beautiful creature, and relief that she had never gone through with it. But those days of lying in bed with a sick bucket and a rag just within reach had taken its toll on their marriage.

Musabi was young. He wasn't ready to have to look after a sick wife, or even just to tolerate one. He was impatient. He still wanted to be out having fun and enjoying life. Gradually Madina had watched the look of concern in his eyes turn to that of annoyance, disgust, and, eventually, contempt.

There had been a reprieve. At around six months, she had started to feel better and the sickness gradually subsided, but by then the damage to their marriage had already been done.

When was it that Musa had first started sleeping with other women? She wasn't so naïve as to think that she had been his first, but she had hoped that marriage would change him. That she would be enough for him. Perhaps, in the early days, he really had just been out drinking with his friends, but then the signs had appeared. A whiff of a feminine perfume on his jacket that wasn't hers. A smudge of lipstick on his shirt that couldn't have come from her pale and vomit-stained lips.

She had begun to obsess over proving his unfaithfulness. She found herself checking his wallet when he was in the shower or rummaging through his coat pockets looking for hotel receipts. It hadn't been long before she'd found one and, in anger and humiliation, confronted him with it.

"What's this, Musa?"

"I don't know. It looks like a receipt. Have you been going through my things?"

"It's a receipt for a dinner for two. With wine. Last Friday."

"I told you, I had dinner with Andrei to celebrate his birthday."

"Alexei. You told me it was Alexei."

"I mixed up the names, so what? What, you think I had dinner with some woman, do you? Is that what you think?"

"Yes, actually, that is what I think. It's not just the receipt, Musa; it's the late nights, the perfume, the lipstick marks…"

There was a pause, and Madina had known that whatever he said next had the potential to destroy their marriage.

"Okay, fine, yes, I've been hooking up with a few women. What do you expect, Madina? I can't get any from my own wife. She's at home throwing up in the toilet. A man has needs."

He'd grabbed his jacket out of her hands and stormed out of the room, slamming the door behind him. Madina had crumpled up on the bed, clutching her swollen belly, and had dissolved into loud sobs.

She'd had no choice but to be resigned to the revelation that her husband was sleeping around with other women. All her hopes had instead turned to her baby. Perhaps if she gave birth to a beautiful, healthy son, Musa would come back to her. He'd want to be a family together. He'd be different when he was a father. He'd have responsibilities.

But it hadn't been the longed-for son. Madina had lied to Musa and her parents-in-law when she said that the ultrasound had showed it was probably a boy. She had been so desperate to win Musa back to her again and to regain the favour of his parents. Besides, these machines weren't a hundred percent accurate anyway, and there were plenty of stories where people had expected one sex and it turned out to be the other. However, in her case, the baby had turned out to be a girl, just as the ultrasound had said it would be. A girl! A girl was lovely and beautiful and a miracle, but in her culture, it was the boys who were the pride and joy. Every family needed male heirs: sons who would carry on the family name and care for their parents in their old age. Sons were a sign of strength and virility.

Alyona murmured in her sleep, and Madina gently rocked the cradle again. *Your Papa has barely even looked at you, lapochka.* More tears started falling now. When her forty days of seclusion were up, she would be expected to return to her household duties and Galina would be the one rocking the cradle and watching Alyona sleep. But would she do so with eyes as loving as the baby's own mother? Madina didn't think so.

Azamat sat on the stone wall of the disused building, casually taking swigs from a bottle of Baltika Seven beer, one leg propped up next to him, the other swinging idly below. The sun was beginning to set, and the group of teenagers hanging out in this part of the town park was growing. Vadim and Tamik were next to him, laughing about something rude one of them had just said, but Azamat wasn't listening. He had his eyes fixed on one of the girls opposite.

She was with a group of friends too: six or seven of them, all dressed in tight jeans and tight tops, carrying pretty, little, leather handbags. Their heavy eyeliner and bright, glossy lipstick made them look several years older than they really were. The girl he couldn't tear his eyes away from was definitely the prettiest. He knew her name, Milana, because they'd spent time together in the dance troupe when they were younger. He'd dropped out a few years ago, but she still danced, he knew. She glanced his way, coyly, and he guessed that she hadn't forgotten him either. She turned to her girlfriend and whispered something in her ear, then they both looked at him and laughed. Azamat wasn't the kind of guy that people made fun of, so it didn't bother him. He had the reputation of being a bit of a tough guy at school, no doubt helped by his father's position in the government. He was the kind of guy people were happy to have in their friendship group, although he himself had never been the leader type. He was also aware that girls found him mildly attractive, and this gave him more confidence in gatherings like this one.

He kept his gaze fixed on Milana, willing her to make the first move. Sure enough, a couple of minutes later, she sauntered up with two of her friends in tow.

"You're Azamat, aren't you?"

"Yeah, that's right."

"We used to dance together."

"I remember. Milana, right?" She seemed really pleased that he'd remembered her name. "Yeah. This is Alisa, and this is Oksana," she said, introducing her friends with a wave of her hand towards each. Azamat nodded to each one, and they giggled back, but he quickly turned his focus back on Milana. Vadim and Tamik had stopped talking next to him and were now taking an interest in the group of girls. Azamat suddenly felt the need to stake his territory. He jumped down from the wall and put his arm around Milana's shoulder, gently steering her away from the others.

"Do you want to go for a walk?"

"Sure," she was trying to look casual, as if she'd remembered she ought to be playing hard to get.

He walked her down the pathway, dimly lit by a soft glow from the various lampposts planted alongside. There were benches every thirty metres or so, and some of them were occupied by kissing couples. Milana didn't seem fazed by that, and he wondered how many times she might have sat on those benches doing the same thing. He'd kissed quite a few girls, but none that he'd really cared about. He couldn't even remember most of their names now, although a few of them were at his school. Milana went to School Number Seven, she told him. She chatted easily and confidently, and he found himself listening with interest. The air was cooling rapidly, and as they approached the top of the path, she shivered slightly. He put his arm around her, and she leant into him. It wasn't long before they were locked in a long, passionate kiss. She was a good kisser. Certainly not her first time, but that didn't bother him.

Eventually, they started walking back towards where they'd left their friends.

"I should be getting home, my parents will start to freak out," she admitted, checking her watch to see what the time was. "I'll be here next Saturday." She looked up at him, a kind of expectancy covered over with pretended nonchalance.

"I'll meet you at the fountain at six," he replied, also trying to feign slight disinterest, as if it wouldn't bother him one way or the other if she turned up or not.

"Sure," she replied, a little too quickly, and hurried off to re-join her friends. The girls quickly picked up their bags, clearly a bit annoyed with Milana for taking so long, and the three of them headed off in the direction of the park exit. She didn't look back at him, but then he wasn't expecting her to. This was how the game worked. And yet, it felt different this time. There was something about Milana that made him really hope that she would be standing by that fountain at six o'clock next Saturday, waiting for him.

Zalina was trembling; she couldn't believe what she was about to do. She was in her room at home, the door shut. Her mother was in the kitchen and her father, well, she wasn't quite sure where he was. She suspected he was out drinking somewhere. His depression had worsened and he'd started drinking a lot more than he used to. It hadn't got too bad yet. Not like Bela's uncle Artur. Papa tried to hide it, tried to look sober when he came home, but it wasn't a thing that was easily hidden. She and her mother could smell it on his breath, see the slightly glazed look in his eyes, and watch him try to balance his steps as he walked down the corridor to the bathroom. But neither of them said anything. Like the hitting and the bruises, this was a shameful but unspoken family secret. Fortunately for Zalina, the alcohol had diverted her father's attention away from her and her grades for a while, and it had been a few months since he'd last hit her. However, his anger and his pain were only worsening underneath. No amount of alcohol could take that away. There was still no job, nothing permanent anyway. Nothing of significance or social standing. And there was still very little money coming in. Zalina kept her head down and kept out of his way.

But here she was about to do something that could earn her a beating from her father. She took the piece of paper and the small Bible that Natasha had given her and that she'd hidden right at the bottom of her schoolbag. On the paper was a simple prayer that Natasha had written out for her.

For several months now, Zalina had been secretly attending the small gathering of Circassian believers. She'd listened and thought a great deal. She'd asked many questions, both of Natasha and of Slava. Every time, her questions had been answered in a way that made sense. Every one of her objections seemed to meet with a reasonable explanation, and while she understood that not everything could be answered completely—after all, there had to be an element of faith here—eventually she'd had to admit that she'd run out of excuses. Everything she'd learned seemed to point in one direction: this was the truth. And if this was true, then it was worth giving her life to. It was worth the possible rejection and beatings. It was worth the taunting and the finger pointing. It had to be.

It was more than truth. It was beautiful. She'd never seen such peace and joy in other people's faces. In some of the meetings, God's presence near her had been almost tangible. She'd felt her heart move, and she'd wanted to reach out and grab whatever it was for herself. But something had always held her back.

Until now.

Zalina looked down at the little piece of paper. She got down on her knees beside her bed: it was probably the appropriate thing to do. She started to pray the words that Natasha had written out for her.

Father God, I'm sorry for the wrong things I've done in my life.

She thought about that for a moment. She'd not done anything really terrible, but she'd said hurtful things, been disobedient, told lies, been selfish. The list could go on. A year ago, these things wouldn't have mattered to her, but now that she'd been so close to the presence of a perfect, holy God, she could see that these things mattered deeply. She was part of what was wrong with the world. She was part of the reason why Jesus had to die.

Thank you, Jesus, that you died for me to take away my sins.
Thank you that I'm now forgiven.

As she spoke those words to herself, an immense sense of peace and calm flooded over her. A tension in her shoulders that she hadn't realised was there seemed to lift and disappear. Her body felt lighter, her mind felt free, and her heart filled with love and gratitude towards God.

Send your Holy Spirit now to fill my life and help me to live for you.

She paused again and felt that God's Spirit had indeed taken up residence in her heart. It was a sign that she belonged to him now.

I acknowledge that Jesus is now Lord of my life and that I belong to Him. Amen.

Tears began to roll down Zalina's cheeks. The fear melted away, and a knot in her stomach unclenched and was replaced by a great sense of relief, a knowledge that she had done the right thing. She was a new person now, about to embark on a new journey in life. She didn't know where it would take her, but she wasn't afraid.

She didn't know how long she stayed there, kneeling on the floor, but it was dark by the time she finally got into bed and fell into a deep, peaceful sleep.

Chapter 15

2004, April

Bela was enjoying working for Michael. He didn't have quite enough work to offer her yet that she could give up her job at the phone shop, but she was hoping that he could see how invaluable she was and find more things for her to do. For now, she was content just to come round for an hour after work, three times a week. Already though, his flat-mate, Cody, had expressed an interest in her helping with his new tourism business. She'd rather be working for Michael, but a job was a job, wasn't it? Wasn't that what she'd wanted in the first place? It didn't really matter which foreigner she worked for. Maybe it was just Michael's Britishness that drew her to prefer working for him. At school, she'd been fascinated by all things British, and had dreamed of going to London one day to see Buckingham Palace and the changing of the guards. And then of course, there was that missed opportunity to go to England when she'd been studying in Moscow.

But why did her heart get all fluttery whenever he was near? She was always aware exactly where he was in the room at all times, and she found herself trying so hard to present the best side of herself whenever they were talking. If she was honest, then yes, she did find him attractive, with his blue-green eyes and dark brown, floppy hair that she wanted to run her hands through and smooth down. He was nice to look at and kept himself in good shape too. Not too muscular, like many of the local guys who liked to lift weights in front of the mirrors down at the gym, but he was toned and athletic from his regular runs in the park. There was something about his manner as well. A gentle humility and over-politeness, which was really endearing. She'd never once seen him angry or moody, not like Azamat. Perhaps that was because of his faith. He'd made no secret of the fact that he was a committed Christian, and often brought God into the conversation almost without realising he was doing it. His Bible on the coffee table looked like it had been well read, unlike like the pristine copy of the Koran her family had at home on the top shelf of the bookcase.

Cody was nice too. He was a big character, always the centre of attention, with a generous smile and lots of jokes. It would be good to work for him. With Michael, she was just translating and typing up his notes into Russian, but with Cody, she'd have a more regular job as a personal secretary. They'd spoken about it a few times, trying to work out what kind of assistant he needed. She would probably be involved in fielding phone calls, writing emails, and dealing with all the paperwork that came with visa applications and registration. There was the possibility of setting up a website, so she'd be learning new skills. In many ways, it would be the perfect job for her. She sighed. But it could only be truly perfect if she got to work in the same room as Michael.

Michael set a mug of black tea down next to the computer where Bela was working. She looked tired, as if her mind was somewhere else.

"Here you go. Take a break; you've been staring at that screen for over an hour."

"Thanks," she said gratefully, swivelling around in her chair and taking the warm cup in her hands.

"How's it going?"

"Good. I think I'm about halfway through. It's actually really interesting; I'm learning so much about my own language. I mean, I know how to speak Circassian, but I've never really thought about how it all fits together, how it works."

"You didn't study it in school?"

"Oh yes, a little, but nothing like in as much detail as this. And to be honest, I'm wondering if what I learnt in school was actually correct. Your analysis of how the verbs split up makes much more sense."

Michael laughed. "Oh yes, your verbs! I never knew a language that could add so many prefixes and suffixes to just one central letter!"

Bela smiled. "It's an amazing language; I'm coming to see that."

"I'd love to learn more about your culture too. It sounds so fascinating." He watched as her face lit up.

"I have so many stories to tell you that my grandmother passed down to me, all about the Narts and our people's history. Our culture and traditions. She's so passionate about preserving it all."

"Your grandmother sounds like an amazing person. Do you think it might be possible for me to visit her and record some of what she says?"

"Oh, that's a great idea. I'm sure she'd enjoy that. I'll talk to her about it."

They both paused to take a sip of their tea. Michael was beginning to get used to having tea without milk, although he couldn't help adding a spoonful of sugar just to sweeten the taste a bit. He wondered what to say next. He had so many questions to ask. He found himself wanting to know all about Bela, about her family, her childhood, her life in the village. Was it just a purely professional interest? He kept trying to tell himself that it was, but if he was being honest with himself, he found her totally captivating. She was beautiful, intelligent and good-natured, not like the pouting, self-absorbed girls that tried to throw themselves at him at the university. Perhaps it was the fact that she *wasn't* throwing herself at him that drew him to her. Come to think of it, why wasn't she throwing herself at him? Okay, that sounded rather conceited. He wasn't *that* good-looking. But his very Britishness seemed to flash the words 'rich Westerner' and 'new, comfortable life overseas' at prospective admirers, and that was usually enough to set the eyelashes fluttering.

Lord, I really like this girl. I don't know if that should make me back away from her or not. I know she's not a believer, Lord, and I couldn't go out with anyone who didn't share my faith. However, I'd really like to get to know her better. Please help me not to take things too far or give her the wrong idea.

Bela broke the silence, which was beginning to become a bit awkward.

"I'd better carry on. I have to be back at the phone shop in half an hour."

"Yes, of course. Let me know if you have any questions."

"Questions?"

"About the paper. Linguistic terminology and all that."

"Oh yes, of course."

Bela looked back at the screen, a flush of heat rising in her cheeks. When he'd asked if she had any questions, a whole host of possibilities had rushed into her brain. "Whereabouts in England do you come from?", "What is your family like?", "How long have you been in Russia?", "How do you like it here in the Caucasus?" She found herself daydreaming about sitting in a café with him and being able to ask all those questions. Just spending time getting to know each other. She thought about how he would ask her questions about herself, how they would laugh at each other's jokes, smile at each other, become really close.

The way her heart was racing and her palms were a bit sweaty was a new experience for her. She'd spent so long running from boys and now men. She'd been so scared of settling for second best, or worse, being forced into a relationship she didn't want to be in. She'd been trying to run away from the kind of life Madina had fallen into. That Mama had fallen into, even. But why shouldn't she allow herself to fall in love with Michael? She was so desperate to show him that she wasn't like the other girls, like Larissa for example, that maybe she was hampering her chances of genuine happiness. Michael could offer her so much. Surely her parents couldn't be opposed to the match. He would rescue her from a potentially loveless and miserable life with Alim. He could rescue her from her boring job at the phone shop. She began to imagine a life in England, doing what she loved, being free. Of course, she'd visit her family and keep in touch, but she could make a real life for herself. One that didn't involve alcohol, like Uncle Artur, or divorce, like Madina, or run-ins with the police, like Azamat. If her Uncle Albert could take his family to Germany, maybe she could start a new life in England?

She checked herself, aware that her imagination was running a little too far in one direction. He had only brought her a cup of tea, for goodness' sake, and now he was proposing marriage? She laughed inwardly and willed herself back to the land of reality. However, she couldn't deny that, though she might be imagining it, he did seem to like her. The way he lingered a bit too long at the end of the conversation, as if he'd got himself lost in her eyes. His thoughtfulness towards her, treating her as more than just an assistant typist. His eagerness to visit her grandmother.

Her grandmother! That was it. She'd set up a meeting as soon as possible to take him to her grandmother. Nana would tell her what she should do.

Michael was quite excited to be visiting a Circassian village at long last. Bela had talked to her family and her grandmother, and they were looking forward to meeting him, apparently. He wondered what kind of reception he'd get. Would they be slightly guarded and defensive around a foreigner, or would they just be open and welcoming? He noticed that his throat was quite dry and his hands a little shaky. It wasn't like him to be so nervous.

The *marshroutka* jolted as it crossed the train tracks, and Michael narrowly avoided bumping his head on the ceiling. It was hard to stand in these minibuses. The best place was just by the door, where you could stand down a step, but another guy had already got that position. He looked out of the window as more fields and trees came into view. On one side was an old concrete building. He guessed it had been a factory at one point, but it looked like it had been deserted for over a decade. Many of the windows were smashed or missing, and there was graffiti on one side of the wall. Further down the road, they passed a roadside café. A pack of stray dogs were hanging around the temporary building. A little further on, a middle-aged woman sat next to a large wooden table covered with a red, plastic table cloth. She was selling crudely-made brooms, which looked like a jumble of sticks tied together, as well as a few jars of something homemade. Houses were now coming into view on the other side of the road. Some were in disrepair, but others had been newly built by owners with more money. Several other plots were in the middle of being built on. He was intrigued that the first step in building a Circassian house seemed to be the outer wall with its large, ornamental gate. It wasn't the first time that Michael had noticed how the elaborateness of someone's outer gate seemed to determine their status and standing in the community. The gates were high, making it impossible to look over, but there was usually a small gap underneath where village dogs could squeeze in and out.

The *marshroutka* suddenly turned left and Michael had to brace himself to avoid losing his balance. This must be the main street of the village. There were houses on either side now, and the road stretched a long way into the distance. Bela had told him to get out at the first crossroads, which he could see was coming up. He hated this bit: having to call out to the *marshroutka* driver to stop, his accented Russian immediately giving him away as a foreigner and therefore causing all eyes in the bus to turn to him. He waited another second, and thankfully a woman called out the stop first. The guy standing by the door obligingly swung it open and Michael and the woman stepped out, slamming the door behind them. The woman headed off along the side road, a heavy market bag in one hand. Michael looked around for Bela. As the *marshroutka* began to move away, he saw her. She lifted a hand in greeting from the other side of the road and smiled at him. He smiled and waved back and crossed over to her.

"Hi, Michael. Welcome to Awush."

"Hi, thank you. You know, I'm really looking forward to meeting your family."

The two of them started to walk down the road. This road, although fairly wide, was not tarmacked like the main road, but rather was covered in gravel. Large potholes in the road at regular intervals made it look like a difficult place to drive a car down. Neither of them spoke for the first couple of minutes. Michael desperately wanted to break the silence but wasn't quite sure what to say. He sensed that Bela was feeling a bit awkward too. Was she worried what people would think of her being seen with a foreigner? Or was she just a little shy, like him?

Half way down the road on the right, a little kiosk was built into the side of one of the houses. Outside there was an old wooden bench, which had been painted blue at some point in the past, presumably to match the shutters on the kiosk window. A young boy was playing with a toy truck and was being watched by an older lady who was presumably his grandmother. The lady looked up at Bela and smiled. She bobbed out of her seat in greeting. Bela went over to her and gave her a side hug.

"How are you, Rima?"

"Good, thank you."

Michael was pleased that he had understood this exchange in Circassian.

Bela switched to Russian. "Rima, this is Michael. He's English and is studying our language. He's come to meet my family and talk to Nana about our history."

A big smile broke out across the lady's face. She heaved herself onto her feet and came over to shake Michael's hand. She was wearing what looked like an old, patterned dressing gown with slippers, and her hair was tied back under a patterned headscarf. Michael spoke a greeting in Circassian, and this only made the lady smile even more widely.

"You speak our language, how wonderful!"

"Well, only a little," he clarified in Russian. "It's not an easy language to learn."

"No, it's very difficult. But a very rich language."

"Absolutely. I'm really enjoying studying it. Do you speak it at home with your family?"

"Oh yes. Zaur here," she motioned to the little boy, "he only speaks Circassian. But when the young people go off to school and then go off to Moscow or St Petersburg looking for jobs, they forget our language and don't speak it so much."

"That's really sad."

Rima took his hand again and looked into his eyes intently. Then she turned and disappeared into her shop, emerging a minute later with a plastic bag full of one of the local kinds of biscuits that Michael had often seen in the market.

"Here," she said, placing the bag in Michael's hand, "for you."

Michael and Bela said their goodbyes and continued down the street. Bela laughed. "I hope you've got a lot of room in your bag. I suspect you'll be leaving with a huge pile of presents today."

"I have," Michael smiled, "but only because I have a few gifts for your family too." He was glad he'd remembered the local custom of not arriving empty-handed at your host's family.

Chapter 16

1994, August

"Is everything okay? You seem, well, different."

Zalina and Bela were sitting on Zalina's bed at home after another tiring day at school. It had been four months now since she'd prayed that special prayer in this very room, and Zalina had been expecting her friend to say something. If she felt as changed and as different as she did on the inside, then surely other people might notice something on the outside.

The morning after the prayer, she'd expected to be a completely changed person. Instead, she noticed herself still snapping at people she found annoying, or thinking selfish thoughts. She'd been a bit surprised, and had wondered if she'd said the words right, but then she remembered the very real feelings of relief and peace and freedom that had washed over her that night. Natasha had been able to explain that it was like she was still wearing the same, old clothes on top of her new self.

"Underneath we may be a different person, but it takes time to take off the old clothes—all our old habits and sinful ways of thinking and acting—and put on the new clothes that God offers instead," she had told Zalina.

Zalina looked at Bela, feeling a little nervous. "I do? In what way?"

"Oh, I don't know. You seem calmer, more peaceful somehow. Happier, I guess."

Zalina paused. She hadn't yet told anyone outside of the Circassian believers about her conversion. In some ways, she'd been dying to tell Bela, her best friend, and yet something had always held her back. Fear of rejection, probably. She'd been afraid that Bela would laugh at her and think her weird and then, even worse, stop hanging out with her so much. But Natasha had encouraged her to gradually start telling those close to her, so perhaps now was a good time.

Zalina got up, opened the top drawer of her bedside table and pulled out a little black book. She handed it to Bela.

"What's this?"

"Open it."

Bela opened it and read a few of the Russian words. She looked up, confusion and shock in her eyes. "Is this a Bible?"

"Yes. I read it every night. I've done so for over four months now."

"Are you... Are you a Christian now, then, like Natasha?"

Zalina laughed nervously. "I guess, yes. Yes, I am."

"Oh," said Bela, looking back at the book again, clearly not knowing what to say.

"It's changed my life, really Bela." Zalina sat down on the bed next to her friend, feeling relief now that she finally knew. "It's amazing. It's all so clear to me now. God really speaks to me as I read the words of the Bible. I feel my whole life has changed. I have peace that I've never had before."

"Oh," said Bela again. "I…um… that is… I'm glad for you, I suppose. If that's what makes you happy."

"It does." Zalina was about to say more, but sensed her friend backing off. This was probably not the time to try to persuade her to become a Christian too.

"Do your parents know?" asked Bela, after another silence. She awkwardly fingered the pages of the Bible and then placed it back in the drawer.

"No, not yet." Zalina looked down at her hands. "I haven't had the courage to tell them yet. You know they won't be happy. I don't want to risk it with my father especially."

"Perhaps you don't need to tell them. Just keep it to yourself."

"Yes, perhaps, but it's really hard not to. I think they've noticed a change too. And I so want to talk to them about it. Just like I'd love to talk to you about it sometime, Bela."

"Oh, I don't think that kind of thing is for me," Bela said quickly.

"That's what I thought too, at first. But it's the best decision I've ever made. Perhaps we can talk about it sometime."

"Perhaps."

"Look, I don't want this to come between us. We can still be friends, can't we?" Zalina looked at her with wide, hopeful eyes.

Bela looked down. "As long as your friend Natasha thinks that's okay."

Zalina gave Bela a big side hug. "You'll always be my best friend, Bela, nothing will change that, ever."

"Even if I'm not a Christian like you?"

"Of course not. And I hope that you'll still want to be my friend too?"

Bela's look told Zalina all she needed to know. Her friendship with Bela was one of those friendships that lasted, no matter what life threw at it. She smiled with relief. One down, two to go.

"Shit, are you sure?" Azamat ran his fingers through his hair and felt a sudden strong urge for a cigarette. Things had been going so well with Milana these past few months, and naturally their relationship had progressed to the stage where they'd been sleeping together. It hadn't been easy, since neither of their families would have approved, obviously. The first time had been on the back seat of Vadim's car, while he'd sauntered off somewhere 'leaving the two love birds alone'. Other times had been at friends' apartments, friends who were at university and lived away from their parents in glorious freedom. Always it was rushed and slightly uncomfortable, always with the threat that someone might walk in on them at any moment, but that had only fuelled their passion and lust for one another.

For Azamat, though, it had been more than lust. It was even more than purely physical. He couldn't stop thinking about her; he couldn't wait to be with her. She seemed to understand him, believe in him even. At home, his parents reminded him constantly that he hadn't lived up to their expectations, that he was a great disappointment to them. But Milana didn't seem to care that he was just tinkering around as a car mechanic. He loved the way that she was so carefree, so unhindered by expectations. She never talked about the future, she just enjoyed living in the present. She made him smile and laugh and enjoy life. He'd never felt so liberated, so free. With Milana, he was allowed to totally be himself. He really cared for this girl, and it had been going through his mind that she would be the one to marry when the time came. But not now, not this way.

"I thought we'd been careful, you know, used protection?"

"There was that one time, do you remember, when it slipped off."

"Shit!" said Azamat again. Why did everything have to get so complicated? Why did these things always happen to him?

"I'm not going to keep it." Milana forced him to look at her. She seemed panicked, like him, but also determined. She'd had longer to think about it. Relief suddenly flowed through Azamat.

"Are you sure? I don't want to force you to do anything you don't want to do."

"Yes, I'm sure. We're too young; we're not married. It was a mistake. Lots of girls have abortions, it won't be a problem."

"Will your parents find out?"

"No, I don't think so. I have a friend whose cousin works at the hospital. She can get me an appointment. No one needs to know."

"Okay. Well, let me know when… when it happens, you know. If there's anything I can do."

"Sure. Thanks."

Azamat took her hand and looked into her eyes. "This won't change anything, will it? We can still be together?"

"Yes, of course." They locked into a passionate kiss. *It's going to be all right*, Azamat told himself. He tried not to think about the fact that this was a baby they were talking about. His baby. A little person who would grow up to be his son or his daughter. He pushed those thoughts from his mind as sternly as he could. It was for the best. They were too young. What did he know about being a father?

Chapter 17

2004, April

Michael followed Bela up another gravelled road, smaller than the one they'd just been on. The houses here were closer together, and it was quieter. There were no people sitting on their benches outside their gates, chatting to passers-by, but a couple of dogs lounged on clumps of grass outside their respective territories. They were small, mongrel-like dogs, and Michael knew enough now of local dogs to be wary of them. They were trained to fear people and bark at strangers. A stray dog limped past on just three legs. Michael wasn't sure whether the dog had been born deformed or whether it had had a nasty accident. Dogs had hard lives here. Bela seemed to notice the direction of his gaze.

"It's sad, yes? It's the way of life here. Most people can't afford to pay for a vet for their animals. Very few dogs are spayed, so they often have puppies. If the puppies can't be sold or given away, then either the puppies are killed, or the owner sends the mother dog away to look after her puppies on the streets."

"It's so different from where I come from. I don't think I've ever seen a stray dog out on the streets. Do people not walk their dogs here?"

Bela laughed. "Not really. Certainly not out here in the villages. The dogs live outside all year round. Most of them are free to roam around the streets as they choose. The larger, more vicious guard dogs are tied up in the yard all day and then allowed to run around the yard at night, but rarely let out in case they bite someone."

They approached what looked to be the largest house on the street. It seemed to have the grandest gate, was built of two storeys, and had ornate decorations on the silver-coloured roof. A dog barked from inside the gate.

"That's our dog, Tuzik," she said with a smile. "Don't worry, he's tied up."

She pulled the latch across on the gate and stepped inside. Michael followed her. The front yard was a large, paved area. Two smaller buildings, which had been hidden from the road by the large gate, lay on either side. The main house was straight ahead, with steps leading up to the front door. Two women appeared at the top of the steps. Presumably, the elder one was Bela's mother. The other, he guessed, was her sister Madina. Bela had already told him a little about her family.

"Welcome!" Bela's mother smiled. She seemed genuinely excited to meet him. She shook his hand once he'd reached the front door and ushered him inside. He removed his shoes and slipped his feet into the house slippers that were offered to him.

They walked through a large entrance hall; the kitchen was obviously off to the right and some smaller doors—presumably the bathroom and toilet room—were on the left. From there, a corridor led to a large living room area at the back of the house. A long, green sofa lay against the further wall, curling around the corner to the next wall. In the middle of the room was a brown, wooden table, covered with a white table cloth and already laid out with salads, bread, fruit, and other delicious-looking things to eat.

The sight of it reminded Michael of his gifts. He put his rucksack down and opened it.

"For you," he said, offering a box of fudge and a packet of shortbread biscuits to Bela's mother. "They've come all the way from England."

Bela's mother accepted the gifts and looked at them with interest.

"And this too," Michael added, producing a calendar. "See, these are some of our most beautiful places in England," he said, showing her the photos on the back of the calendar.

Bela's mother thanked him and motioned for him to sit down while she muttered something about food and hurried off down the hallway.

It gave Michael an opportunity to gaze around the room. The television occupied a prominent place in the corner. There was a typical Russian *stenka*—a large assortment of cupboards, drawers, and shelves—that took up the whole of the far wall. One of the shelves housed a collection of old-fashioned-looking books behind the glass front.

"Does your family read much?" he asked Bela, who'd sat down at the other end of the sofa.

"No." She laughed. "They're just for show."

"Are any of the books written in Circassian?"

"No." She looked thoughtful. "Very few people actually read much in Circassian. They say it's too difficult. I think they get that from school, from the Russians, and then they never bother trying. I'm not sure there are that many books in the Circassian language anyway."

At that moment, another lady shuffled into the room. This must be Bela's grandmother. Michael rose from his seat to shake her hand, clasping his other hand around hers too as a sign of extra respect. "How do you do?" he managed to say in Circassian.

Nana smiled and answered using a long phrase in Circassian that Michael didn't understand. He turned to Bela with a look of helpless bemusement.

Bela translated, "She says 'May God bring peace and health and prosperity to you and your family'."

He turned back to face Nana. "Thank you," he said in Circassian.

Bela's mother and sister returned bearing more food and drink for the table, and everyone settled down to eat. The atmosphere was a little awkward and stiff at first, but soon Michael got used to answering their questions and everyone gradually relaxed.

"Papa had to be at work today, but he hopes to see you before you go," apologised Bela. "And Alyona is at school. She'll be back soon."

Michael nodded. The food was delicious. Circassian hospitality really was second to none. It was good, though, that, since it was the middle of the day, he wouldn't be expected to down lots of shots of alcohol. That might change, perhaps, if Bela's father returned home before Michael had left.

After the meal, Bela, Madina, and their mother cleared the table and brought out the kettle to pour cups of tea for everyone. Michael gave Bela what he hoped was a meaningful look, and she understood straight away.

"Nana, Michael has come to hear some of your stories about the history of our people."

"It will really help my research, thank you," Michael added, turning to the old lady with a grateful smile.

It was as if the floodgates had opened, and Nana, who'd previously been almost silent, didn't stop talking for the next hour. She was in her element, it seemed. Michael remembered to press play on his recording device just in time to capture what she was saying, which fortunately was all in Russian for his sake.

Nana told stories of the ancient Narts, the legends of her people. She told how the Circassians had lived in this land for centuries. She spoke of invasions, first by Genghis Khan.

"My people used to be fair-haired and blue eyed," she said, "but now we have the brown eyes and black hair of the Turks."

Then her face darkened as she spoke of the Russian-Caucasian wars of the nineteenth century. "The Russians nearly wiped out my people," she said sadly. "We sent a prince to London to appeal for help, but no help came. Many fled south, over the mountains, to what is now Jordan, Syria and Turkey. Mostly it was the princes and the nobles who were able to leave."

Michael nodded, sympathetically. Her story continued to the time of Stalin, when neighbouring people groups were sent off to Central Asia, and the rest split up. It was a sad story, but their people had remained proud and steadfast, keeping as many of their old traditions as they could.

Michael had been entranced by her story. Some of the history he already knew, but there were many parts that were new to him. It was amazing to him that so few people back home even knew that these people existed.

When Nana had finished her story, Michael got out his notebook and asked some of the linguistic questions that had been troubling him. Mainly about language use, reading and writing skills, and whether or not Nana thought the language was gradually dying out.

It had been a fascinating afternoon, but now Michael could feel his head aching uncomfortably from trying to follow all the Russian. His brain was telling him 'enough!'

Bela's father had been detained at work, but Michael felt he really must get back home. He needed some rest and a couple of paracetamol tablets. Bela offered to walk him back to the bus stop.

"Thank you. It was so good to meet you all," Michael said in broken Circassian, shaking hands with Nana, Madina, and Mama. Bela's mother disappeared into the kitchen and emerged a few seconds later with a jar of homemade jam and a bottle of homemade wine, which she thrust into his hands. He thanked her for the gifts and placed them carefully in his rucksack.

He and Bela stepped out into the yard. A loud *moo* from the other side of the gate startled Michael.

Bela laughed. "That's our cow," she said, opening the gate to let the large animal in. The cow slowly loped past them and disappeared around the back of the house.

"What? How?" Village life in the Caucasus was certainly interesting.

Bela explained. "Each village has a cowherd. Every morning we let our cow out into the street, where it joins the other cows and goes off to pasture. At the end of the day, the cowherd brings them home."

Michael stepped out onto the street, and sure enough, two other cows were slowly ambling up the road. He watched as each of them stopped outside a different house and began mooing to their owners to let them in.

"And they know exactly where they live? That's amazing. I never knew that about cows."

"Your English cows don't do that too?"

"Our cows just live together in farms, I guess. People don't tend to have pet cows."

They reached the *marshroutka* stop and could see the number fourteen approaching.

Michael turned to Bela. "Thank you so much, that was so interesting."

"You're welcome. I know my family would like to see you again, if possible. My father will be sorry that he missed you. Will you come again?"

"Yes, thank you, I'd like that." He wasn't quite sure what the culturally appropriate way of saying goodbye was at this point in their friendship. He opted for a slightly awkward handshake.

"Thank you, Bela. I'll see you next week."

As the *marshroutka* turned the corner at the end of the main road, he looked back and could still see Bela watching him from where he'd left her. He felt a little lurch in his heart.

"A handsome young man," said Nana, who was still sitting on the sofa when Bela returned.

"Yes, I suppose so," she replied, trying to sound nonchalant. There was a pause while Bela wondered what to do next. Should she go and see if Mama needed help in the kitchen, or should she stay here with Nana and dissect the finer details of Michael's visit? She could hear Mama and Madina chatting happily to the clink of dishes and decided it would be okay to stay with Nana a little longer. She sat herself down next to her on the sofa.

"He's very interested in our language, Nana."

"Yes. And you."

Bela recoiled slightly. Nana could be very blunt sometimes. "What do you mean?"

"Oh, I could tell by the way he looked at you. He likes you, *si dakhe*."

"Nana, he was just being polite. That's how the British are with everyone."

"Well, like I said, he's a very handsome young man." She grinned with a twinkle in her eye.

"But, and this is all very hypothetical you understand, just suppose that he did like me, I don't think he'd want to marry me."

"Why not, *si dakhe*? You're young and beautiful and talented."

"Thanks, Nana." She squeezed her grandmother's hand. "But, well, I sense that his faith really means a lot to him. He's a Christian, you see. Not like the Orthodox Christians I know. This is different somehow. He talks about God, he always has his Bible lying open on the table in his apartment, he prays before mealtimes. He's like…" She lowered her voice. "He's like Zalina."

"Hmm, I see."

"Oh, it's not that I think it's wrong, or anything. I kind of admire him for it. But, I just don't think it's for me and, well, if we don't believe in the same things, then how could we be, you know, a couple?"

"Well, perhaps you should look into this Christianity thing."

Bela was shocked. After all that had happened with Zalina, how could Nana suggest such a thing?

"But I'm Circassian, Nana. We're not Christians. If anything, we're Muslims."

Nana was thoughtful for a moment.

"The way I see it, I don't think being Circassian and being Christian are incompatible. Especially given our history."

"Our history? What do you mean?"

"Well, *si dakhe*, before the Turks came, before we became Muslim, our people were Christians."

"Really? I never knew that!"

"Yes, of course. Think about it. What's the Circassian word for Sunday?"

"*Tkhemakhwe.*"

"And what does that actually mean?"

Bela thought for a moment and wondered why she'd never noticed the meaning before. "God day".

"You see. Sunday is the special day for Christians, like it used to be for our people."

"What other evidence is there, Nana?"

"Well, for one, think of the people around us, to the South. The Georgians, they're Christians. The Armenians, they were the very first Christian country, did you know? There are also pockets of our own people who are Christians. Not because they became Christians later, but because they always were. It was us who changed."

Bela was silent, trying to process what she was hearing.

"And one more thing," added Nana, "The name of our village."

"Awush?"

"Some people say that Awush was the old Circassian name for Jesus."

Later that evening, Bela was lying in bed, still unable to get her conversation with Nana out of her head. Everything had suddenly changed. When Zalina had become a Christian, Bela had thought that, in some way, she was betraying her heritage. Yes, she'd helped her anyway, because she was her best friend, but still, Circassians and Christianity weren't supposed to mix. Bela loved her people and loved the history of her people. She hoped she would uphold the traditions of her people when she had a family of her own. But now? Maybe there was room for faith in Jesus after all?

She still didn't believe in it. She would still need to be convinced that it was the truth, that it was necessary.

But maybe, just maybe, the God that Michael believed in was also interested in her and her people, way out here in the North Caucasus.

Chapter 18

1994, October

It had not gone well. She hadn't really expected it to. There had never seemed to be a good time to tell her parents about her new faith, and she'd left it too long, she now realised. Her mother had found her Bible when she'd been cleaning one day. Zalina had usually been careful to hide it away, but that morning she'd been late for school and hadn't noticed that she'd left it on her pillow.

"What's this, Zalina?"

"Um… It's a Bible, Mama."

"Yes, I can see that. But what is a Bible doing in your bedroom?"

In that split second, Zalina was tempted to come up with some excuse. Anything to avoid the inevitable disgrace. She could claim it wasn't hers. That someone had put it in her bag as a prank. That she was looking after it for someone. But in that split second, she knew that God wanted her to give an honest answer.

"It's mine, Mama. I've become a Christian."

A wave of shock passed over Zalina's mother's face, and she sat down heavily on the stool behind her.

"But, why?"

Zalina sat down too and, as calmly and clearly as she could, she told her mother about her journey of faith, about the group of believers and Natasha—although she was careful to leave out names and other details—and about how wonderful she felt now. How it had made a difference in her life. How she honestly felt that she had found the truth. For a moment, she wondered if she might have won her mother over. Made her mother interested to find out more too. But then a cloud of parental concern and anger descended and, for the following five minutes, Zalina had to endure the rant of objections that she'd been expecting. Christianity was for Russians. Circassians, if they were anything, were Muslims. Zalina was bringing shame on their family, on their people. She'd been brainwashed. Everyone knew the Bible was inaccurate. It was a dangerous book and shouldn't be in their house.

Zalina could take all this from her mother, but her father was the unknown element. She prayed silently for help and courage. When her father came home, he was in a drunken stupor, which was a bad omen of what was to come. Surely her mother would wait until Papa had calmed down a bit? Maybe after he'd eaten his food at least? But no, she could hear the conversation happening now. She sat in her room awaiting her fate. There was a pause, but it was just the eye of the hurricane. The worst was about to come.

The door slammed open, and her father stood there with the Bible in his hand. He threw it across the room in disgust and anger. "You're never to bring that into our house again, do you understand?"

Zalina wasn't sure what to say. Should she obey her father or God? Could she survive as a Christian without being able to read her Bible every night? She paused too long.

"Do you understand?" His right hand smacked across her left cheek, knocking her back against the wall, where she banged her head. He hit her again, this time across the other cheek, splitting her lip open. She brushed her finger gently over her lip, mopping up the blood.

"Yes, Papa."

Azamat stared at the scribbled message in disbelief. Milana had finally contacted him, and she wanted to see him. He hadn't heard from her for over a month. Shortly after she'd told him she was pregnant, she had seemed to disappear off the face of the planet. She hadn't turned up at the park with her friends, and he'd had no way to contact her. She'd never given him her home phone number, or even her home address, for fear her parents would find out.

He hadn't understood it. He thought she'd made up her mind about the abortion and was happy with her decision, so why then would she cut him out of her life so suddenly? He hadn't forced her to have the abortion, and if she'd decided not to go ahead with it after all, then they could have talked it through. He'd not been able to sleep properly because he missed her so much. He'd looked for her in crowds, but never caught a glimpse. He'd repeatedly plied her friends for information, but the answers were always vague, and in the end, he'd decided that they too didn't know why she wasn't around anymore or why she'd seemingly dumped him.

But finally, here was a message on a scrap of paper handed to him by Milana's friend Oksana. He read the note again, although with his first glance, he'd already memorised the time and place she wanted to meet. He tried to spot some clue to what she wanted, tried to read between the lines. Her tone felt cold and distant. No explanation for why she hadn't wanted to see him.

What was going on?

Three days later, he was waiting on the bench, about to find out. He was dressed in the best, cleanest clothes he could find. He looked down at his hands, noticing how they were shaking slightly as he waited for her. She'd chosen a bench overlooking the lake, near where they'd had their first kiss. He jumped to his feet as he saw her approaching. She looked more beautiful than he'd remembered. Her skin glowed with health and her eyes were brighter. He looked down at her clothes and realised why. It was just a small bump under her top, but he knew at once. She was still pregnant with his baby.

He looked up at her, his face clearly displaying shock and confusion.

"I didn't have the abortion."

"I can see that, but why? Why didn't you tell me? Why haven't you let me see you?"

"I'm sorry, I really am. I'll try to explain." She sat down, and he sat down next to her. At least it looked like this was just as hard for her as it was for him, which consoled him somewhat. She still loved him, he could tell.

"These last few weeks have not been easy for me." A tear started to roll down her cheek. He wanted nothing more than to brush it away and draw her to him, but he sensed that there was an invisible line on the bench which he should not cross.

She continued, "My parents found out I was pregnant and planning an abortion. They didn't want me to get rid of the baby. They tried to make me tell them who the father was, but I didn't." Azamat looked guiltily down at his feet. He had defiled their daughter. It didn't seem like it at the time, but now he felt ashamed somehow.

"You know that we could never have married. I told you why."

Azamat nodded, his heart full of pain and sorrow. Even though he'd secretly been hoping that things might be different eventually, she'd made it clear a few weeks into their relationship that there was no way her parents would approve. It wasn't because he was still in school and didn't have a proper job yet. It was because of his family line. Even though his father had a respected position in the local government, they couldn't hide the fact that they were originally of peasant stock. All Circassians knew their family trees. Even Azamat, who couldn't remember much of the history he'd been taught at school, knew his family line back to the tenth or eleventh generation. Milana's family were descendants of Circassian princes. One of the rare families who'd not managed to escape to Jordan or Turkey during the Russian-Caucasian wars.

And Circassian princesses were not supposed to marry Circassian peasants.

"They've always wanted me to marry Murat," Milana continued. "His mother and mine are best friends. It's been arranged pretty much since I was born. I thought I could be free for a while longer. I thought I could have some fun and do what I wanted, but, well, this happened." She stroked the small bulge in her belly.

"I never meant to hurt you, Azamat. I really liked you. I do, still, really like you. But, well, I need to marry Murat now, before people find out about the baby. The wedding's arranged for next month. I'm so sorry."

Azamat hung his head. He wanted the ground to open up and swallow him whole. He wanted to run away from this horrible situation and pretend that none of this was real.

"I love you, Milana," he said quietly. He'd never said that to her before, but he'd known it for some time. He laid his heart out raw before her, but there was nothing she could do. The tears flowed more freely down her face. She reached out and squeezed his hand.

"I'm so sorry," she whispered.

"What about the baby? I'm still the father."

"I know, but you have to understand, you can have nothing to do with the child. It's best that no one knows."

"You mean you're going to let the baby think that Murat is his or her real father?"

"It's for the best, Azamat. It's best for the baby too. It will be well looked after. It'll have a stable life."

That comment stung as Azamat took the full force of it. But how could he deny it? What could he have offered Milana's baby? His baby?

"And Murat? He has to know it's not his. Doesn't he?" Panic suddenly swept through Azamat as he briefly entertained the irrational thought that Milana might have been sleeping with Murat all this time too.

"Of course he knows it's not his." She put her hand on his to reassure him. "I wasn't sleeping around, Azamat."

Azamat nodded, relieved but still desperately unhappy. He was about to lose both the love of his life and his child to another man. A better man, perhaps, but another man nonetheless.

"So, you mean he's okay with it?"

Milana let out a cynical laugh. "Not really. But he didn't have much choice. Our parents can be pretty forceful." Her eyes dulled over.

"Are you going to be okay? I mean, he's not the kind of guy who… who might hit you?"

"No, no, it'll be fine. He's not like that." Milana looked convinced of that. She wiped her eyes. "We've come to an arrangement, as it were. He'll bring up my baby as his own as long as I don't let anyone know it's not his, and, in return, I'll do my wifely duty and be a good girl."

She was smiling sadly. Azamat knew that she hadn't planned on her life turning out this way quite so soon.

"Does he know who the real father is?" Azamat asked tentatively.

Milana took his hand in both of hers and looked him in the eye. "I swear, I'll never tell anyone, Azamat. You don't need to worry. I'm doing it for you but also for the baby. It's best that this is just our secret."

A secret they would both have to carry for the rest of their lives. The weight of it was already beginning to bear down on his soul.

"And Azamat, please don't come looking for the baby, will you? Please don't cause trouble. If you ever loved me, you'll leave me alone. Okay?"

She looked as if the thought terrified her. Azamat didn't want to say what an impossible thing she was asking of him. Did she not know how she was breaking his heart? Shattering it into tiny little pieces?

"It's okay, I'm off to the army soon, you don't need to worry." He released his hand from hers and put a little distance between them. So, this was it.

"Azamat…." Milana gave him a long, tight hug, and he could feel her wet tears on his neck.

"Goodbye, Milana." He hugged her back and then pushed himself away. He didn't look at her as she walked away, walked out of his life for good. When he felt that she must be out of sight, he slid onto the ground, curled up into a ball, and sobbed harder than he'd ever cried in his life.

Chapter 19

2004, May

Michael crunched his way through a bowl of cereal. There really was very little choice of cereal in Shekala, and what there was rather resembled cardboard. How many locals actually ate cereal for breakfast? He supposed he could have eaten something else but it was so ingrained in him as a habit that it was hard to change.

Cody had gone off to the gym for a quick workout with his local buddies, so Michael was alone in their little kitchen. He cut himself a slice of bread to put in the toaster. Sliced bread! He missed that too. The longer he stayed in Russia, the more he found it was the little things he missed, and it often surprised him what they were. Even the chocolate bars didn't quite taste the same as they did back home. They looked the same, had the same kind of packaging, but there was something about the taste that wasn't quite right.

The toast popped up, and he absent-mindedly started to smear butter and jam on it. He wondered how his family was doing. He should phone them later today. He hadn't spoken to Claire in quite a while. His mum and dad had been asking when he was planning to come home, even just for a visit, but he couldn't really do anything until the conference was over later this month. He was still preparing his paper, and there was some research he had to finish for it. Besides, the university probably wouldn't let him go until the end of the academic year. He took a bite of his toast.

Azamat was due to come that afternoon for another language lesson, and he would need to prepare for that. And then Bela was popping in for an hour or so after work to carry on with the typing. He'd really enjoyed visiting her family in the village. He'd listened to the recording of her Nana several times now and had got lots of useful information from it. But something inside him told him that he needed to be careful. He didn't want to get too involved with this family. He didn't want to give any wrong impressions.

And yet?

And yet, he couldn't stop thinking about her. Her beautiful smile and lovely eyes. The way those eyes lit up any time she started talking about her people or her language. She wasn't like the other girls he'd met, or rather, the ones who were throwing themselves at him at the university. In fact, he couldn't even be sure if she was attracted to him or not, and he found that a little intriguing, like a bit of a challenge.

He'd prayed a lot about it recently. It wouldn't be helpful to get involved with someone who didn't share his faith. The Bible warned about being yoked with unbelievers, and he'd seen too many friends at university who'd once been strong in their faith, like him, but somehow had drifted away once they'd become involved with or even married girls who didn't believe in the same things. No, that's not the life he wanted. He wanted a wife he could talk to about anything, who shared his passions and principles, who would bring up their children to love God.

But what did Bela think about God? He didn't really know. They'd never really had a proper conversation about it. Perhaps he could find out? Yes, that's what he'd do. It wasn't right to judge people without hearing their opinions first, was it? A picture came into his mind of Bela walking towards him in a beautiful, white wedding dress. He shook his head instantly to make the picture go away. A strong cup of coffee and a good morning's work was what he needed!

Bela turned up for work at Michael's apartment as soon as she was free from the phone shop. Her parents knew about her work and seemed happy enough that she was bringing in a little extra money. Michael was always careful to make sure that there was someone else in the apartment, like Cody or another friend from university, so that they wouldn't be alone and run the risk of people getting the wrong idea. She was glad that he understood her culture and was sensitive to it.

Cody answered the door and let her in with a big smile. She couldn't help smiling back; he gave off such positive vibes that you were automatically swept up into them.

"Hey, Bela, how ya doing?"

"Good, thank you. How are you?"

She bent down to remove her shoes and slipped into her usual pair of guest slippers.

"Hey, would you have some time to talk about my job offer after you've finished with Michael?"

"Yes, sure, no problem."

"Great!"

Bela walked into the living room and saw her work ready for her at the table. Michael had his back to her, checking out some books on the bookcase by the window. He turned around, flashed her a quick smile and said hello, but went back to searching through the books. Her heart gave a little skip, and she sat down quickly on the sofa, focussing her attention on the papers on the coffee table. Did he realise what kind of effect he had on her? He looked so handsome, silhouetted against the window like that.

He found the book he'd been looking for and came to join her. "I've gone through your translation of my talk and made a few notes." He pointed to some places on the papers where there were comments written in red pen. "If you could just add those in where I've marked, then…" He paused. "Then I think we're probably done."

"Oh, okay." Bela's stomach gave a sudden lurch of panic at the thought that her work with Michael might be done. Perhaps she was imagining it, but he had seemed to look at her in a way that suggested he might also be sad to think that their working relationship was coming to an end.

"Of course, I'll need you to help me learn how to pronounce everything properly. I don't want to look a complete idiot up there on the stage in front of all those academics!" He smiled, and she smiled back.

"You won't look like an idiot. They'll all be really impressed, and not just with the content of your paper." She genuinely believed that. It wasn't every day that you came across a foreigner who spoke Russian to such a good level, and the odd mistake here and there would barely be noticed.

She got down to work and forced herself to concentrate on the paper, but all she could think about was what would happen when he didn't need her anymore.

An hour later, Cody came in to find Michael and Bela laughing side by side on the sofa.

"*Vzai…eemo…za…myen…yemi.*"

"No. *Vzai-eemo-za-myen-yai-yemi!*" Bela laughed again as she tried to teach Michael how to pronounce the Russian word for 'interchangeable'.

"But that's what I said, wasn't it? You have no idea how hard it is for a foreigner to learn Russian!"

"But what about English? All those different words ending in o-u-g-h? At least Russian is phonetic. What you see is what you get."

"True, true. But don't even let me get started on Circassian!"

"Hey, are you guys nearly finished, or shall I come back in ten?" interrupted Cody with a grin.

"No, no, we're done for today. Thanks, Bela." Michael handed her her payment, which she quickly tucked away in her handbag. She felt awkward being reminded that she was being paid for helping him. She would have been happy to do it for free. Michael got up to go into the kitchen and put the kettle on, while Cody took his place.

For the next hour or so, Bela and Cody discussed the terms of her potential employment as his personal assistant. It was beginning to look like a real possibility. Cody's business was now officially registered, and he would be able to pay her a proper salary. The prospect of her actually being able to leave her job at the phone shop was becoming a reality. She could start as soon as she'd worked out her notice with Irina Petrovna.

As she left that evening, in the taxi that Cody and Michael had called for her, she felt jittery with excitement.

Finally, a job she'd always wanted, where her skills would be recognised and valued. A job with status and good prospects. She couldn't wait to tell Mama.

Her phone beeped, and she looked down to check the message that had just come in. It was from Michael, asking her if she'd like to go for a walk in the park on Saturday. Her heart started beating faster, and she quickly typed a reply, saying she would look forward to it. Could she dare to start dreaming about her and Michael being a couple? Why else would he want to meet her in the park?

The moment he'd sent the text, he wondered if he shouldn't have done it. Perhaps he'd been too hasty. After all his cautions about not giving her the wrong idea, what better way to do so than to ask her to go walking with him in the park? He suddenly felt a bit panicked. It had been a spontaneous decision. As he'd watched her taxi pull away from the yard below, he just knew he needed to see her again. It had been a knee-jerk reaction. He probably should have prayed about it first, but he'd been praying about nothing else for the past week or two.

Oh Lord, I'm sorry if I've done the wrong thing. Please give me wisdom to know what to say and do. Please guide me. I like this girl so much, God. Please, if there's any way she would be interested in becoming a Christian, please would you reveal the truth to her. And yet I need to know, Lord, that she's not just saying what she thinks I want to hear. I don't want to get involved unless she really is the person I could spend the rest of my life with.

The rest of his life with? How would that work out? He couldn't picture himself wanting to move to Russia permanently, and yet she probably wouldn't want to leave her home and her family either. Would she be happy living in England? Could he ask her to do that for him? Was it fair?

Michael, Michael, you're getting ahead of yourself again, he chastised himself. *You barely know the girl. You don't know where she stands in terms of faith in God, and you have no idea if she'd even want to go out with you anyway!*

He slumped down on the sofa and clicked the remote for the DVD player. An episode of *24* would be just the thing to help him take his mind off a certain captivatingly beautiful Circassian girl, wouldn't it?

Chapter 20

1994, December

Zalina sat on the floor, in the dark, in the corner of her bedroom. She gripped her hands tightly around her knees and rocked herself backwards and forwards, tears falling freely down her cheeks as she prayed silently.

It had been two months since she'd told her parents about her new faith. Her Bible had been taken away, probably thrown into the rubbish bin. Her room had been scoured for other sources of 'Christian propaganda', but there had been none. Thank goodness she hadn't ever written down the names or contact details of the people in her church group. Her parents had wanted her to give it all up, this new 'religion thing' as they called it. Her mother had plead gently with her, trying to appeal to Zalina's 'better side', whatever that might mean. She'd talked about family harmony and family honour. Zalina's marriage prospects would be severely hampered if it were known that she was a Christian. No one would want to marry her, and under no circumstances was she to marry anyone other than a Circassian. It was so unfair that it was totally fine for

Russian girls to become Muslims and marry into Circassian families, like Natasha's mother had done, but it wasn't okay the other way around. Not that she had anyone Russian in mind to marry, but still.

Her father's approach had been much more heavy-handed, sometimes literally so. He had taken away privileges and laid down harsh rules, all in an effort to get her to 'come to her senses'. She was allowed to go to school each day, but her mother had to see her off at the bus stop and meet her there as soon as school was over. She was to come straight home and see no one, not even Bela. Her father had ordered that all her clothes be taken away except her school uniform and her village *khalat* and slippers, to prevent her from running away. As an extra measure, the front door was not only locked at night, but the key was also removed and hidden.

At first, she'd doubted that her fledgling faith would be able to survive such treatment: not being able to read God's Word, not having been a believer long enough to know any passages by heart, and not being able to meet up with other Christians, especially Natasha and Slava.

And yet, she'd found, her parents couldn't take away her ability to pray.

Zalina spent nearly all her time praying now. She prayed wherever she was. At school, she prayed for help with her school work. At home, she prayed that she might still be able to show something of God's love to her parents. She prayed about her homework, that her parents could be proud of her grades. She prayed for courage to survive her new prison life. She prayed for her faith to remain strong, and that she wouldn't give into the pressure to conform and reject God.

And something amazing had happened. The more she'd prayed, the more peaceful she'd felt. She could feel that

God was really there with her, watching over her. She prayed to Jesus like he was her best friend. She felt God talking back to her sometimes. Nothing miraculous and out of the ordinary, just words or phrases that became imprinted on her mind in such a way that she knew it must have come from God. Words of comfort and grace. Sometimes she knew that Bible verses were coming to her mind, even though there was no way she could possibly have known them herself. She wrote them down and read them often. When this was all over, she would check them out and see which part of the Bible they came from.

One night, she'd had another vision of Jesus. She'd recognised him immediately from her previous vision. Still the same kind face, full of love. Still the same bright, white light and the hand outstretched to her. She'd felt so much joy to be with him that she'd woken up with a big smile on her face.

It hadn't been easy, though, especially on those occasions when her father arrived home drunk. He didn't seem to notice that her grades had got better, or that she was doing as much as she could to help her mother around the house. He didn't notice the way she was being an obedient daughter in all other respects. He only noticed that she still hadn't recanted her faith, and the longer the stand-off went on, the more incensed by it he became.

And then this evening, the unthinkable had happened. It was a Saturday, and her father had come back from town more drunk than usual. She'd heard him arguing with her mother. She'd heard lots of doors slamming, and then she'd heard the all too familiar heavy footsteps coming down the corridor towards her room. The door had been flung open, and she'd sat up in bed only to come face to face with a shotgun pointed straight at her.

She'd seen the gun many times before. Her father used to take it hunting, sometimes looking for deer, other times for rabbits. Once or twice it had been used on stray dogs that had looked rabid or had bitten someone. But never had he pointed it at her, never.

"You tell me right now that you've given up this Christianity thing or I'll shoot you, I swear I'll shoot you."

He'd swayed and stumbled a bit, the effects of the liquor making him unsteady. Zalina had prayed silently for her life.

"I love you, Papa, but I love God too."

Her mother had appeared behind her father, her face ashen with fear and horror. She'd reached out a hand tentatively to stroke her husband's arm and calm him down, not wanting to alarm him or jolt him into pulling the trigger by mistake.

"Hasan, no! She's your daughter, Hasan, your only daughter!" Her gentle voice had shaken with fear.

After several seconds that seemed more like minutes, Zalina's father had gradually lowered the gun. He'd allowed Zalina's mother to take it from him, and she'd quickly left the room. Hopefully, to put it in a place where he'd never find it again.

He'd looked at Zalina one last time, running his fingers through his hair, as if it were only just occurring to him what he'd been about to do. He'd stumbled backwards slowly and left the room, slamming the door behind him, but with a little less force than before. Zalina had heard her mother sobbing further down the corridor.

That had been over an hour ago. Zalina had turned off the light and crawled into the corner of the room. She wanted to be in the dark, hidden, where no one could find her again. And here she was, still in the same foetal position, still rocking backwards and forwards, forwards and backwards, tears of terror and relief streaming down her face. She thanked God over and over again for sparing her life. But now, an hour later, she had come to a new resolve. She understood what she must do. She had no choice now.

Bela knew that something was wrong. Zalina had seemed withdrawn and distant for several weeks now. She desperately wanted to talk to her and find out what was wrong, but Zalina's mother was always there at the bus stop, and their paths didn't cross much at school. Finally, one day, just as they were getting off the *marshroutka* in front of the school entrance, Zalina slipped a note into Bela's bag.

"Zalina, wait!" she called out, but her friend was already disappearing into one of the school buildings, and Bela had to head in the other direction or she'd be late for class.

She fingered the note nervously during the day, not daring to open it until she'd got home and even then there were chores to do, and dinner. When she was finally on her own in her room, she shut the door and tore open the envelope.

Dearest Bela. I'm sorry I've not been able to spend time with you recently. I was hoping things would get better at home, but they haven't. They've got worse. I told Mama and Papa about my new faith, and they took it badly. I'm not allowed to speak to anyone. I'm not allowed to leave the house except to go to school and back. They've taken away my clothes and lock the front door each night so I can't run away. Something happened last night that made me realise I'm not safe here anymore. I have to leave. I'm sorry but you're the only person I can turn to. I know you don't share my faith, but please, as my best friend, will you help me? Come to my window tonight at ten o'clock. Use the gate in our backyard. Bring some money and some clothes and shoes for me, and I'll forever be in your debt. Your friend, Zalina.

Bela looked up at her clock. It was nine thirty. Half an hour to wait. She read Zalina's letter over and over again. She knew only too well how controlling Zalina's parents were, and how unpredictable her father was, especially now he'd started drinking more. He might have hidden it well from the other neighbours, but Bela had noticed. Something like this was bound to happen; it had only been a matter of time.

She quickly gathered some clothes that she knew would fit Zalina well enough and put them in a plastic bag. She opened her bedside drawer and took out all the money that was tucked inside it, money she'd been building up from her own savings. Would it be enough? She didn't want to steal from her parents.

But what could have happened to make Zalina so afraid that she would want to leave home? She started to think through how she could creep out to Zalina's unnoticed. Her bedroom was on the ground floor, but the foundations of the house were so high that it would be quite a jump to get to the ground. She probably wouldn't be able to do it without spraining an ankle. Ah, that was it. She would go outside, pretending she was checking on Bobik or something like that, and quietly move the garden table to just below her window. She could easily climb down onto that.

Ten minutes later, she was back in her bedroom, mission accomplished. Mama had seen her go out, but had also seen her come back in again, so no one would suspect that she wasn't in her room. The moon was out, so thankfully she would be able to see enough of her surroundings without needing a torch. She felt her heart thumping—she'd never done anything like this before. She looked at the clock again. Ten more minutes. She waited five and then quietly opened her window and lifted herself over and down. It worked. She let out a sigh of relief and then silently chided herself for making a noise. She crept over to the back gate, gently lifted the latch, and squeezed through into Zalina's backyard.

Zalina's dog, Jack, padded up to her. She ruffled his fur and gave him a quick pat. Thank goodness he hadn't barked his welcome. Carefully, she crept over to Zalina's bedroom window. The window opened, and Zalina looked down at her.

"I'm so glad you came," she whispered.

"I brought what you asked for," Bela whispered back, handing up the bag of clothes and money.

"Thank you! Can you help me escape through your front yard? There'll be someone waiting for me at the end of the road."

"So, you're really running away from home?"

"I have no choice. Believe me, I've thought this all through, Bela."

Suddenly, doubts started flooding Bela's mind, and she considered backing out. What kind of trouble would she be in if she were found out? Was she doing the right thing, helping Zalina disobey her parents and run away? What would her own father say or do if he found out? But then she remembered that Zalina was her best friend. She thought of the many bruises she'd seen on Zalina's face and arms over the past year or so. She knew that something awful must have happened for Zalina to even contemplate running away from home, leaving her only family. Especially since she was so close to finishing school. Her life would never be the same after this, she must know that.

Zalina had disappeared from the window, and, in just a minute or two, she was dressed and had started to swing her legs out over the window ledge, a small bag of belongings slung over her shoulder. She'd obviously climbed out of the window like this before, because the jump didn't seem to worry her. The grass underneath broke the sound of her feet making contact with the ground, but the two girls still froze for a few seconds to make sure no one had heard. There was silence.

They crept slowly through the gate into Bela's garden, then they made their way as soundlessly as they could along the wall, past the side of the house, and into the front yard. Bela hurried over to pat Bobik to make sure he didn't bark a friendly, curious bark at them, and it seemed to do the trick. Ever so carefully, she eased the catch on the front gate and pulled it back just enough for them both to squeeze through, pulling it closed just as carefully.

Keeping to the shadows as much as possible, the two girls hurried down the lane. Soon they were around the corner. They were safe; no one had seen them. They allowed themselves to smile at each other in relief.

A car was waiting a little further down the road, and Bela saw a man get out. A woman, perhaps his wife, was in the passenger seat, waiting. He took Zalina's bag and opened the back door of the car for her. Zalina gave Bela a quick hug.

"Thank you! I'll be in touch, somehow. Thank you!"

"Take care," was all Bela could manage before the car's engine switched on and it started slowly down the road, taking Zalina away to a new life, whatever and wherever that might be.

Chapter 21

2004, May

Azamat had noticed the digital camera sitting on the window sill, slightly obscured by the net curtains. There wasn't much of value in Michael's apartment, he had to admit, but the camera would fetch a few roubles. He tried to shake off Vadim's voice in his mind. It was Vadim's idea, of course, to take something from the 'rich Westerners'. He hadn't exactly used the word 'steal', and he'd almost made it sound like Michael would be doing them a favour.

"Oh, they've probably got insurance and will be able to upgrade to new models of anything that might... go missing. It wouldn't bother them much. These Westerners are rolling in it. They might pretend not to have much money, but they do. It's only fair that they should share some of that. Who do they think they are, coming to live in our country and not helping us out?"

He tried to concentrate on the lesson that Michael had prepared for today. They were working on the past tense, and Michael had drawn various pictures of things he might have been doing yesterday, like 'I went for a walk in the

park', 'I watched television'. It was easy money, this
language helper thing.

Azamat glanced back over at the window sill. Exactly
how much he would get for the camera? Vadim was a few
thousand roubles in debt, and his dealer was getting on his
back about it. He'd just been messing around with drugs,
but drugs were expensive, and Vadim kept wanting to get
more. At least Azamat had seen enough sense to stop after
his first few tries. He'd been called many derogatory names
by his father already, but he wasn't going to let 'drug addict'
be one of them.

Michael's voice brought Azamat's attention back to the
lesson. "Are you okay, Azamat? You seem a bit distracted
today?"

"Yeah, sorry. I'm fine."

"Well, it's okay, I think we're done for now. Thanks
again. I'll just go and get your payment."

Azamat barely knew what he was doing, but the
moment Michael had left the living room to find his wallet,
Azamat had jumped up and swiped the camera off the
window sill. He covered it with his jacket, which had been
lying beside him on the sofa, just as Michael returned.
Azamat took the money that was held out to him, a wave of
guilt flooding through him at what he'd just done. Vadim's
assurances about how rich these Westerners were didn't
really seem to fit. Azamat knew plenty of local families who
seemed to be rolling in more money than this British
linguist. He knew people who had designer clothes and
fancy cars, none of which Michael or his American friend
seemed to have. But he'd done it now. He managed to put
his shoes on without letting go of his jacket, shook
Michael's hand and bounded down the stairs and out of the
door of the apartment block. His heart was beating loudly
in his chest.

He'd stolen many things before, always at Vadim's instigation, but this one seemed more personal somehow. Michael was a friend, wasn't he? Perhaps he hadn't done the right thing. He wouldn't tell Vadim he'd done it, not yet.

"Azamat! Mama needs some help getting the potatoes out of the cellar," Bela called out. She knocked once on Azamat's door but didn't wait for an answer. She pushed the door open just in time to see Azamat push something hurriedly under his pillow.

"What's that?" she said, walking up to his bed.

"Nothing! Stop snooping in my room, Bela."

"Oh, come on, show me. What have you got?" She lunged at the pillow and managed to grab whatever it was before Azamat could stop her. She looked at it, curiously, turning it over in her hands.

"What's this? A camera?"

"Give it back, it's mine."

"I didn't know you had a digital camera?"

"Yeah, well, I got some money, didn't I?"

Bela looked at the back of the camera case. There was something familiar about this camera. Had she seen it before somewhere? She opened it up, and inside there was a small piece of notepaper, embellished with flowers. On it, written in English, were the words: *"To Michael, May you make many happy memories on your travels. Love Claire."* She looked up at Azamat, her eyes wide with shock.

"This is Michael's! What are you doing with Michael's camera?"

Her brother looked down guiltily. She could see he was trying to come up with some reasonable, believable answer, but she already knew the truth.

"You stole it!"

Azamat said nothing, but she could tell that she was right. She sat down next to him on the bed.

"Why, Azamat? Michael's our friend. You're his language helper. Why would you do this?"

"I… I don't know. Vadim said he wouldn't even notice. These foreigners are all so rich."

"Vadim! Azamat, Vadim is a stupid idiot, and you need to stop listening to him. He just gets you into trouble, that's all. Why do you listen to him?"

"I don't know." Azamat turned away sulkily. Bela gently placed the camera in her pocket and Azamat didn't object. She would find a time to return it to Michael, but she'd have to think about what she would say to him.

She looked at Azamat. She felt sorry for her brother. They'd been close when they were younger, but Azamat had been following the wrong path for many years now, and it was leading him to greater danger.

"What's happened to you, Azamat? You've been so different, ever since you came back from the army. You've always done lots of stupid things," she laughed, and saw the corners of his mouth edge up into a weak, acknowledging smile, "but lately you've seemed, well, depressed."

Azamat looked at the wall. Would he open up to her at last, or just push her away again?

"I just feel like there's no point to life anymore," he said quietly. "There's no future, nothing worth fighting for, nothing to look forward to."

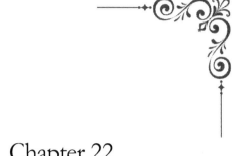

Chapter 22

1996, May

"What's that?" Bela asked, wide-eyed, pointing to his arm. Azamat shot her a fierce look and quickly pulled his sleeve down.

"Is that a tattoo?"

"Maybe."

"Why do you have a tattoo?"

"All the guys in the army were getting them. It's no big deal. Just don't tell Mama, okay?"

Bela paused. "Okay," she agreed reluctantly.

Azamat managed to get rid of his little sister and close his bedroom door. She'd looked hurt, and he felt a bit bad, but he just couldn't deal with any more questions right now. His year in the army had been a mixed experience. At first, he had to admit, he'd been a bit homesick. Most of the new recruits had in some way, although they'd tried to hide it. One guy from Stavropol had even wet his bed a few times, and he'd been completely humiliated by the other recruits and by the officer in charge. Azamat was glad that he'd been able to look strong. The Circassian recruits had a reputation for that.

In many ways, army life had suited him. He liked not having to think for himself or make his own decisions. He just did what he was told and kept his head down. At first, the physical demands—the early mornings, the chores—had been exhausting, but his body had got used to it and, in time, he had started to thrive in the army atmosphere. He'd been commended at the end, and even encouraged to consider a permanent career in the army later on.

"We could use guys like you," they'd told him, and Azamat had felt a sense of pride and achievement that he hadn't felt for a long time.

The army had also toughened him up. He'd had a couple of tattoos done, one that Bela hadn't seen yet, and he was now sporting a scar on his left leg from a weapons exercise that had gone slightly wrong. He'd learnt to talk tough and to act tough and to hide any possible signs of weakness.

But all through that long year, he'd carried the pain of his broken relationship with Milana in his heart. Sometimes, the pain had been so bad that he'd physically felt his body ache with the wretchedness of the situation. Perhaps he should have fought for her? Perhaps he shouldn't have walked away? Perhaps he should have demanded his rights?

She would have had the baby several months ago now, just before he'd gone off to do his military service, but he'd heard no news. He didn't even know if he had a daughter or a son. She'd be married too. In the arms of someone else, someone who might never love her the way Azamat would have done. Had done.

Mama had phoned a few times to fill him in on what they were doing back home, but the news that Azamat desperately wanted to hear had never been there. How could it be? He'd told no one about it, not even Vadim. He was broken, yes, but also ashamed. He had failed in his first role as a father—to stand up for his child.

Would Milana ever tell the child the truth? Would she ever tell the child that his or her father was not the man that he or she thought he was? Would the child eventually come looking for him? He doubted it. He'd been pushed out of Milana's life for good, he was sure of that.

Milana had left a massive hole in his life. When he'd thought about his future, it was always with her, but now? Now he had no idea what he should do with his life, where he was heading. Perhaps he *should* consider making a full-time career in the army? However, he knew deep down that, as youngest son, it was his duty to stay in his parents' home and be there to look after them in their old age. Deep down he was proud to be Circassian and proud to uphold his people's customs. No matter how much he hated his father sometimes, he knew that he would do his duty as a son.

Part of him wanted to make something big of himself. He wanted to show Milana and her parents that they'd been wrong. He would have been the better choice. He would have provided Milana and their child with a very comfortable life. He wanted to show them, make them feel sorry.

It was strange how he could love Milana so much and yet hate her at the same time.

Besides, he was back home now. Perhaps he should try to find out where she lived? Just to see her one more time. To catch a glimpse of the little child she'd be carrying in her arms.

Madina wiped a bead of sweat off her forehead, rinsed out the rag in the bucket, and stood up. The laminate on the kitchen floor shone with newly washed cleanliness, but she knew it wouldn't last long. She'd be back here on her knees with the same bucket in a couple of days. She looked outside the kitchen window. It was a beautiful day in early summer, and she longed to be outside. She hurriedly emptied the dirty water, put away her cleaning materials, and smoothed down her house coat. She would take Alyona out for a walk.

She found her daughter in the living room, playing with the plastic blocks that some well-meaning neighbour had bought for Alyona at the market. Galina was in the room but wasn't paying much attention to her granddaughter. She looked up as Madina came in. Always with an air of disapproval, always with an expression of contempt.

"I'm taking Alyona out for some fresh air."

Galina nodded her acceptance and returned to her sewing. Alyona left her blocks and toddled towards Madina with a big smile on her face. Madina smiled back.

"Let's go for a walk, sweetheart," she said, swinging her daughter onto her hip. Her heart felt lighter already. Alyona was the joy of her life. Perhaps the only real joy, if she was honest.

Madina dressed Alyona in suitable clothes. Was it still necessary to have so many layers on at the beginning of May? She dared not incur the wrath of some watchful *babushka* on a street corner. The last thing she needed was to be told that she was a bad mother. It was enough to be reminded every day by Musa and his family that she wasn't much of a wife.

Madina placed Alyona in the large, cumbersome pushchair that had once been a pram. There were newer, lighter ones in the market these days, but the wheels on this one were large and sturdy and well-suited to the gravelly village roads where they lived. She strode down the street, feeling her lungs fill with the fresh, mountain air, and enjoying the warmth of the sun on her face. She felt almost happy.

Musa had started paying her a bit more attention recently, or rather, he'd been demanding more of her wifely nighttime duties, but Madina wasn't fool enough not to realise that it was because he wanted her to get pregnant with a son this time. During the day, she barely saw him, and in the evenings, if he came home, he treated her more like a housemaid than a wife. Why had he grown bored of her so quickly? Had he never really loved her in the first place? She stifled a small sob and focussed her mind back on the present moment.

All around her were signs of new life and new starts. The apple blossoms were out in full force, and the walnut trees sported shiny, new, green leaves. One woman was out watching a brood of chickens, and Madina paused, letting Alyona smile with delight at the little chicks who were running around looking for food.

She turned down another street and realised that, subconsciously, she'd been heading for the house of her new friend, Milana. She'd met Milana a few times when they were both out with their prams. Milana's son, Alikhan, was exactly a year younger than Alyona, but already the two children played together like they were best friends. In Milana, she'd sensed a kindred spirit; another young bride uprooted from her family home and brought to this quiet village far from anywhere remotely civilised. She sensed Milana was finding it harder to adjust than she had, and suspected that her new friend had been much more used to the delights of clothes' boutiques, cafés, cinemas, and the bright lights of the big town.

As she approached Milana's house, she saw her struggling out of the front gate with her own cumbersome pushchair. She'd obviously had the same idea on this beautiful morning. Madina quickened her pace.

"Milana!" she called out when she was within earshot.

Milana turned around and smiled. She closed the gate behind her and waited for Madina to catch up. They gave each other a quick hug.

"You also going for a walk?" asked Madina.

"Any excuse to get out of the house and away from all the chores!" replied Milana with a light laugh that was a little too forced.

"Your mother-in-law treating you like a housemaid too?"

"It just seems to get worse! I really wish I'd spent more time watching my own mother when I was at home. Nothing comes naturally to me." Milana sighed. "One of the disadvantages of marrying into a respectable family is that there are so many more rooms to clean."

"You don't have domestic help?"

"They haven't needed it up till now, but I'm trying to pester Murat about it. I'm exhausted. I keep telling him there won't be any more children at this rate; I'm too worn out."

"That should do it." Madina smiled in sympathy. She hesitated before asking the next question. "Is he a good husband, your Murat?"

"Oh yes, he's good to me. I have no complaints."

"But, does he love you?"

Milana let out a cynical laugh. "Love? We didn't marry for love. It was all arranged, ever since I was a baby. But I could have done a lot worse, I'm aware of that."

"Do you think you'll ever learn to love each other?"

Milana was thoughtful for a minute, and a deep sadness crossed her pretty face. "Perhaps. I was in love, once. I know what it feels like, and I know we're not there yet. But there's more to marriage than love; at least, that's what my parents kept telling me. How about you?"

Madina shook her head. "Perhaps we were in love in the beginning, but it's all changed now. I think… I think he's just grown bored of me."

Milana nodded understandingly. "It's often the way. Are there other women?"

"I'm pretty sure, yes."

"I'm so sorry." Milana gave her shoulder a supportive squeeze.

Alikhan started fussing in his pushchair, and Milana stopped to give him his water bottle. An old lady approached. She paused to look at the two children and raised her hands to her face in delight. She pulled down the edges of their hats, making sure their ears were well-covered, and muttered some words of appreciation and blessing in Circassian, followed by the customary spitting to ward off the attention of the evil eye. Madina was glad that she'd paid equal attention to both children, even though Alyona was a girl. Why couldn't Musa's family be more like that?

When she was gone, Madina commented, "You know, Alikhan reminds me so much of my brother. I don't remember him much from when he was a baby, of course, but we have photos, and he looks so similar."

Milana stiffened a little. "Oh really?" She laughed. "What's your brother's name?"

"Azamat."

Milana's face paled as if she'd seen a ghost.

"Is something the matter?"

"No! No, nothing. I... I just suddenly don't feel too good. Shall we turn back?"

"Sure, no problem."

For a moment Madina wondered whether it was the mention of her brother's name that had made Milana look so strange, but then she chided herself. There were so many boys with the name Azamat that the chances of Milana and her brother actually knowing each other were very small. He'd certainly never spoken of a Milana before. Her friend was probably just feeling a bit ill, like she said.

Madina tried to think quickly of something to say that would lighten the mood. "You don't think you're pregnant again do you?"

"Oh God, I hope not!" Milana laughed, the colour in her cheeks returning. "Imagine having to go through all that again!"

They laughed and started sharing horror stories from their respective pregnancies and births.

Madina was so grateful she'd found Milana. She didn't know what she'd do without her. She would have slowly spiralled down into depression, that's for sure.

Chapter 23

2004, May

Bela waited anxiously on the bench near the park entrance, where they'd agreed to meet. She clutched her handbag tightly on her lap. Michael's camera was safely inside, and she didn't want to lose it again until she'd handed it back to its rightful owner. What would Michael say; how would he react? Would he be angry when he found out that it was Azamat who'd stolen it? Would he blame her too in some way, think that she'd been an accomplice somehow? Stupid Azamat, why did he always have to get himself in trouble?

She saw Michael arrive under the entrance sign to the park, and she had a moment or two to look at him before he noticed her. He didn't seem to be angry. He just seemed to be his usual, affable self. His usual, *handsome*, affable self.

He looked over and saw her. She waved tentatively, acknowledging him, and rose out of her seat. He increased his pace and was almost jogging by the time he reached her.

"Hi." He smiled, clearly not knowing if he should hug her, kiss her cheek, or shake her hand. He did none of them, simply kept smiling at her.

"Hi," she replied. "I have something of yours." Best to get it over and done with quickly.

"Oh." He looked surprised. She sat down, and he sat down next to her. A young family walked past, two parents pushing a small child along on a tricycle. She reached into her bag and handed Michael the camera. It took him a moment to work out what it was.

"My camera? But, how?"

"It was Azamat. I'm so sorry. He took it. Stole it, actually, I guess. On Friday, when he was at your lesson." She glanced down at the ground, ashamed, as if she too was implicated in the theft.

"Oh, I see." Michael paused looking at the camera in his hands, his expression a little confused. "Did he say why?"

"My brother has a few troubles at the moment. He's not all bad, he just has bad friends that persuade him to do bad things. One of his friends dared him to steal something from you. They figured that you had so much money, being a foreigner, that you wouldn't even notice. They were planning to sell it and get some money. I'm so sorry."

"Oh, I see," said Michael again. He paused, taking in what she'd just said. "How did you get it back?"

"I saw it in his room last night and knew that it was yours. I made him give it back. I think he was genuinely sorry. I don't even know if he was going to go through with it, selling it that is. Please forgive him. Us. Please don't tell anyone."

Michael looked a little taken aback. "Of course, I forgive him. I can see how it would be tempting, I shouldn't have left it lying around. And you, well, Bela, there's nothing to forgive. You're the one that got it back, right?"

Relief flooded through her. He wasn't angry. He wasn't going to report Azamat to the police. Or to their father.

"Thank you," she said, looking up at him gratefully.

Michael stood up suddenly. "Hey, let's put this all behind us. The whole thing's forgotten. Shall we walk?" He put the camera into the small rucksack he was carrying and slung it back over his shoulder.

Bela got up too. "Yes." She smiled. "Let's. Actually…" She paused.

"Yes?"

"Can I ask you one thing? About the camera?"

"Sure."

"I couldn't help noticing the little note inside the case. It was what told me that the camera belonged to you."

"Oh, yes?"

"I was… I was just wondering. Who's Claire?"

"Claire's my sister. Have I not mentioned her before? She loves photography, and she wanted me to get some great shots of interesting places." His smile faded. "Places she can't go to herself, that is."

Bela sensed that Michael didn't really want to talk about his sister, so she didn't ask any more questions. Why had she been so worried about who Claire might be? And why was she so relieved to find out she was Michael's sister?

They walked side by side up the central alleyway of the park. The path had been newly paved over this past year, and the old benches were gradually being replaced by new ones. A new café was being built just by the entrance, and the park employees had been doing a great job on the huge flower displays at the intersections of the various paths. She was proud of their town park; it really was a beautiful place to walk and relax. There were a lot of other people also walking, which wasn't surprising for a Saturday. She wondered if she would meet anyone she knew, and if so, how she would introduce Michael. She'd cross that bridge if she came to it. She was just relieved that he still wanted to be friends.

She resisted the strong urge to link her arm under his and focussed instead on trying not to trip in her high heels.

Michael felt nervous. He hoped that Bela wasn't still feeling bad about the camera incident. He hadn't even noticed that it was missing. And when he did, he probably would have guessed that it was Azamat. He hoped his friendship with Azamat could be restored; he'd hate to lose a perfectly good language helper, and he sensed that he was being a positive influence in Azamat's life in some way.

He couldn't help noticing how lovely Bela was looking today, and he wanted more than anything to reach out and hold her hand, but he knew that he shouldn't. They walked along in silence for a while, watching all the other people out and about on their Saturday strolls. They reached the central fountain, and Michael noticed a little ice cream cart on the left.

"Would you like an ice cream?"

Her eyes lit up like a young girl's, "Yes, please."

He chose a couple of ice creams, and they sat down on a nearby bench to eat them.

They broke the silence at the same time.

"I've…"

"I…"

They laughed over the confusion.

"You first," he said, smiling, glad that the awkward silence was broken.

"I was just going to say that I've enjoyed working with you. I hope you enjoy the conference next week."

"And I was just going to say how much of a help you've been. I'm sorry to lose you to Cody, but I was hoping I might be able to call on your services every now and again. If he doesn't work you too hard, that is."

She laughed. "Yes, of course. I'd like that."

"Bela." He paused, trying to formulate what he was going to say.

"Yes?" she looked up expectantly, wiping a bit of ice cream away from the corner of her mouth.

"I hope you don't mind me asking, but I was wondering what you thought about God? About religion? I guess I don't really know whether you're a Muslim or an atheist or what."

"Oh, okay." She obviously wasn't expecting that question. Michael wondered if he shouldn't have brought it up, but after a few seconds, Bela answered.

"Well, my family say they are Muslims, like all good Circassians should be. But I guess it doesn't really mean anything in day-to-day life. I mean, we don't go to the mosque or say *namaz* or anything."

"Namaz?"

"The daily prayers."

"Oh, yes, of course. Go on."

"Well, I suppose we have lots of our own traditions. Things we believe in. Like the evil eye, spirits, and things. We say prayers for the dead."

"And what about you? What do you believe?"

Bela paused again, giving his question some thought.

"I guess I've just always gone along with what was expected of me, what my family believed, but I realise now that perhaps I've been avoiding having to think it through for myself personally. I believe in God, I think. I don't believe we're all here just by accident. I believe that something, someone, must have made all this." She gestured to the beautiful park surroundings, and then took another lick of her ice cream.

"I remember going to the mountains with my Uncle Artur and having this intense feeling, like there was something powerful that made the mountains. I even felt like I heard a voice, but since I was just a little girl at the time I was probably making it up."

Michael looked up, interested. "A voice? What did it say?"

"It said 'Lift your eyes to the mountains'. I guess that's why I believe there must be a God. Every time I look at the mountains, I can't help thinking that God must have made them, and He must be an amazing God."

A small jolt of excitement shot through his body, and he sat up straighter. "Did you know that that's a verse from the Bible?"

Bela turned and looked at him, startled.

"No. What do you mean?"

"That line, 'Lift your eyes to the mountains'. It's from the Psalms. Look."

Michael reached inside his rucksack and pulled out a small copy of the Bible that he usually carried around with him. He deftly turned to the right place. It was one of his favourite verses, all the more so since coming to live in Shekala.

"See?" He handed it to her, pointing at the place.

She read it aloud. "Lift your eyes to the mountains. Where does your help come from? It comes from the Lord, the maker of heaven and earth."

"Wow," she said. "I had no idea." She held the little book in her hand, and he wasn't sure whether she felt intrigued or terrified or both.

After a while, she handed the Bible back. "My friend, Zalina—have I mentioned her? She's a Christian."

Michael said nothing but willed her with a slight nod to go on with her story.

"She became a Christian when she was seventeen. She tried to get me to read the Bible, but I didn't want to. I wish now I'd asked her more questions about it. She was my best friend."

"Was? Did something happen?"

"Oh, she's not dead, if that's what you thought I meant. It's just, she had to go away. Her parents didn't like the fact that she'd become a Christian, and she had to leave home. I... I helped her escape."

"Oh, gosh. That must have been frightening for you both."

"Yes, it was. I've not told this to anyone before, other than Nana."

"And how's Zalina doing now? Have you seen her since?"

"Oh yes, I visit her from time to time. She moved to a town a few hours away. She married a great guy called Ruslan, and they have two adorable little children. I should visit her more, but it's hard to get away. I don't really want my parents to know I'm still in touch with her. They wouldn't approve."

"I see." Michael felt disappointed. Of course her family would disapprove.

"They didn't mind that I was a Christian?" He had to ask.

"Oh no! You're a foreigner. Of course, you're a Christian, it's understood. Despite what many people think, most of us Muslims want to live in harmony with other religions. We don't want to cause trouble. We all worship the same God, don't we?"

Michael was silent, thinking how best to answer.

"I don't doubt your family's good intentions, but I worship the God of the Bible. I suspect that He may be a little different to what many of your people understand God to be like."

"Oh?" Bela seemed genuinely interested.

"Well, for a start, He loved us so much that He sent His one and only son to die for us so that we could be forgiven. We can never earn our way to heaven by doing good works. It's a gift from God. All we have to do is accept it by having faith in Jesus."

"Zalina said some similar things to me, but I never quite understood. Surely it's okay just to live a good life?"

"And have you? Do you think you're good enough to go to heaven?"

Bela looked down awkwardly, and Michael suddenly regretted what he'd said. Maybe he'd gone too far.

"I'm sorry," he said hastily. "I'm not judging you. It's just that we've all done things that we regret, things that we need to be forgiven for. The Bible says that 'no one is good, not even one'."

Bela finished her ice cream and stood up to put the empty wrapper in a nearby bin. "Let's carry on walking," she offered brightly, clearly wanting to change the subject. Michael got up and smiled in agreement. He desperately wanted to talk to her about the truth, about God and Jesus, but at the same time he really didn't want to lose her friendship.

"Do you fancy a ride on the chair lift over the lake?" he offered. "I've always wanted to see what was at the top of that hill."

She nodded happily. "Oh, it's a wonderful view, right over the whole of Shekala. You can even see my village in the distance."

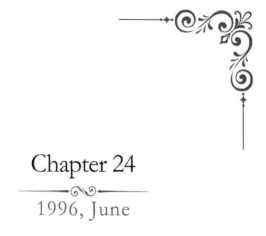

Chapter 24

1996, June

Zalina closed her Bible and took a sip of her tea. She looked around her and felt her heart welling up with love for God and thankfulness for how her life had turned out. The terrifying days preceding her escape from her parents' house were long behind her, and she'd been living with Rosa in a neighbouring republic for over a year now. The lovely older lady was also a Circassian Christian, and, being a good friend of Slava's wife, she had agreed to take Zalina in when she'd fled Shekala.

She smoothed her fingers over the cover of her Bible. It felt so wonderful to be able to read her Bible freely, without worrying about who might come in and catch her doing it. She'd grown in her faith so much since living with this kind and generous woman, who'd answered all her questions patiently, to the best of her ability. Zalina had insisted on making herself useful by helping with the chores around the house and in the garden, and in turn, Rosa had made her feel like this was her home.

In fact, this really was going to be her home very soon. Rosa's son, Ruslan, had returned from a job in Moscow a few months after Zalina had moved in. They'd both been attracted to each other straight away and, after a few months of shy glances and secret smiles, they'd finally admitted to each other that they were falling in love. He was a full ten years older than her, but that didn't matter to her one bit. He was kind and gentle, and a wise, godly man. He was also a committed Christian, like his mother.

Zalina trembled with excitement. Their wedding was only a couple of weeks away. God had been so good to her, not only looking after her and placing her here in a safe family, but also in the way that he'd brought Ruslan into her life. She almost laughed. The old Zalina would have been shocked to be looking forward to getting married, but here she was. She hadn't counted on how wonderful it would feel to actually be in love with someone. She got up and fingered the net curtain as she looked out over Rosa's back garden. What she hadn't counted on was that neither of her parents would be at her wedding. She hadn't been in contact with them since the escape, other than a letter to say that she was safe, but she knew from occasional phone calls from Bela that her father still hadn't forgiven her and was still fuming. Perhaps it would be best to wait until after the wedding to try to get in touch again. She didn't want another run-in with her father to spoil her happiness right now. Besides, once she was legally married, he wouldn't have any rights over her anymore.

The only person from Awush who knew where she was living was Bela. Knowing that she could trust her, Zalina had written to Bela soon after her escape to let her know that she was safe and being looked after. Bela would have worried about her, even if her father didn't seem to care. Her mother hadn't been making much of an effort to track her down either, apparently. Was it because her father had forbidden it? Perhaps she shouldn't have left her mother to face her father's angry moods on her own, without a daughter to deflect his rage. Perhaps she hadn't done the right thing in running away? It had seemed the only option at the time, but looking back, she hadn't really given it much thought. Or prayer.

Either way, it was too late now to change anything.

Zalina picked up the phone and dialled Bela's home number again. She'd already rung a couple of times, but someone else had always answered, so she'd hung up immediately. For weeks she'd been dying to ask Bela a question. Would Bela, her best friend in all the world, be willing to be her bridesmaid? Would she risk being found out by her family to make the trip all the way over here in two weeks' time? The phone was onto its third ring. Zalina prayed that it would be Bela who picked up this time.

The atmosphere in the simple bedroom at Rosa's house was charged with excitement and nervous happiness. Zalina twirled in front of the mirror in her simple but elegant, ivory wedding dress, smiling and bursting with joy. Bela watched her friend, her heart full of happiness too. She'd never seen Zalina look so beautiful and radiant.

She'd noticed a change in Zalina ever since she'd arrived at the house yesterday morning. She seemed so happy and serene. It was more than just being in love. There was something about Zalina's faith that made her glow too. It was so good to see her friend happy and safe. It made the frightening events of that night several months ago, and all the lies and deception since, worth it.

When Zalina had called to ask Bela to be her bridesmaid, Bela had said yes straight away, although it had taken her a while to work out how she would make the trip without her family or neighbours finding out. In the end, it had been Nana who'd come to the rescue. Good old Nana. She was the only one who knew what Bela and Zalina had done that night. She'd caught Bela sneaking back into the house after Zalina had been driven away and had made Bela tell her everything. Bela had been relieved, actually, not to have to shoulder this secret alone. Fortunately, Nana had been sympathetic and had agreed that it was all for the best if no one knew that Bela had been involved in Zalina's sudden disappearance. Bela and Nana had tried their best to look surprised when Zalina's mother had told them over the fence that a letter had arrived saying that Zalina was safe.

She felt a bit sorry for Zalina's mother. It must be awful to lose your only daughter and not know where she was, but for Zalina's safety, Bela knew it was best not to tell. Zalina's father was still drinking heavily, and his anger hadn't dissipated at all, though it was now tinged with slight regret. It was up to Zalina to choose when to tell her parents where she now was.

The wedding ceremony was to be held in Zalina's church, and Bela was intrigued to know what that would look like. The official service at the registry office had taken place yesterday afternoon, but Zalina and Ruslan wouldn't consider themselves properly married until they'd taken their vows in their church the following day. At least that meant Bela got to dress up twice, so she was quite happy about it, although Zalina had reserved her wedding dress for this special day alone.

Zalina was chatting away happily to Rosa, who was putting the finishing touches to the flowers in her hair. As a child, Bela had often thought about what it would be like to be the bridesmaid at Zalina's wedding, even if Zalina herself hadn't been too keen to play along at the time. She couldn't believe that the day had finally come. Funny, she'd always supposed that she would be the first to get married. But that was before her rose-tinted glasses had been shattered.

Before Papa's affair and Madina's unhappiness.

And yet, there was something about this marriage that told her it would be different to Madina's. Bela had warmed to Ruslan the moment she met him and could tell straight away that he loved Zalina and would be a good husband to her.

"The Bible has high standards for husbands!" Zalina had assured Bela with a laugh the previous night as they'd talked about what it would be like to be a married woman. "He's supposed to love me as much as he loves himself. To love me like Jesus loved his people and gave up his life for us. That's quite a tall order!"

Bela really hoped that things would work out for Zalina this time. She certainly deserved some happiness in her life, given all that she'd been through. Bela's hands still shook when she thought of all the details surrounding Zalina's escape. They'd talked about it last night, and Zalina had filled her in on the rest of the details which had prompted her to run away. Bela hadn't known about the gun and she was still shocked, hours later. How could a father pull a gun on his own daughter? Her Papa had his faults, that was for sure, but she didn't believe he'd ever do a thing like that.

The church turned out to be an ordinary-looking house on a street just a short car ride away. The basement had been converted into a large meeting room with rows of chairs, and today it was beautifully decorated with garlands of flowers tied with white ribbons. It was full of people, including families with children. Bela looked around. These people seemed friendly and, well, just ordinary people. She also thought that the marriage service itself was quite lovely. There were songs sung about Jesus and God, beautiful songs, and parts of the Bible were read aloud. Bela listened with surprising interest to the speech given by the pastor of the church and found herself agreeing with a lot of what he was saying.

An hour or so later, she was enjoying the delicious meal which had been laid out on tables outside in the front yard, and she laughed along with the others at the funny speeches and games. She didn't know anybody present other than Zalina, but these were good people, and she could see why Zalina was happy here among them.

Later that afternoon, when the time came for her to make her way back to the bus station, she hugged her friend fiercely.

"Congratulations, Zalina! I'm sure you're going to make a wonderful married couple!"

"Thanks, Bela!" Zalina laughed. "Did you ever think this day would come? Me, a married woman! But seriously, I'm so glad you could come. It meant the world to me that you were there as my bridesmaid today."

"Me too. Thank Nana for that. She's been covering for me, saying that I'm visiting some elderly friend of hers."

Bela waved, watching Zalina as long as she could from the bus window as it pulled away.

She envied Zalina, she realised. Would she also be that happy one day?

Chapter 25

2004, June

She had never felt more miserable in her whole life. Sadness flooded through her body, leaving nothing behind but emptiness and a huge hole.

A hole where Nana had once been.

Nana had died during the night after a brief but potent illness. Thankfully, her grandmother hadn't seemed to suffer much, but it had been so sudden that it was still a huge shock. She'd had no time to prepare for Nana leaving. Had she asked all the questions she wanted to ask? Had they had all the talks Nana wanted to have with her? What would she do now without Nana's gentle and wise guidance in her life? She had been the one rock in Bela's life, the one person to keep her grounded while everything else seemed to be sinking sand.

And now she was gone.

There wasn't much time to dwell on the sadness. Nana's body had to be buried within twenty-four hours. The Imam had already been notified, messages had gone around quickly to as many relatives and friends as possible. Mama,

Madina, and Bela had already been to the market early that morning to buy the huge amounts of food needed for all the mourners. The house had to be cleaned and swept, mirrors covered over, and chairs arranged. The body had to be washed and prepared too, but fortunately Mama hadn't asked her to do that.

The men were already assembling in the front yard, sitting on long benches, consoling Papa. Inside the house, the women were gathering. Mama sat in the chair in the centre, Bela and Madina on either side. Now and again, a new guest would arrive. She would speak to Mama quietly and sadly, a gift of money would exchange hands, and then the guest would find an empty seat on which to sit for a while and show support to the family in their grief. Conversations were muted out of respect, but Bela didn't feel much like talking anyway.

At about three o'clock in the afternoon, the Imam arrived in the yard. The men, in their black, flat caps, gathered around in a circle, holding up the palms of their hands. Ceremonial words were spoken and prayers were said. The women watched in silence from the porch steps or from behind the windows. Eventually, the body was brought out on a simple stretcher, wrapped in a white cloth and covered in an ornate blanket.

Nana!

Bela let out a sob as the stretcher was carried out of the front yard. She ran down the steps and watched in tears as the men slowly processed down the street and around the corner on their way to the village cemetery.

Nana!

Eventually, she turned to go back into the house with Mama and Madina and the other women. They needed to have the meal ready for when the men returned.

Michael heard the news the following day, when Azamat rang to explain why he couldn't come to his language lesson. The incident over the camera had never been mentioned, but Michael had been expecting Azamat to find some excuse to cancel the lesson. He'd been prepared just to let the matter drop completely, but also knew Azamat might try to stay away from him now, out of embarrassment. It was so important in this culture to save face.

However, the death of a grandmother was a fair enough reason for not coming. Michael passed on his condolences, then found himself asking if he, too, could come to pay his respects. Somehow, he felt as if he owed it to the old lady who'd been so wonderful in telling him all about her people's history and language. There was another reason, of course. He wanted to see Bela. She must be devastated; he knew how close she was to her grandmother. She'd not mentioned her being ill before, so maybe her Nana's death had been unexpected. He wanted to tell her how sorry he was for her, to be there for her.

Azamat had agreed to meet him at the bus stop, and Michael was planning to ask him exactly what was culturally expected at a Circassian funeral on the short walk through the village to the house. There were so many things to learn about the way people conducted their lives and deaths here. He was sure to put his foot in it many times but hoped people would forgive him. As he rode in the *marshroutka*, holding in his hands the black, flat cap that was appropriate to wear on such occasions, he thought about the fragility of life, and his mind went back to a time when he'd been standing next to someone else's bedside, not sure if they were going to live or die.

It had been a wonderful summer. Michael had been almost ten at the time and Claire five. They'd spent the whole month out in the country at his uncle and aunt's house. It had seemed like a mansion to the two children, who were used to their smaller, detached house in Bristol. Uncle Edgar and Aunt Sophie had no children of their own, and although they were very welcoming to their loud and energetic nephew and niece, they always seemed to hold themselves with an air of bemusement and slight horror when regarding the workings of young children.

Michael and Claire spend most of their time outdoors anyway, well away from fragile china vases and cleanly polished mahogany furniture: a situation that seemed to suit everyone quite well. Their parents came to visit at the weekends but had to return to work during the week. It was an arrangement designed to keep the children out of too much mischief or expensive child care during the long summer holiday.

The grounds of the country house were quite extensive, and in one corner, at the top of a small hill, there was a small, brick building. A kind of summer house, was what Uncle Edgar called it. Michael, who loved to climb, had been eager to see the view from its roof, and it had been surprisingly easy to climb up, helped in places by a creeping clematis plant that provided some useful footholds. On this particular day, Michael had persuaded Claire to climb up too.

"Come on, you're nearly there."

"I'm not sure I want to do this, Michael."

"Oh, but you have to see the view. You can see over the whole grounds. Come on, just a little bit further." He held out his hand to help his sister up the last, tricky bit. Finally, she clambered onto the flat roof next to him and sat down with relief. They played up there for about half an hour, making up stories about princes, princesses, and dragons who might have lived there. Eventually, a voice called out from the house. It was Aunt Sophie telling them it was tea time.

"Let's go. I bet there's going to be cake. I saw a yummy looking chocolate gâteau in the kitchen earlier!" said Michael eagerly. Without a second thought, he jumped straight down from where he was to the soft ground below.

"Michael!" wailed Claire, who had been left behind.

"You can do it, Claire. It's really not that high. Just remember to bend your knees, and you'll be fine."

But Claire looked petrified. "I can't do it, Michael. I'm afraid."

Michael was a little impatient. He wanted to have a piece of that cake. He spoke to Claire with a sterner tone.

"Stop being silly, Claire. Just jump. I'll catch you."

Claire, sensing her brother's displeasure with her, braced herself to jump. Michael could still clearly see the next few seconds in his memory even now, years later. As she jumped, she somehow caught her foot in the clematis. Her body turned as it fell, now headfirst. She landed awkwardly on her back with a sickening crack, and lay in a crumpled heap on the ground, unmoving.

"Claire!" Michael screamed. He touched her lightly, but she didn't respond. His heart beating at double speed, panic rising in his throat, he ran as fast as he could back to the house to fetch his Uncle and Aunt.

The memory still brought tears to Michael's eyes, even though it had happened fifteen years ago. It had all been his fault. If only he hadn't been so greedy for that piece of cake. He should have climbed back up onto the roof and then helped his sister down slowly.

Standing by his sister's body in the hospital, Michael had been convinced she was going to die. But she hadn't, thank God. She'd broken her lower spinal cord, but she was still alive. However, she was now paralysed from the waist down and would have to spend the rest of her life in a wheelchair, all thanks to him. The memory of the accident, and the guilt that he experienced over it every day since, was a wound that Michael would always carry in his heart. It had nearly cost him his faith, and he had gone through a long period of doubting God during his time as a student. If it wasn't for his friend Mark, who'd pulled him back from the brink, quite literally, he would have been a very different person today. A very bitter, twisted, and angry person.

But even though Michael had long ago made his peace with God over the tragedy, he couldn't understand why Claire had never seemed to be angry with him. She had to know the accident was all his fault. Maybe—probably— deep down, she did blame him, but on the surface she didn't show it. In fact, after the accident, she'd seemed to dote on him even more. She'd needed him more than ever, not just to push her chair around for her, but also to entertain her, to cheer her up, to give her some sort of life in place of the one that he'd taken away from her. That was why Michael knew that no matter how interesting life was here in the Caucasus, no matter how attractive a certain, local young woman, there was no way he could stay here long-term. He needed to go back home. His sister needed him, and it was the least he could do.

Bela sat next to Nana's chair in the living room, looking at how empty it seemed. It had only been four days since her death, and the cushion still had Nana's imprint in it. A couple of pats and it would be gone, but the imprint that Nana had left on her life would never be gone. Nana had given her a love for her people and their history. Nana had made her feel proud to be Circassian.

Now that she was gone, the future looked so bleak. Without Nana holding them all together, her family would fall apart, she was sure of that. Azamat was inexplicably angry and brooding and clearly had his secrets. Papa was distant, and she'd lost a lot of respect for him ever since the revelation of his affair with Maria. Mama was weak and lacked ambition, and her life was basically tied to cooking and cleaning and not much more. Madina's life was in ruins—a divorced, single mother, living back home with her parents. Uncle Artur had managed to hold himself well at the funeral but had quickly slipped back into drinking more than ever. One of these days, he'd wander out in front of a car or fall into a ditch. The family didn't seem to know how best to help him, and they didn't seem to be making much of an effort, either. The only person in her life who seemed to be happy was Zalina. Maybe it wasn't just her faith. Maybe it was because Zalina had managed to escape. She'd gone somewhere else. Started over again. Perhaps that's what Bela needed to do too. There wasn't much left for her now in Awush.

She thought about Michael. He'd been so good to turn up at the funeral, with his quaint British humility and tactfulness. He was a good man. Not the kind of man you should let go of. Perhaps she should do everything that she could to win him. He could be her escape route. It was obvious that he liked her. There were just two things holding him back, she suspected. One was his politeness, wanting to respect her and her culture. That was one of the things she liked most about him. The other, no doubt, was his faith. What would she have to do, she wondered, to make that not an issue? Perhaps if she showed interest in Christianity, that would be enough? Perhaps if she looked sincere, read a bit of the Bible, asked more questions? Surely he didn't expect her to convert to his faith? It would be enough to know that she respected what he believed. She could easily do that.

But she felt uneasy about that option. She wasn't a manipulative, deceptive person at heart. She didn't want to pretend that she was someone she wasn't, even if it enabled her to become Michael's girlfriend in the process.

She wiped the tears from her face. She'd been crying almost constantly over the last few days. She missed her grandmother so much. Nana would have known what to do. Nana could have given her the right advice. She remembered that Nana hadn't been as opposed to the idea of conversion as Bela had expected. Maybe she really could become a Christian? No, Bela drove that thought away. It would have to be a totally genuine conversion, and Jesus would literally have to appear to her in person for her to believe in him the way that Michael did. All she had at the moment was a warm, fuzzy feeling that God, in some form, really did exist and that perhaps Michael and Zalina had been lucky enough to find him.

They had both talked about eternal life. Initially, she had readily agreed with them. Of course, good people went to paradise when they died. But it seemed that perhaps that wasn't quite what Michael and Zalina believed in. They suggested there had to be some kind of faith in Jesus to be absolutely sure. So where did that leave Nana? Had she believed in Jesus? Probably not, at least not in the way that her friends did. But surely Nana was in heaven, wasn't she?

She'd asked Nana about heaven before, once, the other time she'd struggled so hard with grief. At least that time, Nana had been there to comfort her.

Chapter 26

1997, March

Bela held the bowl of food in front of Bobik's head, but the old dog barely lifted his chin in acknowledgement. He'd not eaten his food from yesterday, either. He'd been slowing down over the last few months, but this was the first time Bela had seen him looking quite so exhausted. She tousled his head fondly and stroked his ears. He closed his eyes and put his head back on his paws.

"Nana, I'm worried about Bobik." She found her grandmother weeding the potatoes in the back garden. "He's not eaten his food for two days now."

Nana put down her hoe and looked sadly at Bela. "Perhaps his time has come, *si dakhe.*"

Bela looked down at her feet, holding back the tears. Nana was right. Bobik was at least fifteen years old, which was a good old age for a dog. She shouldn't be so upset about a yard dog, but of all the family, she'd been the one closest to Bobik over the years. She'd known him all her life, from as far back as she could remember.

"Should we call out the vet? Do you think he's in pain?"

Nana shook her head sympathetically. "I don't think so. He doesn't seem to be in pain, and I don't think there's a lot the vet could do. You know, *si dakhe*, death is just a part of life. It's sad, but it's something we all have to face at one time or another."

Bela went back to check on Bobik. The dog's breathing was fairly laboured now, and he hadn't opened his eyes when she'd approached him. She sat down next to him and released him from his chain. She didn't want him to die chained up like a prisoner. She wanted him to know he was loved like a member of the family.

She shuffled closer and helped the old dog lift his head onto her lap. He opened his eyes briefly as if to show her that he appreciated her being there, and then he closed them again and returned to the effort of keeping alive just a little longer. Bela stroked him gently, thinking back to all the times they'd played together in the yard when she was younger. The times when he'd patiently let her dress him up in an old shawl and hat and pretend he was having a tea party with her dolls. The times he'd run around chasing after the ball she threw at him. His delight at bouncing around in the newly fallen snow at the beginning of the winter. The way he made her feel safe at night, knowing that he was protecting their home from intruders. He'd been a good dog. A tear silently made its way down Bela's cheek. The dog's breathing was shallower now.

She whispered to him, "Goodbye, Bobik. I love you. You've been a good dog. I'm going to miss you."

As if he'd been waiting for her to say those words, Bobik licked her hand weakly one last time, and then breathed out one long breath.

There were no more.

Bela held his still, stiffening body for a further five minutes, the tears now freely falling down her face. It was a while before she noticed that Nana was sitting on a stool a little distance away, watching her. She turned.

"He's dead, Nana," she sobbed.

"I know, *si dakhe*. I know."

Later that evening, Papa and Azamat dug a deep hole right at the back of the garden, under the evergreen tree. Bela and Nana stood a little distance away, watching. Even Mama had come out to pay her respects. Bobik's body had been wrapped in some old cloth and was lowered into the hole. Papa and Azamat started shovelling the soil back into the hole, and Mama turned to go back into the house. Bela and Nana stayed until the job was finished and the men returned their spades to the garden shed. Bela placed Bobik's dog collar on top of the mound of freshly dug dirt.

"Goodbye, Bobik. I hope you're at peace now."

"Do you think dogs go to paradise, Nana?"

Azamat gave a snort from the chair where he was watching television, but Nana didn't seem to find Bela's question something to laugh at.

"It would be nice to think so, *si dakhe*. I think the next life wouldn't be quite the same if there weren't some dogs running around."

"Is that where Dada is?" asked Bela, speaking of the grandfather she'd never known.

"Yes, I'm sure. He was a good man," Nana said wistfully. "A good man."

"How do we make sure we get to paradise, Nana? Do we just have to live good lives?"

Nana thought for a while. "I think, if you believe in God, if you're open to all he tells you about Himself, if you try your best to live a good life, loving others and showing mercy to those in need, then you'll be in paradise."

Bela nodded thoughtfully. Nana would have no problem. But what would happen to her? She wasn't sure if she believed in God like Nana seemed to. She did her best to live a good life but couldn't think of the last time she showed mercy to someone in need, unless rescuing Zalina counted.

As Bobik was taking his last breath, many miles away, Zalina was waiting for someone to take their first. The contractions had started the night before. They were easy at first, and Zalina had pottered around happily, packing a bag of things she would need for the hospital. She was buzzing with happy expectation that she would be seeing her son at last, that they would soon be a proper family. Ruslan had done enough worrying for the two of them, constantly asking her if she shouldn't be sitting down and resting, and asking when she would be ready to go to the hospital.

"Just wait a little longer, Ruslan. I don't want to get there too soon."

"Yes, but what if the baby comes before we get there?"

"Relax." She laughed. "I'm sure we have plenty of time yet."

She'd been right. Long after Ruslan had anxiously left her at the door of the hospital, watching her being ushered inside by the nurse, the contractions had continued, growing more and more painful. After a few hours of labouring by herself on a makeshift bed in the corridor, Zalina had actually started to feel a little afraid. It took a lot to faze her, but she'd never known pain like this before. The hospital was busy and short-staffed, and it was a while before a proper bed was made ready for her.

The doctor was there now, promising her that it wouldn't be much longer. She looked to be in her fifties, a brisk, proud-looking woman, and had probably forgotten what it was like to give birth to children. Why had no one told her that it hurt this much? She tried to control the screams coming out of her mouth, knowing that the doctor wasn't impressed with how she was handling this. Her legs were up in stirrups now, in a most uncomfortable position which fought against every natural instinct that Zalina had.

At last, the time had come to push. Zalina wasn't sure she had enough energy left, but everything in her wanted to get this baby out as quickly as possible so that it would all be over. She felt a rush of warm water flooding down her legs as her amniotic sac was burst, and then came the assurances that the head was crowning. A few more pushes were all that it would take, she was told. At last, the head was out. Just a couple more pushes. She prayed to God for strength to keep going, and finally it was all over. A sensation of relief washed over her as the rest of the baby slithered out of her body into the arms of the waiting doctor. The baby was immediately whisked off to be checked over. Zalina rested her head back on the pillow, panting with exhaustion. "Is he alright?" she asked as soon as she'd caught her breath.

"He looks very healthy," said the doctor after a giving the baby a brief check.

Thank you, Lord, thank you!

The baby was wrapped in a blanket and returned to Zalina. This was the moment she'd been waiting for: the moment she got to look at her son for the first time. His eyes were closed and his fists tightly clenched, his little body wrinkled and crusty from the ordeal of being born. She counted ten little fingers. He was perfect.

"Welcome to the world, Adam," she whispered over him. Already, she felt her heart so full of maternal love she thought she would burst.

A few hours later, Adam had been washed and checked again by the nurses, and she'd also been checked over as soon as the placenta was delivered.

"It's all looking good," the doctor had assured her. "A healthy baby boy. Three-point-four kilograms and fifty-five centimetres in length. You just need to rest now."

Adam had been taken to the nursery with the other babies so that Zalina could get some sleep. She longed to see him, to have him with her, but didn't dare to question the wisdom of the hospital staff. Instead, she did as she was told.

Ruslan wouldn't be able to see his son until she was allowed to leave the hospital in a few days' time, so she needed to concentrate on recovering as quickly as possible. Tomorrow, she'd be allowed to start breastfeeding. She couldn't wait to bond with her son again. *I'll be the best Mama to you*, she promised herself, *with God's help*.

Azamat sat staring at the bottle of beer in his hand as he waited on the park bench, trying to muster up courage to walk to the bus stop and catch a *marshroutka* home. He used to feel nothing but contempt for the drunks that he saw staggering around at night, vomiting on street corners and pissing themselves. However, now he was beginning to understand how easy it might be to fall into the trap of alcoholism. He swore to himself that he'd never allow himself to start getting drunk on vodka, but his beer consumption had been growing steadily over the past few months. People talked about needing to numb the pain, but he'd never understood that until now. Never understood how you could carry almost physical pain in your heart constantly, with no relief and no chance of relief. Alcohol certainly did help a bit, and Azamat quickly finished his second bottle and tossed it into the trash can next to the bench.

His life was broken, he knew that, but he couldn't work out how to get himself out of this pit. After he'd returned from the army, he'd enrolled on a college course studying computer science, but he just couldn't focus, and his teachers had been on his back almost from day one. Eventually, he'd had enough and quit, knowing that his parents would be deeply disappointed in him. He tried his best to make it sound like it was a positive move, like he needed to follow some other career path, and had even got his father pushing a few doors on his behalf, trying to get him into some sort of entry-level job, but nothing had remotely interested him. He was running out of time, though. Soon his father would give up, exasperated, and start shouting at him again.

Many of his peers at school had headed up to Moscow after their military service. There were more jobs up there, he was told. More money to be had. He'd considered it once or twice, but he just didn't have it in him at present to make those kinds of decisions. He felt like he had no energy to do anything anymore. Maybe one day he would pack up and head north, but for now, it was all he could do just to hang out at the park with the guys and tinker around fixing up his friends' cars with Tamik, who lived a few doors further down the street in Awush.

About half an hour later, he pushed open the front gate and nodded a greeting to Uncle Artur. It occurred to him that the two of them had a lot more in common now, but he wasn't ready to talk about it with anyone. At least Milana and his baby were alive, he presumed. He felt a newfound sympathy for Artur. Maybe this was what pain did to you; it made you more empathetic, more understanding.

He heard a flurry of women's voices coming from the kitchen. Madina was visiting with her daughter. She always came on her own, never with her husband. That guy was a waste of space, from what Azamat could tell. He didn't seem to treat Madina right. Not like he would have treated Milana. If he'd been lucky enough to marry Milana, he would have made her happiness his top priority.

He entered the kitchen and tried to seem pleased to see everyone. Little Alyona ran towards him and gave him a big hug.

"Azamat!"

"Hey, beautiful! How's my favourite niece?" he asked, swinging her up onto his shoulders. "Did you know you're going to be three next month? You're getting so big!"

"Azamat! She'll bump her head on the ceiling!" protested Madina, but there was a twinkle in her eye. Azamat wondered if Musabi ever swung his own daughter onto his shoulders. He carefully put Alyona back down onto the floor and pulled up a stool so she could sit on his lap. Alyona chatted away happily to him in baby gibberish while he half listened to the conversation of the women. Suddenly, something Madina said made him stop cold. He could have sworn she'd mentioned the name 'Milana'. He blocked out Alyona's voice and concentrated on Madina's instead.

"If it weren't for her, I think I'd be going mad!" Madina was saying. "I'm so glad I have at least one friend in the village. I'm hoping that her son Alikhan will be a good friend for Alyona. They certainly get on really well. He's such a sweet little boy."

A shiver slithered down Azamat's spine. "Who's this Milana?" he asked, trying to sound vaguely disinterested.

"Oh, just a friend of mine. She married into one of the richer families down the road about two years ago. I think it was a bit of hurried wedding, if you know what I mean!" She winked at Mama and Bela.

Azamat knew exactly what she meant. Milana's pregnancy would have been showing sufficiently for people to talk a little, no matter whom they passed off as the father.

"She has a son, you say?" he barely dared ask.

"Yes. Alikhan. He's a gorgeous little thing." Madina looked at him in a funny way, as if she'd just remembered something. She was about to say something else, but thought better of it and kept quiet, still looking at him with a confused look on her face.

He'd better change the subject quickly. Milana had promised she wouldn't tell anyone the truth about her child's father, but Azamat didn't want to run the risk of Madina working it out for herself. He stood up, lifting Alyona into his arms.

"Now, I'm sure we have some chocolate somewhere in the house. Can you think of anyone who might like chocolate?"

"Me, me!" sang Alyona gleefully, as he whisked her off towards the living room, where he knew a bowlful of sweets would be sitting on top of the television.

Later that evening, while Madina was putting Alyona to bed in the guest room, Azamat allowed himself to think over what he'd just learnt. He had a son. A gorgeous, healthy son, called Alikhan. More than that, he now knew where Milana lived, and he even had a reasonable excuse for just so happening to be walking down the same street someday. If he dared.

Chapter 27

2004, June

"So, do you think you might be able to come?" Cody's words broke her out of her daydream. The summer had rolled around again, the students had finished their end of year exams, and Michael and Cody's visas would soon run out. She'd been thinking about what the future held. They would both need to leave the country and get new visas if they wished to return. She couldn't believe that her time with them might be coming to an end.

Cody was hoping to come back on a business visa, and he and Bela had been working hard to get his new business up and running. He'd managed to find enough sponsors back in the States to pay her a reasonable salary, so she'd finally been able to leave the phone shop.

Michael's presentation at the linguistic conference had gone well, and he was tying up his research now. Bela got the impression he wasn't sure if he would return in the autumn. The revelation had come as a bit of a shock to her, and she'd redoubled her efforts to win his heart and persuade him to stay. But time was running out, and she still wasn't sure where she stood with him, especially since she wasn't planning on becoming a Christian any time soon.

She'd considered her job with Cody and had briefly thought about whether they would make a couple, but, much as she liked Cody, she couldn't see herself falling in love with him. After all that she'd seen Mama and Madina go through, she knew that she wouldn't settle for anything less than being truly in love with her future husband. Besides, there was no hope of starting a relationship with anyone while Michael was still on the scene. He occupied all the empty spots in her mind, all the pauses in her daily life. She found herself thinking about him constantly, daydreaming about spending time with him. Perhaps she really was in love with him, but it was probably best she didn't let her mind go there. He might be leaving for good, and she didn't want to be nursing a broken heart afterwards. Besides, the pain of Nana's death was still so raw, and grieving the absence of the person who'd been the closest to her in her whole life would take time.

"Bela?"

Cody had been saying something about America.

"Sorry, what?"

"Do you think you might be able to come to Philadelphia with me?" He had her full attention now.

"You want me to come to the business launch with you?"

"Of course." Cody laughed. "I'm sorry, I thought I'd made that clear. You've been doing such a great job helping me to organise it. You simply must be there if possible. You are my personal assistant after all."

"But I don't have the money!"

"I'll find someone to sponsor you, don't worry. But we should start work on your visa. You'll have to go up to

Moscow to hand in your forms and get the visa stamp in your passport. You do have a passport, don't you?"

Bela nodded, remembering the missed trip to London a few years ago. She'd had everything ready. But America! She was being given the chance to visit America! Her face broke into a big smile as it began to dawn on her that this was actually real and might truly happen.

"I can't thank you enough; that would be so exciting."

"Well, it's not totally a holiday," Cody grinned, "and you'll have work to do there, but I'll make sure there's plenty of time for sightseeing."

Cody's family lived in Pennsylvania, not too far from either New York City or Philadelphia, two places that Bela was eager to see. Cody handed her some rough plans for the trip, and she started reviewing them with a new energy. Her hands tingled with excitement as she held the piece of paper.

"Here are the possible dates I had in mind, and this is the list of potential sponsors I'd like to visit. Some are friends of the family, some are people who've been suggested to me by others in the travel business."

Bela nodded as she scanned through the notes. Most of the meetings were pencilled in for August.

"You should get working on your visa application as soon as you can. If you can come in July on a three-month tourist visa, that would be perfect."

"I'll get on it first thing tomorrow. I'll need to check with my father of course but I don't think he'll have any objections."

"Okay, great. You'll be staying with my family. They can't wait to meet you."

Two whole months in America, maybe three, all expenses paid! Bela couldn't believe it. As she rode home in the *marshroutka,* she wondered why there was a little hint of something other than excitement in her heart. Of course, she was a bit nervous. She'd never actually flown in an aeroplane before. But perhaps what was really making her apprehensive was the thought of being away from Michael and maybe not ever seeing him again.

Michael walked home from the air ticket office with a heavy heart. In his hands, he held definite proof that he would soon be boarding a flight to take him home, away from Shekala and away from Bela. His year at the university had been all he had dreamed it would be. He'd had ample time to study the fascinating Circassian language and had more than enough notes to make a start on his PhD thesis when he got home. He was pleased with how much progress he'd made in Russian too, and hoped he'd find opportunities to keep practising the language once he was back in the UK.

Lord, what plans do you have for me? I'm looking forward to seeing my family again, but I don't want to leave this place either. A piece of my heart is here, it seems. The people, the culture, the mountains. And what about Bela, Lord? I really care about her, but I know she doesn't share my faith, so it's not right to ask for more than just friendship from her. Lord, would you reveal yourself to her?

It was early June and the days were longer than usual, though not as long as they would be back in England at this time of year. Michael found himself walking past the door to his apartment building and towards the entrance to the town park instead. As he walked down one of its side paths, he thought and prayed about the many things that were weighing heavily on his heart.

Lord, I don't understand why this is so difficult for me. I was only planning to be here a year. I have things waiting for me back home. Family who need me. Claire needs me, Lord. Yes, I've met a lovely girl, but she's not a believer, Father. Why am I finding this so difficult?

As he walked he felt God impressing again on his heart the words of Psalm 121:

"He will not let your foot slip -
He who watches over you will not slumber;
Indeed, he who watches over Israel will neither slumber nor sleep."

Yes, Lord, I know you're watching over me. I know you haven't forgotten me. Help me to trust you even when I can't see clearly the path ahead of me. Thank you for helping me not do anything I would later regret, Lord.

Michael thought about Bela and how easy it would have been to have allowed himself to slip into a romantic relationship with her. In fact, how easy it would have been to allow himself to get involved with girls like Larissa, who'd made no pretence of their attraction to him. But he knew that God asked for purity and holiness from him, and he was thankful that God had kept him strong in the face of temptation.

Lord, I pray that you would watch over the people of Shekala like you watched over the people of Israel. Bring them peace and prosperity, Lord. Shine your face into the darkness here and touch their hearts and minds with your love.

Gradually, his anxieties lifted as he laid them at the feet of Jesus, and he was able to return to his apartment with a fresh sense of God's peace.

Cody was already home when he returned. After a quick and easy pasta dinner, the kind that, as two single guys, they'd tended to live off of the whole of this past year, they both cracked open a beer and sat down on the sofa in the living room.

"I guess I'll have to find a new roommate now," said Cody jokingly, although there was an edge of sadness to his voice.

"I guess so," replied Michael. He couldn't believe his time with Cody was coming to an end. For all their differences, it had been great fun sharing an apartment with him, both here and in St Petersburg.

"I know this sounds a bit cheesy, but I'm going to miss you, mate."

"Hey, look, why don't you come visit me and my folks this summer?" Cody's eyes brightened and his big grin returned. "Bela's coming over for a few weeks to help me pitch my business to potential sponsors. It would be great to have you there too. We'll show you around a bit."

Michael's heart leapt at the sound of Bela's name. "Really? That would be great. It's been a while since I've been to the States, and I've not spent much time on the East Coast."

"Sure! Look, you've got my email. We'll be in touch about the details."

Michael thought for a moment. "I know I've got a few things on in July, but I could come the second half of August."

"Perfect!" Cody smiled, lifting his hand up for a friendly high five. Michael smiled too. This wouldn't quite be the end. He'd get to see Cody at least one more time. And Bela too.

Chapter 28

1999, April

Moscow was a huge, grey, sprawling mega-city. Bela had never seen so many people in her life, all hustled together in crowded buses or squeezing into already full carriages on the metro. The first time she got on the escalator to start her descent into the bowels of the earth at Chekovskaya, she actually felt afraid. The moving staircase seemed to be so long she couldn't see the bottom. No one else around her, though, seemed bothered. They were all staring blankly ahead or calmly reading their newspapers.

Eventually, she'd come to love living in Moscow. She'd got a place studying English at Moscow State University, after achieving the top marks in her school in the subject. Mama and Papa had been so proud, and for Bela, it had been a dream come true. She worked hard and soon won the respect of her teachers. She even made a few friends, mainly other students from the Caucasus or from the outer regions of the former Soviet Union. She'd been warned that she might encounter some racism in the city, but found that it was mainly the young, ethnic men who were stopped by the police or hassled by whiter-skinned students. She herself felt safe and generally welcome, that is, as welcome as you can be in a city of ten million people.

The capital seemed full of potential, with signs of progress everywhere. On many days, she allowed herself to be a bit of a tourist and travelled around seeing the sights. She visited the imposing Kremlin building and the beautiful painted domes of St Basil's Cathedral in Red Square. She shopped for trinkets in the market at Izmailovsky Park, she wandered down the touristy streets of the Arbat, and enjoyed seeing the fine art at the Tretyakov Gallery. On her first visit to the McDonald's on Pushkin Square, she was so excited that she'd felt like a little child again. Her first ever Big Mac. There was no McDonald's in Shekala.

But most exciting of all was the invitation to go overseas as part of her course. She was desperate to visit England. She started working part-time as a waitress in a little coffee shop near the Faculty of Foreign Languages, where she was studying, to save up some money and hoped that Papa would be able to give her the rest. It would be another dream come true, maybe even the start of a new life for her, a life away from the drudgery and hopelessness of life in Shekala. She now understood why so many young people moved up here to Moscow from her home town. Why would anyone want to stay in a little, unknown backwater of this huge country when there were so many exciting opportunities here in this huge city?

She wasn't oblivious to the poverty here, though. They had gypsy beggars back home at the market in Shekala, but there seemed to be hundreds more here. There were drunks too, stumbling around the streets. However, what particularly touched her heart were the *babushkas* selling flowers in the corners of the metro stations. *Babushkas* with worn out shoes and stockings with holes. It wasn't right.

Back home there would be family members able to look after the elderly. The older generation was respected and honoured. It would be shameful for a village to have a grandmother begging on the streets. She tried to give small bits of change to these bent-over, little old ladies, whose eyes held so much sadness and hopelessness.

No, it wasn't right.

There was something else that troubled Bela too. It was the packages she had to deliver on behalf of her father. Before she'd left Shekala back in September, Papa had taken her to one side and explained that he had a job for her to do.

"I need to be able to trust you, Bela. Can you do this for me?"

"Yes, Papa, of course. What?"

"I need to send money to someone." He looked shifty and awkward.

"Who?" Bela asked innocently, although she already had her suspicions.

"It's a colleague of mine. A lady. She's doing some work for me in Moscow, and I need to pay her."

"Okay." Bela knew he was lying but said nothing. Her father handed her a large envelope filled with something, and a handful of smaller, empty ones. She guessed the large envelope contained money. She looked at the smaller envelopes. The same address was written on each of them, with the name 'Shatinova, M'.

M? Bela's suspicions were confirmed in her mind. M for Maria. But she said nothing to Papa. Did he not know that she knew? Had he really not seen her there in the yard that day, hiding behind Bobik's kennel? If he had, he certainly wasn't acknowledging it now. Perhaps it was best that she just played along.

"Can't you just put these in the post, Papa?"

"No, it's best not to. I'd like you to deliver them by hand. One every two months. The address is not far from where you'll be staying. It should be just a twenty-minute walk or so."

Bela felt the wad of money inside the large envelope. "And how much should I put in, Papa?"

"Two thousand roubles each time."

Bela was stunned. Two thousand roubles was a lot of money. What would Mama do if she could have an extra two thousand roubles every couple of months? And yet, instead, Papa's money was going to this woman. Bela felt angry and cheated, but she knew she had to hold her tongue. She didn't want to cross Papa, especially when he was about to fund her going to university in Moscow.

"Okay, Papa, I can do that."

"And just one more thing, Bela."

"Yes?"

"Try to deliver the envelopes without being seen."

It was April, and Bela had already delivered three envelopes; one in October, one in December, and one in February. It was time for the next instalment. She opened the large envelope and removed four five-hundred-rouble notes. She placed them in one of the smaller envelopes and sealed it shut. There were enough roubles for one more instalment, and then she presumed Papa would give her more money when she went home for the summer. She hoped he still had enough money left over to pay for her student exchange to England. She'd saved up a couple of thousand roubles herself through her waitressing, but it wouldn't be enough to pay for all the expenses. Papa had seemed reasonably willing when she'd broached the subject on the phone the other week, but there was still time for him to change his mind.

She put the envelope in her bag, along with what she needed for her university classes that day, and went to put on her coat and hat. Once outside the door to her building, she paused. The sun was shining, but it was still cold, and summer wouldn't break through for another month at least. She pulled her coat closer to her body and sighed. It would be warmer down in Shekala. The winter in Moscow seemed to have lasted forever, and although it wasn't unusual for temperatures to reach down to minus twenty degrees centigrade in Shekala, up here in the north of the country, it was the longer nights and shorter hours of sunlight that made the winter months so much more dismal and depressing.

Bela walked around the back of her building and then followed the pavement five blocks further to where Maria lived. She'd never caught a glimpse of the lady, even though she felt she would know her instantly if she did. As Papa had requested, she'd tried to make sure she wasn't seen posting the envelope into Maria's box inside the front door of the building. It hadn't been hard to work out the code on the door. It was easy to see which three numbers were most worn away from the constant use by the residents, and she just had to press them all at the same time to hear the click which would let her in. She walked briskly, trying not to think about that day when she'd found out her father had been cheating on her mother. She'd even tried to convince herself over the years that she'd been mistaken about the little two-year-old boy. She focussed her thoughts instead on the upcoming trip to England. Her whole class was excited about it, and several students had already handed in their money and paperwork. She herself had got her own passport ready and had filled in most of the lengthy forms. It was just a matter of waiting for the money now. The trip would involve two weeks staying with a family, improving her English and participating with her group in several day trips to places of historical interest. Bela got shivers down her spine just thinking about it. She had longed to go to England, ever since she'd first started studying English at school.

She reached Maria's building, punched in the code and, after a quick glance around, placed the envelope into the post box. She was just turning to leave when a figure approached her from out of the shadows. Bela recoiled in shock. She should have given her eyes longer to adjust to the dark—that's why she hadn't seen the person standing just behind the door. Her body froze, panic rising up inside her. The person came closer and she recognised Maria Shatinova at once. She looked older than Bela remembered. Years of anxiety had stolen her youthful glow and replaced it with worry lines and dark shadows under her eyes. She looked thinner too.

The two women stood silently in front of each other for a few seconds. Bela's heart was beating so loudly that she was sure the woman could hear it. Maria spoke first.

"Are you the younger daughter? Aslan's daughter?"

"Yes," Bela replied, her voice shaking a little.

"And you're the one who's been delivering the envelopes?"

"Yes. Papa told me to, but he didn't say who they were to or what they were for."

There was a pause as Maria reached inside her dressing gown pocket. For one wild moment, Bela wondered if she was reaching for a gun or a knife. How upset had this woman been that Papa had refused to leave his wife over her? How desperate was she to pay him back? Bela wouldn't have a chance to run, Maria was barring her way to the door.

But Maria pulled out an envelope, and Bela inwardly felt a flood of relief.

"Here, give this to your Papa. Tell him it's urgent. Tell him..." Tears welled up in Maria's eyes. "Tell him Pavlik is very ill. He's in hospital." Her voice wobbled and she steadied herself against the door. "He needs an operation, and I can't possibly afford it."

She broke down, sobbing, and Bela almost reached out a hand to comfort her. Was it possible to feel sympathy for this woman? True, she'd had an affair with her father, but she'd definitely paid for that mistake. She looked broken, damaged, and without hope. Pavlik might not be her half-brother, but either way it was only right that Papa should do something. He had destroyed this woman's life. Prevented her from meeting someone else, someone who would have looked after her and Pavlik properly. He had reduced her to this.

Bela took the envelope and nodded. "I'm sorry. I'll tell him."

Maria stood aside, satisfied, and Bela walked out into the daylight once more.

She rang Papa later that day. She told him about the envelope and about what Maria had said. She was careful not to imply that she knew anything more than just what the lady had told her. Papa obviously didn't care to enlighten her. In fact, he didn't really say anything.

After she hung up, she suddenly realised something. Her heart almost stopped in anguish. If Papa stepped up and did the right thing, if he helped to pay for Pavlik's operation and hospital fees, then... Then there would be no trip to England for her. He'd already made it quite clear that there was only just enough money to scrape together to allow her to go, and Bela knew that he wouldn't be able to afford both. Even if the hospital paid for the actual operation, Maria would still need money to pay the doctors and nurses, and money to pay for all the medicines that Pavlik would need. And there was no way that Bela would be able to earn enough money for her trip to England through waitressing, even if she doubled all her shifts. She put the phone down, buried her head in her sleeve, and cried bitterly.

Several weeks later, she returned home. She'd completed one year of her course, but she doubted there was enough money for her to return and finish her degree. There had been no trip abroad. Many of her friends were in London already, seeing the sights that she'd so desperately wanted to see. It wasn't fair. Life wasn't fair. What kind of future stretched ahead of her now? Her year in Moscow had changed her. Shekala suddenly seemed so small and parochial. It was as if the residents were stuck in a time warp, as if they had no idea what progress was being made in the rest of the world. She'd once loved village life, but now it bored her. Papa was distracted, and the secret of what had happened with Maria hung awkwardly in the air between them, unspoken and unacknowledged.

And there was something else to worry about: Azamat had disappeared.

Mama was distraught, but Bela didn't think there was anything immediate to worry about. He'd simply gone off with some friends, although he'd not been in contact for over a month now.

"He's an adult, Mama. He's allowed to do his own thing."

"I know, but I can't help worrying about him. I trust him to stand on his own two feet, but he's so easily swayed by other people, Bela. That's what I worry about. What if he's fallen in with the wrong crowd again? I just want to know where he is and what he's doing. I just want to know that he's okay."

"I know, Mama. I'm sure he'll call soon."

"I just worry, with the war starting up in Chechnya again, that maybe, maybe he'll get caught up in that somehow. He always did like being in the army. Perhaps he and his friends have rallied around the cause and gone to fight? I daren't even mention it to your father or to anyone else, but what if I'm right?"

"Don't be silly. Azamat's too sensible to do something like that, Mama. He's probably just gone off with his friends to look for a job in a bigger town somewhere." Bela put her arm around her mother and hugged her for a long while. As she did, she noticed that tears were falling down her cheeks too. But they weren't tears for Azamat, they were tears for herself. Azamat had gone and Madina was married. That meant that there was only her left. If money wasn't already an issue, or the fact that a new war starting up would again cause huge instability in the region, this was the final nail in the coffin of her dreams and ambitions to work abroad. There was absolutely no way she could leave Mama alone now. Not until Azamat came back. It was her duty. This was her lot in life.

Nana was right, there were some things you couldn't change.

3

The Lord watches over you —

The Lord is your shade at your right hand;

The sun will not harm you by day,

Nor the moon by night.

Psalm 121, verses 5 and 6

Chapter 29

2004, August

America was huge and overwhelming but colourful and fascinating all at the same time. Even though she'd been here for four weeks already, Bela still had to pinch herself that it wasn't a dream. Coming here in the first place had been a much smoother process than she'd anticipated. Her father had readily given his permission, especially when he heard that all her expenses would be paid for. They both knew that it was his fault she hadn't been able to go to England when she was studying in Moscow and, although it was never mentioned, Bela could see that a sense of guilt pushed him to say yes more quickly than he might otherwise have done. She'd packed her suitcase and travelled up to Moscow on the overnight bus to apply for her visa, and a week later, with the coveted stamp in her passport, she'd been boarding a plane bound for Philadelphia.

It was her first experience of flying, but she hadn't been nervous at all. She was too excited that her dream was coming true at last, and she felt like a small child, staring out of the aeroplane window and marvelling at what she could see. Cody had met her at the airport and driven her back to his parents' home. Ted and Kathy Eriksson had been warmly welcoming, and immediately Bela felt relaxed in their presence. She'd soon discovered, though, that there were so many little differences, and so many cultural things to learn, like not having to take your shoes off when you entered a house, or the way people drove everywhere and barely walked. There was no such thing as a local shop just around the corner; instead there were shopping complexes, drive-through banks, and drive-through restaurants. She still hadn't got used to the ferociousness of the air conditioning. Shekala was also hot in the summer, but air conditioning was rare there. In her home in Awush, they had a few electric fans, but outside, on public transport, you just got used to sweating a lot. Here in America, it was as if sweating was avoided as much as possible, which meant that you had to adapt to extreme changes in temperature. In the car, she had goose bumps on her arms from the air conditioning, but then they parked and climbed out and she would experience a blast of heat like that of an oven door opening, which felt almost welcome. A few seconds later, they'd enter a shop and she'd feel the need to put on an extra layer of clothing again.

The four weeks had gone by in a whirlwind. Cody had done a great job of packing the timetable with a mixture of work-related meetings and sight-seeing trips. She was exhausted from speaking English non-stop but was already noticing how much her English had improved in just this short time. So far, she'd visited the Statue of Liberty and Central Park in New York and even taken in a show on Broadway with Ted and Kathy. It really was like a dream, and she didn't want it to end. Life was so much easier here than back home in Shekala. People seemed happier. They smiled all the time. They didn't have to struggle for the basics, like having enough food to eat or having to grow their own food. They had plenty of money for hobbies and leisure activities. Their houses were filled with useful gadgets and helpful technology. No wonder many of her friends had wanted to move to the West and start new lives over here. She thought of her cousins in Germany—was their life just like this?

The longer she stayed in America, the more she could imagine herself living here permanently. She wanted this life for herself. As much as she loved her people and had her roots in the Caucasus, the lure of the ease and comfort of the West was pulling her in, like a fish caught on a line. She deserved this, didn't she? She could make something of herself here. As the weeks passed, her mind was gradually pulling her heart away from everything she'd left behind.

Something else added to her sense of excitement and restlessness. Not long after she'd arrived, Cody had casually dropped into the conversation the fact that Michael was coming for a visit at the end of August. Bela hadn't allowed herself to think about him much since they'd said goodbye back in June, but she'd missed him terribly. It was like a huge hole had opened up in her life the day that she'd waved him off at Shekala's local airport. No matter how much she tried to convince herself that it wouldn't have worked and that he was gone now, she just couldn't shake off the memories of their time together this past year.

But now she was going to see him again. Her pulse raced just thinking about it. Somehow, they belonged together. Perhaps this was going to be the moment that they both crossed the invisible boundary they'd been skirting around for so long. Perhaps Michael had been missing her as much as she'd been missing him.

Michael had been missing Bela so much so that it physically hurt. She had looked so bereft when she'd given him that final wave at the airport gate that he'd wanted to run back, sweep her up into his arms, and never let her go again. It had taken all his strength to turn his face away from her and follow the other passengers down through the scanners and into the waiting room.

He hadn't told her that he might be seeing her in America later that summer because he wouldn't be sure himself that he was going until he'd spoken to his family first, and he didn't want to get his own hopes up. Besides, he still wasn't sure how she felt about him. They'd never spoken about their feelings for each other, and although he suspected that she cared for him almost as deeply as he cared for her, he knew he could still be wrong. Perhaps he'd misread the signs, misunderstood her body language and the look in her eyes. The sensible side of him told him that it would be good to have this time apart from each other. Perhaps it had been nothing more than a potential holiday fling. An almost-to-be romance, brought on by the exoticness of the country in which he'd been staying. Being back home in England he'd have a good chance to really evaluate his feelings, and maybe he'd be able to hear God's voice more clearly about the path he should take. Michael had done a lot of praying since he'd returned, but no matter how much he sought God, no matter how often he read his Bible, he still couldn't quite discern God's voice in this situation. It seemed that God was asking him to wait. To trust him and to wait.

But as Michael stepped out of baggage claim at Philadelphia International airport and saw Bela standing there next to Cody, waiting for him, he suddenly seriously doubted he would have the self-control to wait for God's leading in his relationship with her. It was as if here, outside of her home context, she stood out from those around her as being even more beautiful and captivating than he had remembered. She hadn't changed much, except that it looked like she had learnt to dress a little more casually here in the States. But there seemed to be a heightened sense of hope and freedom about her. A sense of having found her purpose and her place at last. Obviously, working for Cody had been a good move for her. His smile dropped for a second and a pang of jealousy rose in his chest as he strode over to them. What if something had happened between her and Cody once he'd been out of the picture? What if they were a couple now? Cody was good-looking and a great guy. What girl wouldn't fall for him? They hadn't seemed to be interested in each other when they'd been in Shekala, but who knew what might have changed in the last few weeks? He'd have to find out. He tensed up. What if he and Cody were fighting over the same girl? He managed a smile as he reached them.

"Hi! It's so good to see you both!"

"Hey, buddy!" Cody embraced him with a couple of firm slaps on the back.

"Hello." Bela looked shy and uncertain. Trying to pre-empt the awkwardness, Michael went for a confident, friendly hug. She smelt so good. He had to force himself to pull away.

"So, this is America," he quipped. "Where can you get a good cup of tea around here?" They all laughed, and Cody led the way to where his car was parked.

On the journey to Cody's parents' home, Cody dominated the conversation. Michael, sitting next to him in the front, was battling jet lag already. Bela, who was in the back seat, was her usual quietly reserved self. Michael fought against the strong desire to close his eyes and focussed instead on what Cody was saying, as he recounted all that they'd been up to over the past few weeks. They'd secured enough sponsors already for the business to be able to proceed for at least two years, and Bela's presence, apparently, had been a big hit, adding a novelty factor to their pitches. *More than a novelty factor, no doubt*, Michael thought to himself. What investor could avoid those beautiful, dark, radiant eyes? As Cody talked, he tried to read between the lines, hoping to catch any suggestion of a romantic involvement between the two of them, but he couldn't find one. Not even a hint. His shoulders and face relaxed a little. Perhaps nothing had changed after all, at least from Cody's perspective. Michael would have three weeks to find out what Bela was thinking.

About a week into Michael's stay, for some rare reason, both Cody and his parents had to be out one evening, and Bela and Michael found themselves alone in the house. Cody had ordered a pizza for them and had pointed out where the DVDs were in case they wanted to watch a film. It almost felt like a date, although no one else seemed to have noticed. If Bela was feeling a little awkward, she wasn't showing it. Perhaps she'd become more relaxed about cultural etiquette and potential misunderstandings since she'd been here.

"Did you want to watch anything?" Michael asked tentatively once they'd both settled down in front of the television with a tray of hot, cheesy pizza and tall glasses filled to the brim with Pepsi and ice.

"I don't mind. Do you?"

"Well, why don't we eat first and then watch something later? I can never seem to do both at the same time," Michael suggested.

Bela laughed. "Sure."

They both started tucking in. The pizza was delicious, and Michael waited until he'd polished off the whole of his first slice before he turned to her and asked "So, have you and Cody been getting on okay over the past few weeks?"

Bela finished her mouthful of pizza and dabbed the corner of her mouth with her napkin. "Yes, of course. He and his parents have been very kind."

"Are you looking forward to working with him?"

"Yes." Bela looked a bit puzzled now, clearly wondering where this line of questioning was going. Michael decided to be upfront.

"I mean, let's be honest, he's a good-looking guy, and you're a beautiful woman. Do you think it might end up being more than just a business relationship?"

Bela blushed, and Michael felt the heat rising in his cheeks also. Why had he said it so bluntly? He hadn't meant for it to come out quite like that, but he did really want to know. He couldn't bear the thought of her going out with someone else. He waited for her to take a sip of her Pepsi.

"Cody and I are just friends and I don't see that changing. He's a great guy, but I don't feel that way about him."

Michael breathed a sigh of relief. "Oh, good."

"Good?"

He hadn't meant to say that out loud, and now he was on the spot. "Um, I meant, I was worried it might get a bit awkward for you. You know, working together closely."

"Oh, I see." Bela looked pained, as if she were hoping for him to say something more.

Impulsively, he put down his plate and moved Bela's away from her lap. He shifted a little so he was turned towards her, and took one of her hands in his.

"Bela, I feel I have to tell you this before I burst. I care deeply for you. I always have. I've missed you so much, and then I had this silly thought that perhaps you and Cody might be getting together, and I felt crazy jealous. I'm so sorry. I have no idea if you feel the same way about me, but I just had to tell you. I'm sorry. I didn't mean to embarrass you. And now I feel like a complete idiot."

Bela squeezed his hand back. "Don't be sorry," she said gently, her eyes glistening with emotion. "I've waited a long time for you to say that to me. I love you, Michael. I have for a long time now. I just didn't think it was possible for us to be together."

"Because of my being in England and you being in Russia?"

Bela smiled. "Well, yes, there's that. But also because of your faith."

"Yes, there's that too."

"Your faith means so much to you. It wouldn't be right for us to be together if I didn't feel the same way. I believe in God, yes, but not like you do. I think I would hold you back. You would try to change me and then become annoyed with me if I didn't change."

Michael thought for a long time before answering. He tucked a stray strand of her hair behind her ear and looked deeply into her beautiful, dark brown eyes.

"Bela, you know that I love you too. So much that it's killing me. I've really been wrestling with this whole situation over the past few months. I've been praying that God would give me clear direction, but all he seems to say to me is to wait. I don't really know what that means, but I do know that God hasn't let me give you up completely. I've prayed that he would take away my feelings for you, but he hasn't. They're still there, and stronger than ever. I don't know what to say. I want to honour you and respect you, and as much as it kills me to say it, I know that you're right. We shouldn't get into a serious relationship if you aren't seriously in love with Jesus as much as you're in love with me. On the other hand, it's not fair on either of us just to leave this dangling. I can't force you to have faith, and I certainly don't want you to pretend to have faith just for me. It absolutely has to be your own decision."

Bela took hold of Michael's other hand and held them both there on her lap, studying them. When she looked up, a tear had rolled out of one eye and was making its way down her cheek. Michael removed one of his hands and tenderly brushed it away.

"Oh, Bela."

They gently leaned in together, and their lips met for the first time. It was a beautiful, tender, sad kiss. Not the hurried rush of a kiss of passion, but a kiss of resignation at all that might be but could not, for the moment, be entered into fully. Michael stroked her beautiful, glossy black hair and slowly pulled his lips away from hers. The two of them stayed there for what seemed like several minutes, their foreheads touching, their eyes down, acknowledging the weight and poignancy of the moment, neither of them wanting to let it go.

It was the first of September. Michael was leaving in two days' time, Bela staying for two more weeks. She couldn't believe that she was about to lose him for the second time, perhaps this time for good. That night when they'd told each other they loved each other had been so beautiful and so sad at the same time. It was like they were meant to be together but there was this massive gulf between them and no sign of a bridge being built anytime soon. Faith in Jesus just wasn't something that she could fake in front of Michael, and she didn't want to either. She wasn't quite sure what was stopping her from believing. Perhaps it was that Jesus still felt like someone who belonged to English people, not to Circassian people. Perhaps it was her pride, that she didn't want to give up control of her life to something—or someone—else. Perhaps it was her intellect, telling her that it couldn't possibly be true, that faith was just for weak people, although Michael didn't seem weak. Perhaps she was worried about what her parents and wider family would say. She didn't want to end up like Zalina, estranged from those she'd grown up with. Besides, things were looking up in her life. She had a fantastic job, involving using her English and travelling, with a great boss whom she trusted to treat her well and pay her well. She'd be foolish to throw that all away, wouldn't she? However, here was someone who loved her and whom she loved in return. She'd always dreamed of having a relationship like that. Maybe she'd get to live in England? Hadn't she loved the freedom of living in the West while she'd been here in the States? Did she really want to return to Russia with all the financial insecurity and social problems? At times like this, she really wished she did believe so that she could just let some omnipotent God handle all of this mess and sort it out for her. Sometimes, she didn't know what she wanted more, to be able to escape Russia or to have Michael. Would it ever be possible to have both?

Lift your eyes to the mountains, my daughter.

There it was again, that still, small voice. Or was it just Michael's words echoing inside her head? And what did it really mean anyway?

Bela was just finishing up her bowl of cereal when a shout came from the living room.

"Hey, Bela, Michael. You'd better come see this!"

Bela raced in to find Cody sitting on the edge of the sofa, his eyes fixed on the television screen. She followed his gaze to the news report. Her heart lurched as she recognised the uniforms of Russian policemen.

"What's happening?" she asked, her pulse quickening and her mouth going dry. Michael joined them.

"Terrorists have taken control of a school. They're holding children and parents captive inside."

"Where? Where is it?"

"Beslan. Isn't that near Shekala?"

Beslan? *No! Not Beslan.* That was where Zalina lived. Adam, how old was he now? Bela quickly did the maths, her hands starting to tremble. Oh no, he'd be seven. He'd be starting school today. Could it be true? Could Adam be in there, a hostage? Could Zalina be there too?

"Oh, God, no." Michael said softly beside her, also clearly shaken. "Bela, do you know anyone who might be there?"

"My friend Zalina." Bela burst into sobs. "Her son Adam is having his first day at school today. He could be there." Without wondering how it would look to Cody, Bela instinctively buried her face in Michael's chest and let the tears flow. She was aware of Michael quietly praying in an almost inaudible whisper. Praying to God for the safety of her friend and child. She tore herself away, needing to look at the television screen again. She didn't want to see, and yet she had to.

"Perhaps it'll all be okay," Cody offered, his expression unusually grave and filled with concern but his words tending towards optimism, as usual. "The police know what they're doing, don't they?"

Bela didn't nod. No one could know how this would turn out. Not yet.

The scene outside the school disappeared as the cameras flicked back to the newsroom.

"What? What's happening?" Bela asked.

"They're moving on to other news, now," replied Cody. Sure enough, the report was now coming from a lone, wind-blown reporter standing on some beach in Florida, reporting on the weather. How could anyone be more interested in the weather right now? She couldn't believe it.

"What about the other channels?"

Cody flicked through them quickly, but none of the others were reporting on the Beslan situation anymore.

"I'm sorry, Bela. Beslan is a long way away from us, in a place most Americans have never heard of. Until something happens..."

Bela spent the rest of the day fixed to the television, hopping from channel to channel, trying to get more information. Cody had kindly allowed her to use his phone. There had been no reply from Zalina's phone, which only made Bela more terrified. Why wasn't she answering? She didn't know who else to call, who would know anything about her friend. She phoned her family, but they didn't know any more than she did, and, since she couldn't tell them about Zalina, they didn't seem to share the intensity of her anxiety. She forced herself to exchange a few words about nothing in particular before she told them she would have to hang up.

As the day wore on, reports of a few fatalities began to come in, as well as scenes of some people fleeing the scene. A few terrified mothers with babies had been allowed to leave. It still wasn't clear how many people were being held inside, and Bela wanted to scream with frustration. The school was cordoned off and military police surrounded it. Hundreds of anxious parents, relatives, and other townspeople looked on helplessly, weeping and in shock.

Eventually, Bela could bear it no longer.

"I have to go," she said to Cody. "I have to go home."

"Are you sure? Perhaps you could wait and see how things play out? It might all be over soon," Cody pointed out.

"I know, it's just that I have a really bad feeling about this. I just really feel like I need to be there, and I won't be able to concentrate on anything here until I find out what's happened to Zalina. I'm sorry, Cody."

Cody nodded. "It's no problem. We don't have anything important scheduled for your last two weeks, nothing I can't easily handle without you. Tell you what, I'll call the airline and see if we can book you on the next flight to Moscow. But hopefully, you'll hear from your friend that she's okay before too long."

Bela smiled her thanks, but wasn't sure that she could share Cody's optimism this time.

Chapter 30

2004, September

Adam stifled a sob and inched even closer to Zalina. Neither of them dared make a sound. They sat on the hard floor, hands clutched around their knees, heads bowed, avoiding eye contact. Zalina's tongue felt dry against the roof of her mouth, and she was desperate for water, but she dared not do anything that might attract the attention of the masked gunmen that held them and hundreds of other children and their parents hostage in the school gymnasium.

The temperature inside the building was unbearably hot, and Adam, like so many of the other children, had stripped down to his underwear. She watched him drift in and out of consciousness, her mother's heart crying. She wanted to scream for help but there was nothing she could do for him. No one was allowed to eat or drink.

It was already the third day, and the air was muggy and stale; the pungent smell of sweat mingled with the putrid smell of blood and decomposing flesh. She tried not to think of the people she'd seen killed right in front of her eyes, but the bodies and blood stains were still there in plain sight. The first had been the most shocking—a father who was just trying to calm everyone down. A masked man had shot him in the head. After that the rest was a blur. Details of the following events were already fuzzy in her memory, as if her mind were trying to protect her from the full terror of what was playing out in front of her eyes. Some men, including her own husband, had been taken away and had never returned. Gunshots and explosions left no doubt as to what their fate must have been. She grieved silently for Ruslan, her stomach knotted with the unbearable pain of it all, and tried not to look at the masked man just a few feet away whose foot was resting on a bomb trigger.

She had been doing the only thing she could, and that was to pray. She'd been praying silently next to her son almost continuously throughout the whole ordeal. Even now, she leant into him, rocking ever so slightly backwards and forwards, the way she used to do when she would hold him and rock him to sleep at night. Only now there were no sweet lullabies, no words of comfort.

Every now and again, when the gaze of their nearest captor was averted, she was able to whisper a few words to him.

"God is watching over us, Adam. God is with us." She stopped short of saying what she really wanted to say. How could you tell your son that everything would be all right and that God would protect you when you weren't sure that you were ever going to escape from this hell hole alive?

Just two days ago, the three of them had entered this building, excited and proud that Adam was starting school for the first time. How he'd longed for that day, his First Bell. How quickly he'd dressed that morning in his brand-new school uniform. Hundreds of others had gathered there too, equally excited and proud. No one knew that a few minutes later, their world would turn upside down as terrorists seized control and forced them all inside the school building.

Suddenly, something startled Zalina out of her half-comatose state. A loud explosion ripped through the building, causing shock waves to ripple through the floor underneath them. Adam clasped his hands over his ears and curled up more tightly into a ball. Zalina wrapped her arms around him and pulled him as close to her as she could, panic and terror swelling inside her. The origin of the blast was unclear, and it seemed to catch the gunmen unawares because they were thrown into confusion. Another loud explosion tore through the building, and then a stream of gunshots started. People began screaming, children crying. There was deafening crash above them, and Zalina looked up just in time to see the roof above her on fire. As if in slow motion, it started to collapse right on top of her and Adam. Her limbs were frozen, her mind too slow to process what she should do. Something inside her yelled 'Run!', but it was too late. A searing pain tore through her head, and then, blackness.

Chapter 31

2004, September

On Thursday morning, there was still no good news concerning the hostage situation in the school. It was speculated that the terrorists had made certain demands and the authorities were discussing those, but nothing was certain, not even the exact number of people being held in the school gym. Bela couldn't get rid of the tight, anxious knot in her stomach. Zalina still hadn't answered her phone, despite Bela leaving dozens of anxious messages.

God, I know I don't really believe in you, but if you are there like Michael says, then please help. Please, let this all end okay. I don't even know for sure if Zalina and Adam are there, but if they are, oh God, please protect them. You know how much Zalina loves you.

Zalina loved this God of hers so much. If he was real then surely he would look after her, wouldn't he? But even as she thought this, she knew that there wasn't any guarantee. Zalina herself had told her that Christianity wasn't a ticket out of suffering; it was a way of having peace within that suffering.

Then let her feel peace, God. Don't let her and Adam be afraid.

That morning, Cody drove both Bela and Michael to the airport. Michael's flight wasn't due to leave until evening, but it made no sense for Cody to make two trips. All three of them were mostly silent on the journey, each subdued by the news of the events taking place not too far from the place where they had all lived, met, and worked together. Bela noticed how Michael kept turning around in his seat to check on her in the back. She sensed he would rather have been sitting next to her with his arm around her, but neither of them had wanted Cody to suspect that there might be anything between them. How she would have loved him to hold her though, at this moment.

When they'd had that talk, she knew she would lose him again, but she never thought she wouldn't have time to say a proper goodbye. Now, her mind was panicked and jumbled. Fear was attacking her on both sides: fear of losing both Michael and Zalina. Part of her kept reasoning that she didn't know for sure that Zalina was even there. Perhaps they'd managed to escape before it all started. Perhaps she was wrong about Adam being about to enter that particular school. Bela tried hard to be optimistic, like Cody, but no matter what plausible possibilities she tried to entertain, they didn't succeed in driving away the awful anguish she felt in the pit of her stomach. She just had to get home, and then she would take it from there.

At the airport, Cody and Michael helped her find the correct desk and then came with her as far as they could, pointing her in the direction of the gate from which her plane was due to leave. The airport was noisy and confusing, a jumble of people from all different nationalities and cultures, all dragging suitcases or tired children, or in some cases both, behind them. She felt like she wanted to cry.

Her goodbyes were short and sober. A quick hug and a kiss on the cheek for both of her friends, although she gripped Michael harder and took in the scent of him as she wrapped her arms around his waist. A rather sad, apologetic wave, and then she was walking away, turning her back on them. She'd never felt so alone.

By the time the plane touched down in Moscow's Sheremetyevo airport several hours later, she was exhausted. She hurried through to the domestic terminal, noticing as she did so how the glitzy, civilised feel of the international terminal was replaced with a more worn, more Soviet-looking one. She was back home. Fewer smiles, darker clothing, a larger number of red-checked market bags tied up with masking tape or string, and a higher percentage of travellers who felt it necessary to wrap their suitcases tightly in reams of cling film to protect them from the dangers of air travel.

The plane down to Shekala was smaller and older. She was surprised how much she'd already got used to the luxury and higher standards of the West. Passengers crammed bags into the overhead lockers and stuffed them under chairs. The seats were cramped and worn, and the plane shook and creaked as it headed down the runway for take-off.

She'd not flown in her own country before, having taken the bus up to Moscow every time previously. She looked around her. Who were these other people who could afford the luxury of flying? Most of the passengers appeared to be ethnic Caucasians. Some were clearly wealthier businessmen. Others, presumably, had been visiting family. In some ways, it was nice to be back among the familiar, almost comforting. How wonderful it felt to hear her own language spoken again.

Her father was there to meet her at Shekala airport when she eventually touched down. The flight itself had been an amazing experience, being able to see the twin peaks of Mount Elbrus in the distance, and then recognising towns and villages the nearer they got to the ground. The touchdown was a little shakier than on her previous two flights, and the passengers all subsequently burst into spontaneous applause as if they were surprised that they were still alive. She smiled to herself as she watched them all scramble out of their seats and start taking bags out of the overhead lockers even before the seatbelt sign had been switched off or the plane had come to a complete stop. The passengers on the international flights had certainly been more law-abiding.

Her father greeted her politely. "We didn't expect you back for another couple of weeks. Is everything okay?"

"Yes, Papa, I..." Bela realised she couldn't explain why the situation in Beslan had affected her so badly that she'd had to change her travel plans. "We finished the work we needed to do, and I was a bit homesick." She smiled weakly, apologetically.

Had she been homesick? It had been strange being in another country, but she had honestly loved every second of it, and not once had she wanted to go home. At least, not until she saw that news report.

Her father drove through familiar streets. It was as if Bela were seeing them through new eyes, perhaps how Michael might have seen them when he first came to Shekala. She noticed the myriad of potholes in the roads, the dirty pavements, the stray dogs. She noticed how drivers jostled each other impatiently to get ahead, and how crowded the *marshroutkas* were that they passed. Houses in Cody's neighbourhood in America had all looked fairly uniform, but here there were stark contrasts between the poorer, more run-down houses and the brand new, gated mansions of the rich.

The car turned the corner onto their street and then came to a halt outside their house. As she got out, the gate opened, and Mama came running out to give her a big hug. "Bela!"

"Hi, Mama."

"We missed you so much, but we can't wait to hear all about it!"

"I missed you too, Mama."

Had she? Had she really? She wasn't sure she'd really thought much about her family back home. She'd been too excited experiencing her new life in America.

"You must be tired, *lapochka*."

As Mama spoke these words, it was as if Bela's body finally understood the exhaustion that it had been under for the past thirty-six hours, and a tsunami of tiredness washed over her.

"I think I'll lie down for a bit first, Mama. It's been a long journey."

She must have slept for a good couple of hours, because by the time she woke up and stumbled her way sleepily to the kitchen, Mama was already preparing the midday meal.

"There you are. You must be hungry. Lunch will be ready in a minute."

Bela's stomach growled a little as if it had understood Mama's words, and the reason she hadn't been able to eat much on her journey home came flooding back into her consciousness.

"Mama, has there been any more news about the terrorist situation in Beslan? We saw it on the television in America."

"That? Oh yes. Terrible business."

"What's the latest? Have the hostages been rescued yet?"

"I don't know. We could turn on the television after lunch if you'd like. But first you need to eat."

Mama set a plate of fried potatoes in front of Bela, and placed a basket of rye bread and a plate of pickled cucumbers within her reach. Home cooking. Had she missed this? Probably. Feelings of familiarity and comfort came over her as she tucked into the simple meal. The food in America had been good, but much of it had come out of boxes or packets and tasted a little artificial. They'd eaten out a lot too, and Bela had been overwhelmed by the amount of food available and the portion sizes on the plates. Cody's mother had been a good cook, but she hadn't needed to cook very often. Bela's mother, on the other hand, spent so much time in the kitchen and cooked three meals a day for the family from scratch. She couldn't remember the last time they'd all gone out to eat together, and there was no such thing as pizza delivery to their house in Awush.

Bela was desperate to turn the television on, but she needed to stay and make polite conversation with Mama while she ate. She tried to talk a little about her trip and her impressions of America. She passed on her greetings from Cody's family. She didn't mention Michael being there, there was no need. Or maybe she was just tired of pretending that her feelings for him were simply a vague, polite respect for the British linguist who had given both her and Azamat some income for a few months.

At last, her mother seemed satisfied by her account of her travels and she was free to go. She tried not to run into the living room, but her hand was shaking as she grabbed the remote. She glanced at the clock. Two o'clock. This crisis had been going on for two and a half days already.

She found a news report almost immediately. It was worse than she could possibly imagine. Scenes of crying children, stripped to their underwear and covered in blood, being escorted from or carried out of a blackened shell of what was once the school gymnasium. Lines of bodies, some covered in sheets, others completely visible. Women weeping and hugging each other. Men looking shocked and stunned with grief and unbelief.

Bela stayed glued to the television for almost an hour as more information came pouring in. Tears fell silently down her cheeks as she learned that the crisis had ended only at about one-thirty that day. There had been some confusion. A couple of explosions. Someone had opened fire, and then it had turned into a full-on gun battle. Any attempts at negotiation had failed and no one had been able to protect the hostages. Many of them had been shot in the back by their captors as they tried to escape. There had been over a thousand men, women, and children held in there, without food or water or medical care for nearly three days. Early estimates were that as many as three hundred of them had died, and half of them were children.

Her chest sank with a heavy weight within her and her hands throbbed with pain and heartbreak for the people she was seeing on the television screen. It was almost unreal, like she was watching a movie. Anger surged up inside her, and she clenched her fists. Surely this sort of thing didn't happen in real life? Surely human beings, even terrorists, couldn't be so horribly cruel? *They were only children, for goodness' sake! What kind of monster can kill children?*

And then she saw her. It was only a brief glimpse, as the camera panned down the side of the school wall again. She couldn't be sure, but it had looked like Zalina. Bela's heart stopped and she held her breath as she craned forward to get a better view. It was only a split second before the camera had passed on, but the woman had looked familiar. A large, dark red patch of blood almost totally covered the left side of her face. She had been lying on the ground with the rest of the dead.

"No, no!" Bela called out.

What is it, si dakhe?

Bela was startled to hear Nana's voice. Only Nana used that Circassian term of endearment with her. Her mother always used the Russian word, *lapochka*. But it couldn't have been Nana, Nana was dead. Suddenly, Bela had an intense longing to run to her grandmother and bury her face in her lap, just as she used to do when she was little and had fallen over in the yard and scraped a knee. She must have imagined it, but how she wished her grandmother were here. Nana was the only one who knew about Zalina. She was the only one Bela could confide in about where Zalina was and what had really happened on that night that she had run away. She realised with horror that Zalina's parents had no idea that Zalina might have been caught up in the tragedy of Beslan. Zalina had been in contact with them by phone a few times to assure them that she was okay, but she had never disclosed her address for fear that they would come for her and force her to return home. What if they'd just seen what Bela had seen on the television? Would they have recognised the face of their daughter?

She had to find a way to be sure that it really was Zalina. It might be days before the authorities contacted Zalina's parents with the news, and Bela couldn't wait that long. She couldn't carry this horrible burden alone, this great fear that something terrible had happened to her best friend. She had to go to Beslan and find out for herself.

Chapter 32

2004, September

It had been two weeks since the tragedy in Beslan, and at last, Bela was on the bus on her way to find out what had happened to her friend.

Deep down, she knew there was no hope. Zalina hadn't answered her phone once, and, had she been alive, surely she would have known that Bela wanted to see if she was okay. There was a slim possibility that she was still alive but badly wounded and in the hospital, but Bela didn't want to get her hopes up. Either way, she had to know. She had to know the truth.

The last fortnight had been unbearable. It was normal to show some sadness and concern over the tragedy, but anything more than that would have aroused suspicion. No one must know that she had been involved in Zalina's disappearance all those years ago. How would Zalina's parents react if they knew the truth? What would Papa say? Besides, she'd made a promise to Zalina that she would never tell.

It was mid-September now, and although the temperature was still warm, the leaves on the trees were turning. Bela watched through her grimy window as the bus passed through the familiar countryside on its way to Beslan. It wasn't that long ago that she'd been travelling on buses in Pennsylvania, and now, by comparison, this bus felt old and shabby. She glanced around at the other passengers. The atmosphere on the bus was more subdued and quiet than usual. No doubt there were others here who were also on their way to find out about relatives or friends. She turned her attention back out of the window.

At last, the bus drew into the bus terminal. This time there was no smiling Zalina to greet her. There was no Ruslan waiting with the car. Had he been caught up in the attack too? And what of Adam and Angelina? She had to find out. She stepped down from the bus and made her way past the various fast food sellers and other stallholders. Was it her imagination or were there more flower sellers than usual today? Other passengers had stayed to collect their bags from the hold, but she had no luggage with her. She wasn't intending to stay the night. She didn't know what to expect.

Part of her wanted to go straight to the scene of the tragedy. She wanted to see for herself the blackened shell of the school and the photos of the children and adults who had died. She wanted to leave flowers and shed tears with the other mourners, but she would do that later. First, she had to go to Zalina's home and see who was there.

Twenty minutes later, after a brisk walk that almost broke into a run at times, she knocked on the gate outside the one-storey house where her friend lived. Had lived? She waited a long time. Zalina's dog was barking from behind the gate, his nose and paws just visible in the gap underneath. Had anyone been there to look after him? She was just about to turn away and give up when the dog stopped barking and she could hear someone shuffling slowly towards the gate on the other side. She'd forgotten about Ruslan's mother. Of course, she would be there.

"Who is it?" came Rosa's shaky voice.

"It's Bela, Zalina's friend from Shekala."

There was a fumbling around the lock on the gate and eventually it opened. Bela was shocked to see how much older the poor woman looked. It was as if she'd aged ten years.

"Come in, come in."

Bela followed the old lady into the house. She took her shoes off at the door and looked up to see a shy little girl peering around the door of the living room.

"Angelina!" Bela cried. She barely knew the girl, but she felt so overjoyed to see her alive that she enveloped the five-year-old in a huge bear hug. Angelina looked rather bewildered but seemed to recognise her.

"Tyotya Bela!" she acknowledged in reply, a slight smile forming on her lips. Bela knelt down to her level and looked intently at her. Large red rings around her eyes betrayed many nights of crying, and the girl was thin and pale. Bela turned to Grandmother Rosa, her eyes full of questions. Rosa shook her head sadly.

"They didn't make it. Ruslan, Zalina, Adam. We lost them all."

"Oh!" Bela let out a large gasp and covered her mouth with her hand. Her knees almost gave way beneath her. "All three? All of them?"

Rosa pointed to the sofa, and Bela gratefully sat down. Her legs felt weak and her hands were shaking. She covered her face with her hands. All three? Gone?

"I'll make tea," said Rosa, shuffling off.

Bela opened her eyes. Angelina was still in the room, looking at her with big, sad eyes. She held her arms out to the little girl, not sure if she would trust her enough, but Angelina willingly allowed Bela to sweep her up onto her lap and drop large teardrops into her hair. The little girl's eyes brimmed with tears too. They sat there, the two of them, united in their loss and their grief. Bela had lost a dear friend, but Angelina had lost so much more: a mother, a father, and a brother.

Eventually, Rosa came back into the room with the tea, and Bela went to help her with the tray. Rosa looked very frail. Bela took a deep breath and straightened up. She would have to be the strong one here; these other two had lost so much more. She wiped her eyes and poured the tea from the teapot into the cups. She stirred in some sugar and handed one of the cups to Angelina and the other to Rosa before taking one for herself and sitting down on the nearest chair.

"Tell me what happened, please, Rosa. I have to know."

Rosa nodded, and glanced at Angelina. She wouldn't go into too much detail for the little girl's sake, but at least Bela would know the basics.

"It was Adam's first day of school, his First Bell. He was so excited, standing there in his new uniform. He looked so smart."

She wiped away a tear. Bela nodded, willing her to continue.

"Ruslan and Zalina both took him to school that morning, but Angelina had a sore throat, so she stayed at home with me. They got caught up in the attack. I went to the school as soon as I heard, but I was too afraid, I had Angelina with me. When I realised there was nothing I could do, we came back home and waited and waited. We prayed for them constantly."

Rosa's voice shook, and she couldn't control her tears.

"Every day, I went down to find out what the news was, and then… and then on the Friday, I heard it was all over. It took me hours to find them. There was confusion everywhere. It was awful. So many people had lost someone. Eventually I found their bodies. Ruslan had been shot."

Rosa took a moment to regain control, and Bela reached out and placed her hand on Rosa's arm. The poor woman, finding her son's body like that.

"Zalina and Adam were together. It looks like they were killed when the roof collapsed." Rosa's teacup rattled in its saucer, and she removed her trembling hand.

"I'm so sorry, Rosa," said Bela. What did you say to someone who had experienced what Rosa had been through? What possible comfort could you offer?

"That's all I know for now, but I hope the authorities will be able to tell me more later, when everything has been sorted out," Rosa finished. "So many bodies. So many dead," she added. But then she looked up at Bela with a small gleam of hope in her eye. "But I know that they are all with the Lord now. They are at peace, and one day we will be together again." Rosa looked at Angelina and smiled gently.

Bela was surprised. She nodded in agreement, but the old lady's faith touched her. She knew that Rosa was a Christian, like Zalina and Ruslan had been, but her belief in a heaven, in life after death, was so strong. So genuine. It gave her a kind of peace and comfort that was astonishing, given the tragic circumstances.

After a simple lunch of bread, cheese, and tomatoes, Rosa took Bela to see the graveyard where Zalina, Ruslan, and Adam were buried. Rosa stood quietly, clutching Angelina's hand, while Bela placed a bouquet of flowers she'd just bought on the simple, hurried grave that lay amongst so many other freshly dug mounds of bare earth. There hadn't been time for the grass to grow back, and it all looked so bleak, so desolate. No wonder people brought flowers to graveyards. Somehow the absence of any beauty whatsoever made the loss so much more painful. Her face crumpled, and she wept, unable to hold back the tears that streamed down her face.

Goodbye, Zalina, my friend. I hope Rosa is right, that you're in a better place now and that you're at peace. I'm going to miss you.

On the way back to the house, Rosa pointed the way to the school and Bela went there alone while Rosa took Angelina back home. There was no point in distressing the child more than was necessary. She turned the corner and gasped at the sight of the blackened shell of the school. The full horror of the tragedy came to life the closer she got. The walls were pockmarked with bullets, and the dark patches on the pavement outside must have been bloodstains. Many others were there too, weaving their way around each other, each suffering in their own way, consumed in their own despair. Some grieving relatives had pinned up photos of their dead loved ones, and Bela took time to look at each one. It was the pictures of the children that made her stomach wrench with a deep, guttural anguish. The children had looked so eager, so hopeful and bright. They had the whole of their lives ahead of them. Who could know, when the photos were taken, that they would be cut short so tragically.

Bela spent half an hour there, laying more flowers outside the school gate and reading the messages of sorrow and condolence that others had left.

The road back to Rosa's house was deathly quiet. Something was missing, something was different. It wasn't until she reached the house that she realised what it was. There were no children walking along the pavements. There were no children playing in their yards. There were no children laughing and making their way home from school, their backpacks slung across their shoulders.

The children had gone.

At five o'clock, Bela moved to leave. "I have to be getting back to the bus station now, Rosa," she said gently.

Rosa nodded, but seemed to want to say something to Bela in private.

"Angelina, would you like to watch some cartoons?"

Angelina nodded, and Rosa switched the television on for her, changing channels until she found some cartoons for her to watch. Once she was sure that the little girl was settled in her chair clutching her brown bear and no longer listening to them, Rosa turned to Bela, her voice lowered. "Will you take the girl? It's what Ruslan and Zalina wanted."

"What?" Bela was completely stunned. What did the old woman mean?

"I can't look after her much longer," Rosa said, understanding Bela's surprise. "I'm old and weak, and the shock of the last few days has made me weaker."

"But… There must be someone else. Other relatives?"

Rosa shook her head. "There is no one. Ruslan was my only child."

"But what about Zalina's family? Surely her parents would want to take their granddaughter?"

Again, Rosa shook her head. "I don't think so. They knew about the children, but they never once contacted them. Never once visited. Zalina said they had cut her off and wanted nothing to do with her or the children."

"I know, but surely, when they hear what has happened, surely…"

"Perhaps." A flicker in Rosa's eyes acknowledged the possibility that even the proudest, most stubborn hearts could be changed by tragic news. "But I know that it was Zalina's wish that you should be the one to look after the children in the event of… In the event of…"

Rosa went over to the *stenka*, unable to finish her sentence. She opened one of the drawers and pulled out a piece of paper.

"They left a will, you see, Ruslan and Zalina. I don't think they ever imagined they would need it so soon, but they were well prepared. See, here."

Rosa pointed to a part of the will and handed it to Bela to read. Sure enough, there was the wish that, in the event of both their deaths, Bela was named as the one they hoped would be guardian to their children.

"But she never mentioned this to me." Bela quickly handed the paper back. "Why didn't she say anything if that's what she wanted?"

"I don't know. She loved you very much. She talked about you often, about her childhood growing up in your village. Will you consider it?"

Bela took a step back and clutched the side of the table, her knees weak. She couldn't think straight. How could she look after a child? She looked over at Angelina, still engrossed in her television show. The girl was adorable and sweet and wouldn't be difficult to look after. But…

"I need to think about it, Rosa. It's a big decision."

"Of course." Rosa nodded. "Just don't think about it too long. I don't know how much time I have left on this earth."

"I'm sure you have many years yet, Rosa," said Bela out of politeness, but she could see the resignation in Rosa's eyes. She was right, she wouldn't be around long enough to see Angelina grow up.

Bela went over and kissed Angelina goodbye, then kissed Rosa too. As she walked slowly back to the bus station, she was overwhelmed by everything that had happened that day. It was all too much to take in. She needed to grieve the death of her friend first before she could even begin to think about what Rosa had just asked of her.

Over two thousand miles away, in his old bedroom back in his parents' home in Bristol, Michael closed his computer lid and walked over to the window. He looked out over the garden where he and Claire had played as children. Now, the swing set had been replaced by a gazebo, and the flower beds had been extended. Michael's mother was out there right now, kneeling on a green mat, pulling weeds out from among the rose bushes. It was good to be home, and yet at the same time, his heart longed to be somewhere else. Bela had been on his mind every hour of every day. He just couldn't seem to shake off his longing for her, his concern to know how she was doing. Had she found out whether her friend was okay or not? What was she having to deal with right now? Michael had seen all the BBC news reports about Beslan, and it had been awful, so tragic and sad. All those poor people, those families. He wished more than anything that he could be there for her, and yet, what right did he have to assume that he should be the one to do that? He had no claim over her. But then why did he feel so bound to her? So many times, he had picked up his phone and wondered if he should call her, but each time, it hadn't seemed the right thing to do. He had left a few text messages but she hadn't replied, and there was no other way to contact her since she didn't have email.

Pray, my son, pray for Bela.

Michael bowed his head and closed his eyes. He couldn't be there for her, but he could pray. He'd been praying constantly over the last few days, sensing that God had laid this particular burden on him for this time. He didn't know exactly what was happening and couldn't pray for anything specific, but he prayed anyway.

Heavenly Father, be with Bela right now. I don't know what she's going through, but whatever it is, Lord, please comfort her. Let her know how much you love her, how you're there for her and care for what she's going through. And please, Lord….

He wanted to ask God to make a way for them to be together again but wasn't sure if that was the right thing to ask for. He was still so confused about their relationship, still in the dark about what God was doing behind the scenes. Suddenly, he felt a new resolve.

God, I'm going to apply for a visa again to try to get back to Russia. If it's not the right thing then please let me know, but if it is… then please pave a way for me to get back to Shekala. If only for a while.

Chapter 33

2004, September

The days that followed Bela's visit to Beslan went by in a blur. All she could think about, all that was on her mind was the terrible loss of Zalina, Ruslan, and Adam and the future of their little girl, Angelina.

Oh, Nana, why aren't you here to help me know what to do? I could really do with your wisdom right now!

Michael had texted a few times, but each time her heart had been too heavy to reply to him. She appreciated his concern and would text him when she felt ready. For now, though, she felt pulled in so many directions she didn't know what to do.

October was coming, and Cody would be back soon. His application for a business visa had been successful, and there would be lots of work for Bela to do to help set up the new office and get things up and running. Already, she had started scouting out a suitable office space for him to use. When she thought of her future, working with the business, the possibilities of travel, and all her responsibilities, she couldn't see how looking after a five-year-old girl in the midst of that could work. For one thing, she would have to explain to everyone who she was. There would have to be a good reason why her parents would let her bring another child into the family, and it was already difficult having Madina and Alyona there still. Mama wouldn't be happy to have one extra mouth to feed. Bela could probably pay for Angelina's upkeep from her salary, but she wouldn't be there to look after the girl during the day. It would be impossible for Angelina to come to work with her each day; the little girl would be hugely bored at best and a distraction and a nuisance to clients at worse. No, she was sure that Cody wouldn't be happy with that arrangement. There was the local kindergarten, she supposed.

All these thoughts went spinning around and around in Bela's head until she fell onto her bed and groaned in frustration. She wasn't supposed to be worrying about things like childcare. She was single. She had her whole future ahead of her. And surely any potential, future husband wouldn't be too pleased to have to take on a child who wasn't his. He would probably run in the other direction. A wry smile formed on her lips as she thought that it would be a wonderful way to get Alim off her list of recommended suitors, but then her mind drew her back to the gravity of the situation. Oh, that poor little girl. She did love her, for Zalina's sake, but it wasn't fair to put this burden on her, no. Zalina should have talked to her about it before she wrote it down in the will.

The only possible solution she could see was if Zalina's parents could be persuaded to look after their granddaughter. Yes, that was it. Bela would just have to talk them into it. As she determined in her mind to pursue this option she tried to suppress the nagging thought that it hadn't been Zalina's choice. *She* had been Zalina's choice.

Perhaps Zalina had good reasons for that. Bela had watched how Zalina's father had beaten her and taken away her freedom, driving her to the point of running away from her family in desperation. Could she really send an innocent little girl into that environment again, knowing all that she knew? That would just be cruel. As far as she was aware, Zalina's father still hadn't changed. He was still an angry, bitter man.

But what about religion? Zalina would want Angelina brought up as a Christian, but Bela wasn't a Christian. Perhaps Zalina had known that at least Bela would be open-minded and would allow Angelina to continue in the faith of her parents, even if she herself couldn't help her in that.

God, if you're there, you could at least tell me what to do. Zalina and Ruslan believed in you. They put all their trust in you, and, as far as I can see, you let them down horribly. How could you have done that to them? How could you leave their little daughter without a mother, father, or a brother, and with no one else suitable to care for her?

There is someone suitable to care for her, my daughter.

Bela sat up on her bed in surprise. That last thought had come into her mind so clearly, so unexpectedly. Could God himself have just spoken to her?

Lift your eyes to the mountains. Where does your help come from?

It was that Bible verse again, the one that had come into her mind in a similar way all those years ago when she was in the mountains with her Uncle. Michael had said that it was from the Bible, but how could she have possibly known those words herself?

Her mind went to the little Bible that Zalina had given her a few years ago. She hadn't thought anything of it then. Where had she put it? She searched through her drawers and eventually found it, stuffed down at the back of the top drawer where she'd hoped no one in her family would have discovered it. She got it out and looked at it with a new reverence. Where had Michael said the verse was from? She opened the book to the contents page. Something looked familiar about the word 'Psalms'. Yes, that was it. She turned to the page where the Psalms started and flicked through. There were over a hundred Psalms in total; how on earth was she going to find the right one?

For some reason, Bela found herself compelled to find this verse. She needed to see for herself where it was written in the Bible. She would just have to start at the beginning and work her way through until she found it.

In his room, Azamat was wrestling with his own terrible thoughts. He rubbed his hands through his hair and groaned. How had his life become such a mess? How had he become this person? He just seemed to make the wrong turn at every crossroads.

He was deeply ashamed of himself. He had to tell someone. He wanted someone to tell him that it was okay, that he was forgiven, that they still believed in him. But who? None of his friends would be interested in his problems. He couldn't really trust any of them anyway. He knew he'd chosen badly in that respect. Mama and Papa had been right, but he'd been too hot-headed at the time to admit it.

Bela. She was the only one he could open up to. She had always believed in him, always been on his side, even when he hadn't treated her very well. He thought of how he'd pushed her away when they were younger, feeling embarrassed to have his little sister tagging along after him. He'd been moody and difficult around her, just like he had been around everyone else, but somehow, he knew that she still cared deeply for him.

Without really knowing what he was doing, he got up and went over to Bela's room. He knocked softly on the door. Maybe she was asleep already; it was quite late. But no, there was a light shining from under the door. He heard a rustling and a drawer closing and then he heard her footsteps coming towards him. She opened the door quietly.

"Yes? Azamat! What is it?"

"Can I come in for a bit? I need to talk to someone."

"Sure, come in." She opened the door wider to let him through and then shut it again. He went over to sit on her bed, and she perched herself next to him. "What's wrong?"

"I've not told anyone this before, but I feel like I really need to get it off my chest, out into the open. Can you promise not to tell Mama and Papa? In fact, you have to promise to tell no one."

His words had clearly worried her. "Are you in trouble with the police again?"

"No, no. Nothing like that."

"Well, okay then... I promise, I think."

Azamat took a deep breath, trying to work out where to begin. "You remember that year that I 'disappeared' as Mama calls it?"

Bela nodded sadly. "Yes, I remember. She was worried sick about you. She didn't know if you were going to come home again. I had to give up university because there was no one else at home to help."

Azamat's face fell, and he hung his head. "I'm sorry about that. I had no idea it would affect you as well."

"It's okay. There were other reasons, financial reasons, why I had to come home. Besides, you came back in the end, didn't you? Mama was so relieved."

Azamat frowned. He hadn't known that there were financial reasons for Bela dropping out of university, but this wasn't the time to ask. "I... I was kind of recruited into something."

"Recruited? Like back into the army? Why didn't you tell us?"

"No, not the army. A different organisation."

Bela was silent, waiting for him to continue.

He took a deep breath. "They told me they were freedom fighters. They told me a lot of stuff about how the government had treated them and their people, our people, badly for years. Well, you know, we hear that around here a lot." Bela smiled weakly but didn't say anything.

"I... I guess I got taken in by what they were saying," Azamat continued. "It all made so much sense at the time. They said they'd train me up. They praised me for the skills I'd picked up in the army, and for a while, it was nice to be back doing those sorts of familiar things."

"You mean like weapons training?"

Azamat nodded. "I didn't really think too much about what they were planning to do. It was just kind of fun to be part of something. To feel respected. To have some kind of purpose. They provided accommodation, food, a small wage. It was like having a proper job. The only deal was that I couldn't tell anyone where I was or what I was doing."

"You were able to let Mama know you were okay though?"

"Yes, of course. I phoned a couple of times to let her know I was alright, but I couldn't say anymore, and I knew she didn't like that."

"So, what happened?"

"Well, after the initial year of training, I returned home, but I continued being in touch, meeting up with the local cell group on a regular basis."

"Oh, Azamat."

"But things changed. They started planning a proper hit. There was a target. There were extensive plans. A number of recruits volunteered. I went along with it… for too long. I managed to get out just in time. I never knew the exact details, so they determined that I wasn't a threat. I mean, I had a vague idea, but no names or anything specific had been shared with us up to that point. I was monitored, though. I know I've been followed, that people were checking up on me to make sure I didn't spill the beans."

"That's awful. Are they still following you?"

"No. Not anymore. I don't think."

"Why not?"

He closed his eyes and ran his fingers through his hair. He took a deep breath and looked straight at Bela. "Because they carried out their plans. They did what they wanted to do."

Bela's face turned pale. "Azamat? What did they do?"

"When I saw it on the news I knew, Bela. It was Beslan. I was supposed to be one of the freedom fighters in that school at Beslan."

Huge tears of shame started to roll down Azamat's face. He buried his face in his hands, struggling to hold back his sobs. "When I saw those children. When I saw what I might have done… Oh Bela, I can't believe I was so close to doing something as evil as that."

Bela wrapped her arms around him, and he let himself dissolve into her. The tears that had been pent up for so long flowed freely now. It must have been a full five minutes before his sobbing slowed and the pain in his heart released just enough to help him regain his composure. He was embarrassed his little sister had seen him like this, but Bela took hold of his shoulders and looked him straight in the eye.

"But you *weren't* there, Azamat. You got out. You didn't do anything wrong. You didn't hurt anyone. You made the right choice."

Azamat nodded. "I know. But I still can't help feeling this huge weight of guilt and shame. What if it had been my own son there?"

"Your own son?"

Azamat felt his cheeks colouring as he realised what he'd said. That was another secret he wasn't ready to disclose just yet. He laughed sadly. "That's a whole other story which I'll have to tell you now I guess. But not right now. One terrible secret at a time, I think. Do you forgive me, Bela, or are you ashamed of your big brother?" He looked at her earnestly, waiting for her reply. He was surprised to discover that her good opinion of him really mattered.

"Of course. There's nothing to forgive. You just got in with a bad crowd again. You need to stop doing that!"

They both laughed.

"Besides, do you remember when you rescued me from the cellar steps next door, when I fell and broke my ankle?"

Azamat frowned and racked his brains, trying to remember the incident. Something about Zalina and a doll? Suddenly it all came back to him, and he hung his head again.

"Oh, Bela. It was my fault that you fell in the first place. I threw the doll down there. I even took the ladder away so that you couldn't get to her. I didn't know that you were going to try to jump down."

"It was you who took away the ladder?" Bela gave him a friendly punch. Then she looked serious again. "But I'll always remember you as the one who rescued me. You're my big brother; I'll always love you, nothing you can do will ever change that."

"Thanks. That means more to me than you know."

Chapter 34

2004, October

Bela thought a lot about Azamat's confession over the next few days. For the first time in a long time, she felt that he really needed her. He needed someone stable in his life. Someone who believed in him. They had both agreed that he needn't mention anything to the police. He hadn't done anything wrong, and, besides, the authorities would be sure to root out all the people they determined were responsible in the end. He would always live in the fear that his connection with the cell would get him into trouble one day, but he would just have to trust that none of his former 'friends' would give his name to the police. And there was no point in telling Mama and Papa; it would only worry them.

Remembering the incident with the doll had brought back several poignant childhood memories, many of them happy days spent with Zalina. Zalina's parents had been informed now about their daughter's death, so Bela had had the chance to speak openly about it with them and to finally show her own grief. It had been such a relief to be able to cry alongside Zalina's mother.

"Did Zalina have any other children?" she had asked tentatively, trying not to give away the fact that she already knew.

"Yes, a girl." Zalina's mother had admitted.

"And what's to become of her?"

"My husband will have nothing to do with her. He believes she can be taken care of by other relatives."

"But, what if—" but Bela had realised this conversation was closed. Instead, Zalina's mother discussed their plans to move away from Awush.

"It's time to have a fresh start. Somewhere new. There's a promise of a job working for one of the museums up in the north. It's a long way away, but I think it'll be good for us."

Bela nodded. Perhaps it would.

She had been reading through the Psalms in Zalina's Bible. She still hadn't found her Psalm yet, but it had been interesting reading the others. The author really seemed to understand so many of the emotions she herself felt. At first, it had been a bit shocking to see how openly he had argued with God and complained and expressed his doubts, but then there were other places where the author demonstrated how much he loved God and trusted him. Who was the person who had written such beautiful words? She must ask Michael, he would know.

She searched for the most recent text message from Michael on her phone, and read it for what must have been the one hundredth time. *"How are you? I've been granted a tourist visa and will come next month. I'd like to see you if I can. I'll be in touch. Michael."*

It had taken her a long time to decide exactly how to reply, but eventually she'd written: *"I'm okay. Lots to tell you. Looking forward to seeing you. Bela."*

Her heart had raced as she'd sent it. What she'd really wanted to say was that she still loved him and missed him terribly, but she couldn't. It had been two months since they'd seen each other, and perhaps he had moved on and accepted that their relationship would never work.

That night she found the verse at last. It was in Psalm 121. She read the words slowly and carefully, her eyes brimming with tears. It was as if that voice was speaking them to her all over again.

> *I lift up my eyes to the mountains - where does my help come from?*
> *My help comes from the Lord, the Maker of heaven and earth.*

She thought again of their beautiful mountains in the Caucasus. How many times had she lifted her eyes to the mountains? How many times had she felt their majesty and wondered at their awesomeness? Surely it was true that they did speak of an almighty, all-powerful creator God; she understood that so clearly now. She knew deep down that there really was a God. That he really did exist. Nana had believed it. Many of her neighbours believed it. Zalina and Michael believed it. Was it true that this God was there to help her? Would he care enough about her to help her in the troubles of her life? She read on.

> *He will not let your foot slip -*
> *He who watches over you will not slumber;*
> *Indeed, he who watches over Israel*

Will neither slumber nor sleep.

She wasn't sure why it mentioned Israel, but the words must be meant for her too. This God was not only watching over her, but he was doing so every second of every day. He would always be there to call on for help.

The Lord watches over you -
The Lord is your shade at your right hand;
The sun will not harm you by day,
Nor the moon by night.

Bela stopped short. It was nice sentiment to say that this God wouldn't allow either the sun or the moon to harm you, but then why didn't he stop the bombs from hurting Zalina? Why did he allow her foot to slip as it walked into that school on that fateful day? Why hadn't he stopped them? Why hadn't he protected them? Bela closed the Bible angrily and was about to fling it away but thought better of doing that to a holy book. Instead, she placed it back in her bedside drawer and closed the drawer firmly. How could she believe in a God who would do that to Zalina, a girl who had loved him as much as this author of the Psalms seemed to have loved him? It didn't make any sense.

Michael's limbs tingled with excitement as the Caucasus range came into view from his aeroplane seat. He leaned closer to the window and looked in awe at the twin peaks of Mount Elbrus, the highest mountain in Europe, rising high above the line of clouds, towering over the other mountain peaks.

God, you're so amazing! This world is just so amazing, so beautiful.

The stewardess came round and collected his plastic coffee cup. He returned his tray to its upright position and sat back into his seat. They would be landing soon, and Cody would be there to meet him at the airport. It would be good to see him again and hear about how he was progressing with his new business. It would be good to go back to his favourite cafés and to walk in the park. But most of all it would be really good to see Bela again. He thought of the package he had for her in his suitcase. Would she like it? He'd been so excited when he found it.

But what mattered most of all was that she was okay, and something deep inside him really needed to know. They had agreed to meet on his third day here. It was going to be torture to wait that long, but he still didn't want to raise Cody's suspicions about his feelings for Bela in case it somehow jeopardized her job. He wasn't sure how, but he felt it was best that his former roommate didn't know.

Finally, the day arrived, and Michael found himself in the familiar position of waiting for Bela in the café at the edge of the park. Autumn was nearing its end. Fallen leaves lay in huge piles, swept up on either side of the main walkway, and the trees looked bare and ready for their long winter sleep. The temperature was cold enough to warrant a hat, and the local people who were walking in the park were already muffled up in their winter outfits. He smiled at the waitress. Did she recognise him? He'd been a fairly regular customer most of last year. He ordered an *Americano*. It was good to be back.

Then he saw her. She walked in wearing her black, woollen winter coat, her beautiful, dark eyes shining, and her cheeks glowing after her brisk walk from the bus stop. When she saw him, her face developed the most beautiful smile of recognition and joy. His heart skipped a beat. It belonged to this girl alone and would never belong to anyone else. He rose out of his seat and greeted her with a hug. He couldn't take his eyes off her as she sat down opposite him, removing her coat and placing her handbag carefully on the chair next to her.

"It's so good to see you," he managed eventually, not able to wipe the wide grin off his face.

"You too."

"What would you like? Coffee? Tea?"

"A pot of *Sencha* green tea, please."

Michael called the waitress over and gave his order. He turned back to Bela, his eyes softer, his smile more sympathetic. "How are you, really? What's been happening over the last couple of months?"

Bela sighed, and her eyes filled with pain and deep sadness. She lowered her voice as she related to Michael all that had happened since she'd returned to Shekala at the beginning of September, pausing only briefly to allow the waitress to set her tea down in front of her. Michael spoke very little in the next half an hour. Instead, he just allowed her time to pour out the tragic story of how her friend had died along with her husband and son, and how Bela had been to visit Beslan, and all that she had seen there. She mentioned Angelina, who had been safe with her grandmother, but seemed to stop short of saying something more. Was she holding something back from him? It wasn't his place to ask.

"I'm so, so sorry," he said eventually when she'd finished. He genuinely meant it. He couldn't begin to imagine the pain and loss she must be feeling.

"I've been reading some of the Psalms," she said, after taking a few sips of her tea, which surely must have gone a bit cold by the time she'd had a chance to drink it. But hope surged in Michael's heart at her words. She was reading the Bible, that was a good sign.

She continued, "I found my Psalm, you know, the one about the mountains?"

Michael nodded. "Psalm 121, I remember."

Bela's face clouded over. "I don't understand how such an all-powerful God, who promises to watch over his people, would allow Zalina to suffer what she did."

Michael felt a jolt of disappointment. Of course she would think that. It was the age-old question of 'How does a loving God allow suffering?'; a question which myriads of wise philosophers and theologians throughout the centuries had not been able to answer in a way that satisfied the sceptics. A question which proved to be a stumbling block for so many, and indeed had been a stumbling block for him as well, once. *Please God, don't let it be a stumbling block for Bela too.*

"That's a good question," he said after a moment, "and I've asked something similar for years. Have I ever told you about my sister, Claire?"

Bela shook her head.

He took a deep breath. "When she was five, she had an accident—an accident which I caused—that put her in a wheelchair."

"Oh, I'm so sorry."

Michael nodded gravely. "For years, I pleaded with God to make her better. I prayed for a miracle, but it never happened. She's still in a wheelchair, and it looks like she'll be in a wheelchair for the rest of her life. It was something that I nearly lost my faith over. I was so angry with God. After all, we were a Christian family. We went to church every Sunday, we did all the right things. We were good people. My sister… she was so sweet; she still is. She didn't deserve this."

"No, of course not."

"But I've come to see over the years that God doesn't need us to know the answers to all our questions. I don't believe that God wanted Claire to be in a wheelchair, but somehow he felt it best to allow it to happen. He has his reasons, however impossible or unfathomable they may be, and one day we will understand. But in the meantime, our responsibility is just to have faith. To trust him."

Bela nodded slowly. "I see, perhaps, yes."

"Bela, God never promised that life would be easy. Even for his closest followers, his best friends, Jesus warned that troubles and hardships would be unavoidable. Indeed, most of them died horrible deaths because of their faith. Bad things happen. Life isn't fair. But one day, everything will be put right, and justice will prevail. I believe that, and I'm sure Zalina did too." Michael reached out across the table and squeezed her hand as she tried to blink back the tears in her eyes. "Bela," he said softly, "I honestly believe that Zalina and her husband and her son are in a wonderful, happy place right now, in heaven with Jesus."

Bela wiped away a couple of rogue tears and squeezed his hand. "I'd like to think so."

The light was already beginning to fade outside, and the café lights turned on. Bela looked at her watch. "I need to get home."

"Of course, I'll just get the bill."

After he'd paid and helped her into her coat, they walked in silence towards the entrance to the park. Michael reached into his bag and pulled out the gift he'd been carrying for her all the way from England. He handed it to her, and she looked up, a little surprised.

"I found this for you," he explained. "Please, will you read it, for me?"

"Yes, of course, thank you."

Michael hugged her goodbye, and then, with all his strength, he pulled away, resisting the strong desire to take her in his arms and kiss her properly. "I'll see you again?"

"Yes, I'll be in touch. Thank you, Michael. Goodbye."

"Goodbye." He watched her walk towards the bus stop, and then he turned to walk back towards Cody's apartment, his heart heavy with concern and desire for the woman he loved with every fibre of his being.

Bela wrestled with her own emotions while she waited for the *marshroutka* to arrive and take her back to Awush. Having Michael back in her life, if only briefly, was a mixed blessing. She was just beginning to imagine the possibility of life without him, and now he was back in Shekala and all her old feelings of attraction and longing had come flooding back. She turned the present over in her hands. It was wrapped in tissue paper, and although she was desperate to know what it contained, it was probably best to wait until she was in the privacy of her own bedroom. She placed the package carefully into her handbag when she saw the minibus arriving and held out her hand to indicate to the driver to stop.

It was another couple of hours before she found herself alone again. Alyona had needed some help with her homework, and Madina and Mama were busy in the kitchen, so the task had fallen to her. She didn't mind, really, she was happy to help out. Since the divorce had gone through, Madina seemed more relaxed and more like her old self. It hadn't been an easy time, and there were still many question marks hanging over her future, but for now, she and Alyona seemed content with life here in Awush, and Alyona was doing well at school.

As Bela watched Alyona work on her maths problems, she'd thought how grateful she was to have this opportunity to get to know her niece better. They hadn't seen much of each other when Madina lived in her husband's village, but now Alyona and Bela were becoming good friends. If Bela were to move overseas, she'd miss the chance to watch her niece grow up into a lovely young woman. She might not even be able to be present at Alyona's wedding, whenever that might be. There would be so many things she'd miss.

Eventually, everyone headed to bed, and Bela was able to close her bedroom door and reach into her handbag for Michael's present. She unwrapped it carefully and slowly, trying not to tear the tissue paper. Inside was a small book, as she'd suspected. It was dark green and decorated with a traditional Circassian design on the front. It almost looked like a holy book. Perhaps it was? She carefully opened the cover and read the first page. Amazingly, the book was written not in English or Russian, but in Circassian, her own language. How on earth did Michael get hold of this? It seemed to be the story of a prophet called Yinus. She leant back on her bed and began to read it eagerly.

Yinus had been asked by God to give a message to a group of people who lived in a city called Nineveh, but he hadn't wanted to. He'd tried to run away from God. He tried to sail away on a ship, but he couldn't run away from God. Soon the ship was caught up in a huge storm, and Yinus knew that it was his fault and that the only way to save the sailors on board was to be thrown into the sea, where he would certainly drown. Eventually, the sailors reluctantly agreed. They threw him into the sea and immediately the storm dispelled. Yinus, however, started to sink to his death. But just in time, God sent a large fish to swallow him up.

Okay, well, that didn't sound terribly believable to Bela, but it was still a good story. She read on.

Yinus sat inside the large fish for three days, praying to God to forgive him and give him a second chance. God did so, and Yinus found himself vomited out of the fish onto dry land. Immediately, he did as he'd promised, as he should have done in the first place, and went to Nineveh to deliver God's message.

But there was more. Yinus didn't really want the Ninevites to respond positively to his message. He didn't want them to turn back to God and be forgiven. He didn't want them to have a second chance, like he'd been given. God did forgive them, though, and he taught Yinus a lesson in the process. No matter how much Yinus hated the Ninevites, they were still precious to God and worth saving.

Bela closed the book and sat back to take it all in. That book was part of the Bible, she was sure. And reading it in her own language, in her heart language, had spoken to a deep place within her. As she'd read the words, it was as if God's love and God's presence had invaded her heart and permeated through her soul. Was there a message God was trying to tell her? Was he speaking directly to her through this book?

The more she thought about it, the more she realized she was a bit like Yinus, really: trying to run as far away from her country and her people as she could. Was God trying to tell her she should stay? She thought of the people that Azamat had been linked to and who now had committed horrible, horrible acts of cruelty. Did God still love those people? If Azamat had been with them, would Bela *really* still have loved her brother, like she'd told him she would?

Exhausted from thinking but no closer to an answer or a reprieve from her swirling thoughts, Bela sank into a deep sleep. She dreamt she saw a man shining in a halo of brilliant white light. Somehow, she knew that this man was Jesus himself. She longed to run to him, but when she looked down, she saw that she held a plane ticket in her hand. When she looked at the ticket, she felt like it held the promise of a future of freedom and of a comfortable life in the West, but when she looked at Jesus, she knew that she wanted to be with him more. She threw away the plane ticket and started running towards him, but he suddenly disappeared.

She woke up with a start and took a deep intake of breath. Her heart was pounding. Looking around, she recognised the familiar surroundings of her bedroom. Her shoulders relaxed. It was just a dream. And yet, the dream had been so vivid, so real, almost as if it had really happened. It was still dark outside, and her eyelids felt heavy again. She lay her head back down on the pillow and settled down to sleep. She would think about the strange dream in the morning.

Her sleep was disturbed again. This time, she was looking down the cellar steps at Zalina's house next door. At the bottom, she could see Angelina crying for her mother. "I'm coming, Angelina!" she called, and she scrambled down the steps to get to the little girl. She felt a sharp pain in her ankle, but she kept going and swept the little girl up into her arms. As she turned to look back up the steps, she saw Zalina leaning over, concern written all over her face. "Don't worry, Zalina," Bela shouted up exuberantly, "I've rescued her. I told you I would."

Once again, Bela sat up with a jolt. That dream, too, had seemed so real that she felt quite disorientated for several minutes. Her pulse was racing, and tingles of fear and excitement skittered across her skin. She took a few slow, deep breaths to calm her heart, which was beating so hard she could hear it in her ears. She reached for the glass of water by her bedside, took a sip, and then held it against her flushed face.

Suddenly, it was all clear to her. It was as if her vision had been blurred for so long, but now it was laser sharp. There were two things she was going to have to do, and both of those would be among the hardest things she'd ever done in her life. But there was absolutely no doubt in her mind that they were the right things to do. She would have to act quickly, because if she didn't do them, then she would be missing out on the purpose for which her life was always intended.

Chapter 35

2004, November

Michael was puzzled but encouraged by Bela's text message the next morning. It read: "*Need to see you today. When?*"

He wrote back: "*Sure. 2pm here? Cody will be out until 3pm.*" As he sent it, he wondered whether it was culturally appropriate to be inviting her round when they would be alone together in the apartment, but he didn't know what else to suggest. He sensed that this might be a deep talk, and those were hard to have in cafés or whilst walking in the park.

Waiting until two o'clock seemed like an eternity, but he tried to keep himself busy running some errands for Cody and praying for Bela and their conversation at every possible moment.

Lord, please give me wisdom to know what to say to whatever it is that she has to say.

Finally, two o'clock came, and a minute or two later, someone rang the apartment doorbell. His heart was beating swiftly as he sprang up to open the door.

"Hi."

"Hi." She came in, and he waited for her to change into slippers while he closed the door behind her.

"Tea?"

"Yes, please." Neither of them spoke while they waited for the kettle to boil. Michael placed two tea bags in two mugs, poured on the hot water, and swished the bags around a bit until the colour seeped into the water and turned it the appropriate shade of brown. He knew she took it black with one sugar, like most people he'd come across in Russia. He handed her one of the mugs, and they both walked through to the living room and sat down on the sofa, a respectable distance between them.

"You needed to talk?"

"Yes. Thank you for the book, by the way."

"You liked it? It's the book of Jonah in Circassian. I came across it through one of my linguistic connections. As far as I know, it's the first book of the Old Testament to be published in the Circassian language."

"Old Testament?"

"Oh, yes, sorry. The Bible is divided into two parts—the Old Testament, which is before Jesus was born, and the New Testament, which is after."

"I see."

"So, what did you think?"

"Michael, I want to become a Christian. Can you tell me how?"

He was stunned. He hadn't been expecting that. Finally, the words for which he'd been waiting and praying for such a long time! He couldn't help a broad smile sweeping across his face.

"That's wonderful! Of course I can explain, but first can you tell me what changed your mind?"

He listened attentively and in amazement as Bela told him about reading the book and about the dream of Jesus.

Thank you, God, thank you!

"It was so real, Michael. I knew that God was real, but now I know that Jesus is too. I know that he loves me and my people and that he wants me to let him into my life. Can you tell me how to do that?"

For the next ten minutes, Michael talked Bela through a quick outline of the gospel message and, when she was sure that she wanted to go ahead, he led her in a prayer of repentance and of asking Jesus into her heart by his Holy Spirit. She repeated his words slowly and carefully but spoke them not in English or Russian but in her own heart language of Circassian. When she was finished, she looked up at him with a glow of joy on her face.

"So, that's it?"

Michael laughed. "Yes, that's it. That's the most life changing thing you've ever done or will do. You'll see. It won't always be easy, but there are so many good times ahead of you now. You've started on a journey, but you're only at the beginning, and there's a lot to learn." He looked down briefly and then brought his eyes to hers once more. "I wish I could be the one to help you but I have to head back to England soon."

Bela nodded. "I know. To be honest, I feel a bit frightened. I don't know how my family will react, or whether I should tell them at all."

"You're thinking about your friend Zalina and what she went through?"

"Yes. Although, Zalina's situation was a bit different. Her parents were much more religious than mine. I can't imagine they'd put a gun to my head, but I don't think they'll be too happy about it either."

"I'll pray that God will give you wisdom to know what to do. Do you know any local Christians?"

Bela shook her head.

"Well, look, I don't go back until Tuesday. There's a little church near here that I've been going to. Would you like to come with me on Sunday morning? They're mostly Russians, but they're very friendly, and I could introduce you to some people."

"Thanks, I'd like that."

When Bela opened her eyes after the prayer, it felt like a huge weight of anxiety and concern had been lifted from her shoulders. She felt free, like a whole new future was opening up in front of her. Although she'd done a really scary thing, she knew beyond any doubt that it was right. Perhaps Zalina was smiling down from heaven at her right now.

After their discussion about a local group of believers they could visit, Michael shifted awkwardly in his seat, and Bela instinctively knew what he was about to say.

"Bela?" He took her hand in his and looked deeply into her eyes. "I don't want to jump the gun, but now that you've given your life to Jesus, do you think that the two of us... that we might be able to be in a relationship?"

She laughed. "For a minute there I thought you were going to ask me to marry you!"

He laughed too, but with a slight seriousness which suggested that that thought hadn't been far from his mind. She clarified quickly, "I mean, it's best not to jump into anything. I want you to know that I made this decision to become a Christian on my own, not because I wanted to be your girlfriend."

"Yes, yes, I know that. We can take things as slow as you like."

"But..." her smile faded. There were some things that were still the same as they'd been before. "What would that look like? How would it be possible? You're in England and I'm here. I still can't see how it would work." The feeling of joy and elation had dissipated and now her shoulders slumped with sadness once more.

"You could come to England," Michael said, tentatively, half-jokingly.

Bela shook her head. "I feel like my place is here now, amongst my people. That was part of the dream, you know? I sense that God wants me to stay here."

Michael's face fell. Bela continued, "Maybe you could move here again?"

This time, Michael shook his head. "Believe me, I've thought of that many times. But, well, there's Claire. I don't think I could leave her, Bela. She'll need me. It would be too hard to live so far away. I feel responsible. There must be a way to make this work." For a second, he looked so frustrated and angry that Bela thought he was about to slam his fist down on the coffee table.

She looked down, despondent, not knowing what to say, and feeling equally frustrated.

"Let's pray about it," he suggested eventually. "Hey, come on, we should be celebrating! This is your spiritual birthday after all!"

Chapter 36

2005, February

The snow lay thickly on the ground outside. It was Saturday, and Alyona was having great fun out on the sledge with her friends from the neighbourhood. Bela watched them from the gate, smiling. It didn't seem that long ago that it was her and Zalina out there. It had been so much fun. They would take turns to pull on the string at the front until the person behind fell off into a snowdrift, laughing hard.

She turned to go back into the house and let out a sigh. February was already upon them. It had been several weeks since her dreams and the decisions she'd made. Michael had gone back home to England, but not before introducing her to his friends at a local church. She'd instantly felt welcome and at home there and had been going every Sunday. She was learning such a lot about the Christian faith and about the Bible. She now realised that so many of the things she had thought and been taught when she was younger were just myths or misinformation, or perhaps even deliberate lies. She had made a good friend who was also Circassian and had been a wonderful support as Bela had shared her fears about telling her family. So far, she had kept things quiet. She was old enough to come and go from the house without too many questions being asked, so until now, it had been easy to keep her faith hidden. Maybe one day she'd have the courage to tell them, but not yet.

She'd celebrated her first Christmas with her new church, filled with joy at the thought of that precious baby born into the world two thousand years ago. But in the time before and since, her thoughts had often wandered to another child. A little girl.

She'd written several times to Rosa, not knowing a phone number through which she could contact her, but she'd not had any reply. It troubled her. She knew how anxious the old lady had been for Bela to take the child as soon as possible. What if the worst had happened?

But then she'd been swallowed up in New Year celebrations. First there was the proper New Year on the first of January, and that had been followed by holiday celebrations right up to 'Old New Year' on the fourteenth of January.

Now it had been nearly five full months since the horrific tragedy of Beslan.

Her phone rang. It was Michael. Her heart skipped a beat and she disappeared into her room to take the call in private.

"Hi."

"Hi, Bela. How are you?"

Michael called once a week. She loved talking to him, but always their chats were tinged with an unspoken sadness, both knowing that there was a huge gap between them that seemed impossible to bridge. They talked about their work and about their families. When he eventually hung up, Bela stared at the now silent phone in her hand for several seconds.

God, I don't know how, but can you make a way for us to be together? Should I go to England?

She waited, but as usual there was no sense of God's specific direction on this matter. She knew she just had to wait and trust His timing. That's what Michael had said.

In the meantime, her concerns about Angelina were growing, and she couldn't get the little girl out of her head. She didn't quite know what lay ahead, but she felt that in taking the path that led to Angelina, she would be taken even further away from Michael.

Go to her, my daughter. Go to the child.

There it was again. The voice that she knew now to be God's Spirit stirring in her soul. He wanted her to go to Angelina. She'd waited long enough. She would have to be brave. 'Be strong and courageous'—wasn't that what God had said in that Bible verse Michael had shared with her the other day? She would have to go in person and find out what had happened to Rosa.

Angelina huddled against the lumpy pillow at the top of her bed, clutching her favourite stuffed animal, a brown bear by the name of Mishka. Mishka was a little ragged now, but Angelina didn't mind. He would always remind her of her family. She remembered her mother laughing as she bounced Mishka from side to side, reciting the poem about a lopsided bear collecting pine cones in the forest. "*Mishka kosalapi, po lesu idyot.*" Angelina often repeated the poem to herself over and over again.

She missed her mama so much. And Papa and Adam. And now Nana. Nana had got too ill to look after her. Aunty Rita from next door had looked after Angelina for a little bit while Nana had been in hospital, but then Nana had never come home, and Rita said that Angelina had to go and live in this big house now. She'd helped Angelina pack a small bag of clothes and had taken her here and left her.

Angelina wasn't sure how long she'd been here. There were lots of other children here too. Many were like her. They were very quiet and often cried a lot, particularly at night. The teachers were nice to her, and she had food every day, but they were all very busy and had a lot to do and didn't always have time to play with her. She wished Mama were here. Or Nana. Nana had played with her a lot before she had to go into hospital. A big tear traced a path down her cheek and was quickly followed by another. Angelina buried her head into Mishka's soft fur and let the tears flow freely.

The bus drew into the familiar bus terminal in Beslan. Bela picked up her bag, walked down the steps, and started in the direction of Rosa's house. She made the brisk twenty-minute walk with a heavy heart. As in Awush, there was plenty of snow still along the side streets, but there were no children throwing snowballs or building snowmen in the communal yards. It was all still eerily silent, devoid of the sounds of life, of laughter. A deep sadness engulfed her, and she mourned along with the local inhabitants, invisible now behind their net curtains, for all that had been lost.

She reached Rosa's house and rang the doorbell and banged on the gate, in case the doorbell wasn't working. Silence.

She tried again. Nothing.

She waited a good ten minutes before she began to feel her toes freezing in her boots and realised she couldn't stay here for ever. She decided to try the neighbouring house in case they knew anything.

A large, middle-aged Russian woman answered. At first, she eyed Bela suspiciously, but then when Bela explained the reason for her visit, the woman's eyes softened.

"You'd better come in," she said, and opened the gate wider for Bela to step through. Bela waited patiently on the sofa inside, while the woman instructed her daughter to make a cup of tea for them both.

"Such a sad situation," said the woman as her heavy frame sank into the chair opposite. "You knew the family, you say?"

"Yes," answered Bela. "Zalina was a childhood friend of mine, and I visited them a few times. I last came after…" She swallowed the lump in her throat. "After the tragedy."

They both fell silent for a moment out of respect, eyes down.

"When I came," Bela continued, fiddling with the material of her skirt, "Rosa was not in good health. Can you tell me what happened?"

"I'm sorry to tell you this, but she eventually became too weak to look after the little girl," the woman explained. There was a pause as the tea appeared on a tray and Bela was handed her cup by a pretty, teenage girl with long, blond hair.

"Rosa asked us to take in the little girl, Angelina, for a while, when she had to go into hospital. Sadly, she never came home again."

"Oh!" exclaimed Bela, although she'd already feared the worse. "And so, is Angelina still with you?"

The woman shook her head. "Rosa knew I wouldn't be able to keep her here," she said with a slight air of defensiveness. "I have three children of my own," she continued, nodding her chin towards the door through which the blond girl had disappeared a few seconds before.

Bela nodded, trying to look understanding. "So, where is she then?"

The woman looked slightly ashamed. "I took her to the local orphanage. It was the only place. There were no relatives, apparently. The will is still being settled, and the girl should have some money once the house is sold, I'm sure."

Bela couldn't believe it. Angelina, Zalina's beloved daughter, was now in an orphanage? Oh, why hadn't she tried harder to find her? Why hadn't she brought her home the moment Rosa had asked her too? After all that poor little girl had gone through, she was now even more alone than ever, and Bela was partly to blame for that.

She masked her shock, not wanting to judge Rosa's neighbour for her actions. Who could say that she wouldn't have done the same thing in similar circumstances? She swallowed the last of her tea and looked up at the woman with resolution in her eyes. "I need to find her. Can you tell me exactly where the orphanage is?"

Fifteen minutes later, Bela was in a taxi heading to the address the neighbour had given her. The car drew up alongside a large, austere, institutional-looking building. She paid the fare, telling the driver not to wait for her, and walked up the steps. She'd never been to an orphanage before, but it was exactly as she had imagined it. Rather like a hospital but with no medical equipment on show, and no white coats or blue plastic shoe covers, but still the same long corridors and identical wooden doors leading to identical-looking rooms. Devoid of the usual mixture of beauty, laughter, comfort and mess, this was certainly not a home away from home, no matter how well the children might be looked after.

After a brief conversation with the receptionist, she was instructed to wait outside the door of the Director of the Orphanage. She sat down on the chair outside and clutched her bag, which was resting on her knees. Her limbs felt weak and shaky. In a moment of panic, she felt like she might just jump up and make a run for the door. What was she doing here? But then she thought of Zalina. She was doing this for Zalina. She had a duty.

Oh, God, please give me courage to do what I know I need to do. And pave the way ahead of me to make this possible.

Michael moved the knight to the black square not far from Claire's king. "Checkmate!" he announced triumphantly.

Claire grimaced but graciously acknowledged defeat. "Okay, you got me this time, but I want a rematch!"

Michael laughed. "Are you sure? I seem to be on a winning streak here."

A frown crossed Claire's forehead, and she looked serious. "Michael, when are you going to tell me what's wrong?"

He swallowed and concentrated on packing the chess pieces carefully back into their box. "What do you mean?"

"You know what I mean," Claire replied. "Look at me, Michael. I know you. I know when something's bothering you, and this, whatever it is, is a big one."

Michael sighed. He knew he wasn't going to get away with hiding his secret for much longer. Claire could always read him like an open book.

"It's a girl," he said, half-jokingly.

"I knew it! Go on, tell me about her."

"Well, her name's Bela. I met her in Shekala. She's Circassian, and she was helping me with my research paper. We got... close."

Claire raised an eyebrow. "And?"

"Well, she wasn't a Christian, so I kept my distance, you know. But then she just recently decided to follow Jesus. I just don't know what to do, Claire. I can't get her out of my head. Sometimes I pray that God would just help me let her go so that I can move on, but it's like he keeps prompting me to pray for her."

"Has he told you to pray for her now?"

"Yes, I've felt it all day. I don't know what's happening, but I sense she needs some supernatural help today for some reason, you know what I mean?"

"Then we should pray for her."

"Of course, you're right. I'll call her later and see what was going on."

Claire tilted her head to one side. "Michael, if you don't mind me saying, you seem to be rather head over heels for this girl."

Michael looked at his sister. This time he didn't feel like laughing it off as if it didn't matter. "Yes, yes, I am," he admitted. "She's, well, she's amazing. She's beautiful and good and kind. When we're together, she makes me light up inside like no one else does. I love being with her. I feel like we're connected in some way, and that even this huge physical distance between us can't break that bond. But..." he dropped his head and ran his fingers through his hair, "I just don't see how we can possibly be together. She's there and I'm here and that's all there is to it."

"She doesn't want to come here?"

"She did, at first, but now she feels that God wants her to stay with her own people."

"Well, why don't you go there?"

Michael paused and looked into his sister's eyes. "But that would mean leaving you, Claire. What if something were to happen to Mum and Dad? It's my duty to look after you. Especially... Well... you know."

"Michael James Gregory! Don't you dare let me be the reason you can't be with the woman you love!"

He was rather taken aback by Claire's insistence. She rarely used that tone with anyone.

"It might surprise you, but I'm perfectly capable of looking after myself, thank you very much. And for the ten thousandth time, the accident wasn't your fault." She softened her voice and placed her hand on his knee. "I keep telling you, I don't blame you at all. I forgave you a long time ago for telling me to jump off that roof, and you weren't to know that I'd fall awkwardly the way I did."

"Really?" Had he really been holding onto all this guilt totally unnecessarily? God had forgiven him, he knew that, even though he still struggled to forgive himself. But was it really true that so had Claire? He'd never believed her before, but as he looked deep into her steadfast, blue eyes, he could see now that she really was telling the truth.

Hope began to spring in Michael's heart. He straightened his shoulders. "I think I really needed to hear that, Claire. I think I've been mistaken about what my duty was for a long time."

Claire's voice was soft but strong. "Go to her, Michael. God will work it all out."

Michael looked up at his sister, trying to blink back the tears welling in his eyes.

"Thank you," was all he said as he leaned towards her wheelchair and gave her a big hug.

Angelina looked up as her voice was called by the matron. "There's someone to see you, Angelina, follow me."

The little girl got up obediently, still clutching Mishka, and let the woman take her by the hand and lead her down the long corridor towards the Director's office. As she walked down the faded brown, laminate hallway, she noticed little faces peeking out of other rooms, wondering where she was going. She wondered herself what was happening. Who had come to see her? She couldn't think of anyone. Perhaps it was the neighbour lady again, although she hadn't wanted Angelina to stay with her; she'd made that clear.

"Don't be afraid, dear." The matron opened the door to the office and pushed the little girl inside. A younger lady with long black hair was sitting on a chair next to the Director's desk. She smiled at Angelina, and Angelina recognised her instantly.

"Tyotya Bela!" she called out, running to her.

Tyotya Bela gave her a big hug. When they eventually pulled away from each other, Tyotya Bela seemed to be crying, but Angelina wasn't sure why.

"Have you come to visit me?" Angelina asked.

"I've come to ask the Director if I can take you home with me, Angelina."

The little girl's heart leapt with joy. She looked at the Director, who had a kind, if important-looking, face. "Really?" she asked. "Now?"

The Director shook her head. "Not now, I'm afraid, Angelina. There's a lot of paperwork that must be sorted out first. But I see no reason why Tyotya Bela won't be able to take you home with her in a few weeks' time. Why don't you take Tyotya Bela to the playroom, and you two can catch up?"

Tyotya Bela gave the Director a smile as if to say thank you, and then she took Angelina's hand and squeezed it tightly. "I remember your bear. What's his name?"

"Mishka," said Angelina happily. "Do you want to hold him?" She offered the bear to Bela, who took him reverently and patted his head.

"*Mishka kosalapi, po lesu idyot*," she chanted out loud to herself, as if she were remembering something from her own childhood. Angelina joined in the chant and they finished the poem together, "*Po nogoiyu TOP!*" At the last word, they both stamped their feet and laughed. Bela gathered Angelina into her arms and gave her a fierce hug.

Angelina thought she hadn't smiled so widely in a long time. Everything was going to be okay now, she knew it. Tyotya Bela was going to look after her and Mishka, and they wouldn't need to be sad anymore.

Chapter 37

2005, May

Spring was her favourite time of year. Bela particularly loved the pink blossom of the cherry trees and the white blossom of the apple trees. Everywhere, signs of life were appearing through what had been a cold, barren wasteland just a few weeks ago. The birds were returning and were busy building nests. Dog violets and primroses were peeking out of the ground, following in the footsteps of the daffodils, which had been particularly beautiful this year. There was hope in the air, and, even though it was tinged with sadness too, Bela knew in her heart that all would be well.

Angelina had plucked a lovely bouquet of wild flowers, and the two of them were making their way to the cemetery in Beslan, where Zalina, Ruslan, Adam, and now Rosa were buried. It would have been Zalina's birthday today. Angelina was quiet and thoughtful, understandably, but thankfully the poor child hadn't seemed to remember much of the awful events that had taken away the lives of her family. When she was older, she might see some of the footage on the Internet, but for now, Bela had tried to shield her from the graphic scenes of what had happened at the school that fateful day.

"Here they are, Tyotya Bela, is this the right place?"

"Yes, that's right, Angelina. You can put your flowers down here." The little girl couldn't yet read the inscriptions, but this wasn't the first time they had visited the graves together. A new monument to the victims of Beslan was being built not far away and was due to open on the anniversary of the tragedy. Some people said it was to be called 'The City of Angels'. It seemed fitting somehow, and, one day when she was older, Bela would take her own little angel there to visit.

Angelina lay her flowers down and stepped back, reaching for Bela's hand.

"Do you think they're happy in heaven, Tyotya Bela?" the little girl asked, innocently.

"Yes, absolutely. They're in a wonderful place. They're only a little sad that they can't be with you anymore, but one day we'll all be together again."

Angelina nodded, satisfied for now by Bela's answer. Bela looked at her and smiled fondly, gratitude flooding her heart. The little girl had captured her heart from the moment she saw her in the orphanage, and she loved her as if she were her own daughter. God had helped the paperwork for the adoption to go through in record time, and even more miraculously, Bela's own family had been sympathetic when she'd explained the situation. They still didn't know all the details of Zalina's disappearance or that Bela had played a part in it, but they recognised their duty to welcome into their home an orphan whose parents and brother had died in such horrible circumstances. Bela had been looking for a small apartment where she and Angelina might be able to live together, but for now, Angelina was staying with Bela in her family home. She knew that it was God who had made that possible.

Thank you, Lord!

Bela reached into her pocket and brought out Michael's latest letter. He had been trying to find a way to get a visa to come back to Russia. He was prepared to move here to be with her if that's what it took. There was hope after all that they could be together at last. Bela clutched the letter tightly to her chest.

Thank you, God! You've done so much for me in just the last few months. First Angelina and now, perhaps, Michael too.

They turned to leave the graveyard and walked back towards the main road. Bela was lost in her thoughts and wasn't paying attention to her surroundings.

"Which grave are those flowers for?" Angelina asked someone in front of them. Bela came out of her reverie and looked up to see who she was talking to. There, standing right in front of them, clutching a bunch of beautiful red roses, was a familiar, handsome, brown-haired Englishman.

"Michael!" Bela jumped into his arms.

"Hey, you'll crush the roses!" Michael laughed, swinging her around in a full circle before planting her feet back on the pavement. They gazed into each other's eyes in wonder for a few seconds, and then Michael brushed back a loose strand of her hair and guided her lips towards his in a quick but meaningful 'hello' kiss.

"How did you know we'd be here?"

"You said, remember? It's Zalina's birthday today, isn't it?"

"Oh, yes, of course. But you could have waited for us in Shekala."

"I wanted to see the place for myself," replied Michael, a sad reverence in his voice.

"Who's this, Tyotya Bela?" There was a tug on her coat as Angelina's question broke into the dream that Bela was still trying to understand was actually real. She smiled and took Angelina's hand.

"Angelina, I'd like you to meet a very special friend of mine. This is Michael."

"Pleased to meet you," said Michael formally, shaking the little girl's hand with a twinkle in his eye. Bela could see that Angelina liked him instantly. "I've heard a lot about you," he added.

Bela reached out her other hand and linked it through Michael's arm as they all walked together along the side of the park. She was glad she'd finally told him all about Angelina after her visit to the orphanage back in February. It had been hard keeping the secret from him, but she had been unsure of what she was going to do until that moment.

"Are you going to marry Tyotya Bela?" asked Angelina, with all the innocence and inappropriateness of a young child.

Bela started to laugh but noticed that Michael wasn't. She turned to look at him, her eyes questioning. Michael reached into his pocket and pulled something out.

"Well, since you ask." He went down on one knee, and Angelina giggled. Bela's hands went to her mouth to stifle a gasp of surprise. Surely this wasn't real.

"Bela, I've loved you since the moment we met. It's been torture trying to live apart from you these past few months, and I don't want to do it anymore. I want to share every moment of every day with you from now on. I don't want to lose you again. Will you marry me, beautiful Bela?" He opened the little box he'd been holding, and out shone a gorgeous, diamond ring, the kind that Bela had only seen in magazines up till now.

She paused for a moment, her heart racing inside her so loudly she was sure Michael could hear it. "And Angelina?" She had to ask. Michael wasn't just taking her, he was taking the two of them. They came as a package.

"I promise to love her like she was my own daughter." Michael smiled warmly at Angelina, and the little girl giggled again in delight.

"Then yes, I will marry you." Bela jumped into Michael's arms a second time and then giggled with delight herself as he placed the ring gently on her finger.

The three of them continued on down the street, Angelina skipping excitedly on one side of her, and Bela leaning in close to Michael on the other side, squeezing his arm and staring at the beautiful ring on her finger in disbelief. She couldn't imagine it was possible to feel this much happiness.

As they passed an overhanging cherry tree, delicate, pink petals floated down on the three of them like confetti at a wedding. Their collective laughter intertwined with their feelings of unfettered joy, and floated away on the warm, spring breeze.

4

The Lord will keep you from all harm –

He will watch over your life;

The Lord will watch over your coming and going

Both now and for evermore.

Psalm 121, verses 7 and 8

Author's Note

I hope you enjoyed *Lift Your Eyes to the Mountains.*

If you have a moment, I would be so grateful if you could leave a quick review on Amazon. Reviews help other readers to find the book and are especially important for independently published authors like myself. Thank you so much!

You can follow along with Azamat and Milana's story, as well as more of Bela and Michael, in the next book in the *Mountains of Faith* series, which is coming soon!

For book group discussion questions, local recipes, notifications of when new books are available, and so much more, sign up to join my Readers List at catherinebarbey.com/readerslist

Acknowledgements

My deepest thanks to all those who made the dream of this book become a reality. Thanks to my wonderful husband, for believing in me, encouraging me and giving me the space and time I needed to hide myself away and write. To my four awesome children, for inspiring me and cheering me on.

Thanks to Sarah Furze and Sue Ricketts for your helpful feedback on my early draft. To Christine Dillon and Ali Hull for an initial critical eye and useful book suggestions. To my editor, Arielle Bailey, for being so positive and affirming, and for all your help getting this book into its final form.

Thanks also to Rebecca Priestley, for your inspired artwork for the cover, to Clare Shearing for your photography skills, and to Rob Richards for your amazing work, as always, on the cover design.

I appreciate so much the wonderful online community of independent authors, whose support and advice have helped me so much on my own writing journey.

About the Author

Catherine Barbey writes Christian inspirational fiction with an international flavour. A tea drinking, home educating mother of four, she also loves running and generally being outside in nature, preferably in warm, foreign climes! In a former life she worked alongside her husband in linguistics and translation, living with her family in Russia for eleven years. They are now settled back in their home country of England, on the sunny south coast.

Catherine can be found blogging about her writing journey at catherinebarbey.com

You can also connect with Catherine here:
facebook.com/catherinebarbeywriter
twitter.com/catherinebarbey
instagram.com/catherinebarbeywriter

33913212R00185

Printed in Great Britain
by Amazon